"He ha
"Really
"A crir
"One   *Publishers*
        W
"Ebull
"Com
"Cred   lm of his
     h
"He is   *urg Times*
"Enor   *ne*
"Russ
"This
"Grac   most hard-
     c

OTHER TITLES BY ALAN RUSSELL

The Gideon and Sirius Novels

Burning Man

Guardians of the Night

Stand-Alone Novels

No Sign of Murder

The Forest Prime Evil

The Hotel Detective

The Fat Innkeeper

Multiple Wounds

Shame

Exposure

Political Suicide

St. Nick

A Cold War

LOST DOG

LOST DOG

A Gideon and Sirius Novel

ALAN RUSSELL

Published by Thomas & Mercer, Seattle

www.apub.com

Amazon, the Amazon logo, and Thomas & Mercer are trademarks of Amazon.com, Inc., or its affiliates.

ISBN-13: 9781503935525
ISBN-10: 1503935523

Cover design by Jason Blackburn

Many years ago, and a dozen novels before this one, I wrote these words that I now write again: To Laura.

THEY ONCE WERE LOST, BUT NOW ARE FOUND

Angie's growling awakened her. Heather Moreland didn't know what time it was, but the encompassing darkness suggested it was the middle of the night.

"It's all right, Angie," Heather said, extending a hand to try and make contact with her dog.

Angie was a so-called third-chance dog. After she was brought to the shelter and put up for adoption, two other owners had returned her, and Heather's adoption had come through the day before Angie was scheduled to be put down. Heather was Angie's call from the governor, but there wouldn't be any more chances for her. If Angie was returned to the shelter for a third time, she would immediately be euthanized. Heather had been determined to not let that happen.

More than a year had passed since Angie's adoption. The first six months had been particularly difficult for human and dog. It didn't matter that Angie acted the way she did because of human neglect and mistreatment. For the first two years of her life, she'd been tied to a short chain in a feces-filled yard, with no access to shelter.

Was it any wonder that Angie was still a work in progress?

The dog had been slow to come around. She distrusted humans, and for good reason. All she'd known was neglect and abuse. Neighborhood boys had used her as target practice, pelting her with rocks. She'd gone without water and food for days at a time. She'd chewed on the chain that bound her until her teeth were bloody, but she hadn't been able to free herself from the metal snare.

It took a long time before animal control finally responded to complaints about the treatment Angie was receiving at her first home. Officers had been forced to restrain her with catch poles; she'd fought them every inch of the way. Once Angie arrived at the shelter, no one was hopeful about her prospects. The staff had seen too many throwaway dogs like her before. She was *damaged*, what one of them referred to as a "Humpty Dumpty dog." She couldn't be put back together again.

Heather had taken on the challenge of proving the skeptics wrong. At the time, momentous changes were going on in her life. She'd left her husband and gotten her own place, and she'd felt this need to help the unloved and dispossessed. Angie was the recipient of her goodwill, and Heather never gave up on her. But although her love was unconditional, that didn't mean it was without boundaries. For the longest time, Angie had appeared immune to love and barely responded to treats. She distrusted Heather, growling at her if she came too close. Sudden movements caused Angie to bare her teeth and snap.

Heather knew Angie did this because she felt threatened. At first Angie hadn't even tolerated being in the same room with her. Given any opportunity, she tried to run away. Heather had made her home's small yard escape-proof, but that hadn't deterred Angie. Not a day went by when she didn't dig up the yard and do her best to tunnel under the fence.

"Where is it that you think you want to go?" Heather kept asking her.

Angie invariably responded to the sound of Heather's voice by either skulking or growling.

"I suppose you want to find a world without humans," Heather said. "I'm afraid that isn't possible, Angie. I would have found that world already if it existed."

Anyone else would have given up on Angie. She was a not-inconsiderable expense. On days Heather wasn't able to telecommute, Angie went to doggie day care. Heather learned the hard way that she couldn't be away from the house without Angie damaging it. Most nonsaints don't have the tolerance for coming home time and again to torn-apart pillows, chewed-up carpeting, and dog crap in the most inconvenient places. But Heather wasn't about to give up, even though at six months together there came a moment when she almost lost it. On a day she was supposed to be telecommuting, an escalating situation had required Heather to go in to work. She had assumed everything could be resolved in a short time, but that hadn't proved to be the case.

When she finally made it home, her house looked like a war zone. There were feathers and foam everywhere, intermixed with colored shampoo and gel. The living room resembled a Jackson Pollock painting. Angie had even managed to get through the window barriers Heather had set up and had torn apart the blinds.

"Shit!" Heather had yelled.

From the hallway, Angie was carefully watching her. At the sound of Heather's cursing, the dog growled.

Heather was tired and hungry and drained. Angie's trail of destruction was too much. She fell down into a chair. Of course the armrests on it had been chewed as well. Covering her eyes with her hands, she began sobbing.

"I can barely cope myself," she said. "Where did I get the idea that I could help a crazy dog?"

As a rule, Heather didn't believe in pity parties. She was good about setting goals for herself and following through. She was too busy to feel sorry for herself. But she felt the need for a good cry. Once the tears started flowing, she cried and cried.

In the midst of her waterworks, Heather felt something touch her hand. She cracked her fingers open and saw Angie gently touching her with her nose.

The dog was trembling. Her posture suggested she wasn't sure whether to flee, fight, or stay put. Never before had Angie willingly approached this close. But it was clear she wanted to comfort Heather even if she didn't know how.

Heather stopped crying and slowly dropped her hands. Angie backed away, staying just out of reach. Speaking in little more than a gentle whisper, Heather said, "Thank you, Angie."

The dog's tail, tucked under its backside, didn't wag, but it did slightly unfurl.

"The two of us are in this together. I'm not going to give up on you. We're kindred spirits, did you know that?"

Instead of running out of the room, Angie seemed to be listening to her.

"We were both born with two strikes against us. Neither one of us had much of a first home. Both of us were abused.

"You lost most of your sight in one eye. I think it must have been a stone. That's why you get upset when I pick things up with my hand. You're afraid I might throw something at you. I can see fine, but I'm dyslexic. When I was young, everyone thought I was stupid because I had so much trouble reading.

"I suppose it didn't help being homeschooled. My father was paranoid. He didn't want my brother and me in school. He was probably afraid of what we might say to others. If we stayed home, we didn't have to explain the bruises all over our bodies. But Mother was his favorite punching bag. I've often wondered if she was mentally ill, or if Father beat her so many times she suffered physical and mental damage."

Angie was still listening. She was even making eye contact with Heather, something she'd never done before.

"Everything changed when I was twelve," said Heather. "That's how old I was when I watched my father beat my mother to death. That's when I was put in foster care. My brother as well. He told me that one day we'd be back together, but that never happened. He overdosed within two weeks of his release from foster care. I was there for five and a half years, until I aged out when I was eighteen.

"You and me were passed over by an awful lot of families, weren't we, Angie? No one wanted a funny-looking girl who could barely read.

"The first time I saw you huddled in the back of your cage, you wouldn't look me in the eye, and I was reminded of how I used to be. I couldn't look at other people either. And when I spoke to prospective parents, they must have heard my growl. I know I heard yours.

"That's why I picked you, Angie. And that's why I'm not going to give up on you. I found a way out of my hole. It wasn't easy. I made mistakes. But here I am and life is good. One day you'll wake up and not feel the need to be scared every moment of every day. I know how exhausting that is. And I want you to be able to wag your tail. I want you to be happy, Angie. And one day I hope you'll no longer want to run away, that you'll want to stay right here with me. And this will be our home sweet home."

Heather had never spoken at such length to Angie. The dog had never stayed in her proximity long enough for her to say much.

"I know you want to be a good dog, Angie. I could tell that the first time we met. You were growling and baring your teeth, and I told you, 'Good girl.' And for just a moment you stopped acting like you wanted to eat me.

"Of course I had to change your name, just like I changed mine. Hardly anyone knows that. But I didn't want my father's last name. That's why I changed it to Moreland. You see, heather grows in the moorland, and I wanted to grow. At the shelter, someone must have decided you were a Dalmatian because of your spots. And so they named you Cruella. Do you remember that name? But I knew you were no Cruella. You were Angie."

That night, for the first time, Angie chose to sleep in Heather's bedroom even though she stayed as far away from her as the room allowed. Neither Heather nor Angie knew it, but they'd reached a tipping point in their relationship. As the days and weeks and months passed, instead of actively avoiding Heather, Angie began to seek her out. There came a day when Angie not only didn't shrink from contact, but initiated it. After a year with Heather, Angie was now wagging her tail. It was getting so that Angie was even learning to play.

And to love.

That's why Angie's growling sounded so discordant to Heather. The new Angie didn't growl, or at least didn't growl nearly as much as she had. Maybe Angie was asleep and some bad dream had her growling. But no, that wasn't it. Heather felt Angie's tensed body. The dog was hearing something that bothered her.

Emilio, she thought.

Heather had been separated from her husband for almost eighteen months now. She'd been stupid enough to marry a man like her father. No, Emilio wasn't as abusive, but he was controlling and had a terrible temper. After she'd moved out, Heather had gotten a restraining order against him. Of course he'd promised to change. Since their separation, Emilio had been attending anger-management courses. It was a step in the right direction, but Heather had decided it wasn't enough. More important, she'd decided she didn't love him. On Friday she'd told him that she would be proceeding with the divorce. That news hadn't been well received.

"You really think I'm going to let you split up with me?" he'd said. "That's not going to happen. I'll be coming over to your place. We got a lot to talk about."

"That talking will be done over the phone or through email," Heather said. "If you come within one hundred yards of me or my house, you will be in violation of the restraining order, and I will have no choice but to call the police."

He screamed into the phone, "You think I'm going to let a goddamn piece of paper dictate to me?"

Heather had hung up on him, cutting him off midrant. She reached for her cell phone now, but then remembered she'd left it charging in the kitchen.

Angie's growling grew louder.

Heather needed to act before Emilio came into her room. She was scared of what he might do to Angie. The two of them had been little more than newlyweds when Heather had gotten a kitten, a sweet orange tabby she'd named Perry because of his periwinkle-blue eyes. Perry had been only a few months old when he'd accidentally scratched Emilio. Her husband had gone into a rage, grabbing Perry and throwing him across the room into a wall. Luckily, Perry wasn't seriously hurt. The next day Heather reluctantly gave Perry up. She didn't want Emilio to hurt their kitty.

And she didn't want him to hurt Angie.

Heather ran to the window, opened it, and knocked out the screen. "Angie, come," she called.

The two of them had been working on commands. Angie knew the commands for "Come," "Sit," "Stay," and "Lie down." But at the moment she was growling and not listening. Heather heard footsteps coming down the hallway.

"Angie, come!"

This time Angie reluctantly obeyed. "Good girl," said Heather, stroking her head.

Angie's collar gave Heather an idea. She disengaged the quick-release buckle, then removed a second clasp before attaching it to the inside of her nightgown. It wasn't any bigger than one of those plastic price tags. As the collar dropped to the floor, Heather strained to lift Angie up and over the window ledge. Angie began resisting, her feet scrabbling on the sill, but Heather pushed her out the window. It was at least a four-foot drop to the ground below, but Angie landed on her feet and seemed to be fine.

"Good girl," Heather told her.

The words were no comfort to Angie. The dog ran back and forth under the window. Heather could tell she was readying herself for a running leap to get back into the room. Reluctantly, Heather shut the window.

That's when the bedroom door came crashing open. A spotlight blinded her. Heather raised her hands, trying to ward off the light. She opened her mouth to scream, but the noise that came out was more like a squawk. Something was hurting her. Something was making her lose control of her body. She fell to the floor and began flopping around like a fish out of water. A rag was pressed up against her nose and mouth.

The last thing she remembered was the sound of Angie's howling.

CHAPTER 1

THE 187 CLUB

My partner and I pulled up to the parking lot of the Jim Gilliam Recreation Center on La Brea Avenue. Because La Brea is one of the L.A. street names repeated ad nauseam in the forties song "Pico & Sepulveda," I felt obliged to sing Sirius a few bars. It's a mostly silly song with a Latin beat that repeats downtown L.A. street names. But in the midst of the silliness is a lyrical reminder of the star chasing that brought so many to the City of Angels, and the failed dreams that resulted.

All those fabled streets, and all those failed dreams. There are truisms even in silly songs. At the end of my finale, Sirius gave me a nuzzle with his muzzle. My partner is a generous critic.

I had never spent any time in Jim Gilliam Park, but I did know where it got its name. My father had been a Dodgers fan, and Jim "Junior" Gilliam was a key part of those classic fifties and sixties teams. Gilliam's professional career started with the Brooklyn Dodgers, where he had the unenviable job of taking over for Jackie Robinson at second base. He was the Dodgers' coach when he died unexpectedly from a brain hemorrhage at much too young an age.

Quoting from iconic Dodger announcer Vin Scully, I said, "It's a mere moment in a man's life between the All-Star Game and an old-timer's game."

Scully's musing reminded me of Simon and Garfunkel's "Mrs. Robinson." I recalled their chorus of how Joltin' Joe DiMaggio had left and gone away. I thought about expanding Sirius's musical repertoire and singing a few lines from "Mrs. Robinson," but I was afraid that someone might overhear and bring me up on charges of animal cruelty. When it came to my singing, less was more.

Unlike a lot of L.A. parks, Jim Gilliam Park didn't appear to have been overtaken by gangs, the homeless, or drug dealers. It helped that the park was designated by LAPD as a "stop-in center." That meant cops regularly stopped there to write up their reports, take breaks, visit the water fountain, and nose around. A police presence tended to discourage illegal activities.

Sirius and I got out of the car and went for a walk around the park. There were trails with lots of trees and greenery, and Sirius did lots of sniffing. We stopped to watch hoops being played on several basketball courts. All the players were under twenty-five and black. Not for the first time I wondered if there had ever been a time when I moved that quickly and jumped that high. I thought of Vin Scully's "mere moment" line for the second time that morning. He wasn't just a baseball announcer, he was a philosopher.

No one seemed to mind my watching the games even though everyone knew I was a cop. If the players were wary of anything, it was Sirius. His ears were up and he was tugging against his leash, hoping I'd let him join in the game. What Sirius still had to learn was that sharp teeth and balls were not usually a good combination. Tomorrow I'd make a point of throwing a ball to him, or maybe even more to his liking, a Frisbee.

I was in no rush to head into the community center, even though I knew the meeting was scheduled to start and I was there as its speaker. The truth was that I wished I had begged off. I was way outside my comfort zone. It was the second Monday of the month, it was 5:30 p.m., and this was the 187 Club.

Someone once told me the 187 Club had started out with a more official name, something to do with grief and gathering, but its members had quickly adopted the name the 187 Club. California Penal Code 187 is the designation for a homicide, and it was that terrible bond that the club members had in common. This was a club no one wanted to join. Membership demanded the awful price of losing a loved one to violent crime.

Langston Walker—retired Detective Langston Walker—had started the club after putting in thirty years at LAPD, his last eight with Robbery-Homicide. But Walker didn't found the 187 Club because of his professional status. Like the other members, he too had lost a loved one. His youngest son had been caught in the crossfire when two gangs decided to shoot it out.

Walker started up the 187 Club two years after his son was murdered and right before his retirement from the force. He'd made lemonade instead of hemlock. He didn't have a degree in counseling and knew nothing about grief therapy, but that didn't stop him from organizing monthly meetings. The 187 Club had no elected officers, and Walker didn't have an official title, but club members referred to him as "The Speaker for the Dead." Homicide detectives often say that's their job—speaking for the dead. Running the club probably wasn't the retirement Walker once envisioned, but doing so had kept him busy in the almost four years since.

During the fifteen minutes Sirius and I had been out walking, the parking lot had filled up. From a distance I could see people making their way to the community center. It seemed to me they walked with heavy steps. Individuals who've had to endure the murder of a loved one were invariably marked. There was a weight they carried, a yoke that couldn't be shrugged off.

Several cars in the parking lot displayed the same bumper sticker: "Someone I Love Was Murdered." I also saw the bumper sticker "Guns

Don't Die, People Do," and another that read: "It's Easier to Childproof Your Gun Than Bulletproof Your Child."

Gallows humor, with hard kernels of truth, has always been my way of coping as well.

Sirius and I made our way to the entrance of the meeting room and then stood there waiting for Walker to notice our arrival. I wasn't in any rush to go inside. The room was packed, and that was enough to make me feel hot and claustrophobic. My phobia is a by-product of having been badly burned in a canyon fire set by a psychopathic serial killer who thought no one would be stupid enough to go into an inferno to try and capture him. I had been that stupid. Sirius and I got our man, but we also got shot and badly burned. Even now I bear the scars, including a prominent one on my face. Then again, I was never leading-man material.

I could see Walker circulating through the crowded room. It seemed like he had a word and a hug for everyone. I didn't know him very well; we'd met at a few functions and at one or two crime scenes. Walker was around sixty and powerfully built, with a big chest and thick thighs. He was about my height, but probably had fifty pounds on me. Like half the people in the room, he was African American. Bullets are color-blind, but even though black people make up fewer than ten percent of Los Angeles's population, they comprise almost a third of the city's homicides. That's not to say that every race, creed, and color wasn't represented. In the room were Hispanics, Asians, Native Americans, Persians, Indians, Arabs, and Caucasians. L.A. is polyglot central. Whites are no longer in the majority; almost half of L.A. is now of Latino ancestry.

In the nineties, the LAPD acknowledged the changing demographics of the city, and over the years has come to field a force that better reflects the faces of its community. We're not a Coca-Cola commercial, and the force doesn't sing in perfect harmony, but on the whole we're the same color: blue.

A Hispanic woman who looked to be about thirty whispered something in Walker's ear, which prompted him to turn around and take notice of Sirius and me. He waved and then reversed course. On the way over to us, he stopped to shake more hands and give more hugs. A politician might have learned a few things from him.

He finally reached us and we shook hands. "Thanks for coming, Mike," he said. "Or do you prefer Michael?"

"Either is fine. But most people just call me Gideon."

"Then Gideon it is."

"What about you?"

"These days I'm just plain old Langston. That's the way I like it, even though there are a lot in here who call me Detective Walker."

He had a deep, mellifluous voice, the kind televangelists try to emulate. The difference was that his was the real thing.

"I didn't know you were going to bring backup," Walker said, taking notice of my German shepherd partner.

"Sirius," I said, "meet Langston."

Sirius extended a paw, and Walker shook.

"I know you by reputation, Sirius, and I'm glad we're on the same team."

Sirius must have liked the sound of that; he wagged his tail.

"There's a patio section at the restaurant we'll be dining at later," said Walker. "I'll let them know we're a party of three."

"My partner thanks you."

Walker had told me that he'd be taking me to dinner after the meeting. He'd said it was his way of thanking those who came to speak.

"We have a great crowd tonight," he said. "It will be standing room only."

I nodded and faked a smile, pretending to be enthusiastic about that.

"I'll make a few short remarks," said Walker, "and then I'll introduce you."

"I hope you're still keeping to your plan about this being mostly Q&A," I said. I didn't have much in the way of prepared remarks.

Walker must have heard the panic in my voice. "Don't worry. I'll prime the pump with questions whenever it looks like you've run out of things to say."

"That should occur right after the time I say hello."

"You won't run out of things to say. I guarantee it. And our audience always comes with lots of questions. You'll see."

Walker patted my arm and set out for the front of the room. Sirius and I weren't alone for long. A middle-aged white man with thinning hair and a salt-and-pepper Van Dyke beard came up to us and said, "Detective Gideon?"

"Guilty as charged," I said, extending my hand.

"I'm Arthur Epstein," he said. "I think I'm the reason you're here tonight. My wife was Suzanne Epstein."

The name was familiar to me, but I wasn't able to make an immediate connection.

"Suzie was the Santa Ana Strangler's victim number five," he said.

"I'm sorry."

He nodded. "I'm glad to finally have a chance to thank you in person for bringing Ellis Haines in. It wasn't until he was behind bars that I began to heal. It's possible you and Sirius saved my life by capturing him."

"I'm glad," I said.

"I'm told you see Haines every month," said Epstein.

I nodded. "I'm working with the FBI's Behavioral Science Unit. Haines is part of their serial killer profiling effort."

"I wonder if you can pass on a message from me," he said.

"What would you like me to say to him?"

"Tell him Art Epstein and his son Joel look forward to the day the state of California takes his miserable life. Tell him we'll be the ones smiling at him and waving bye-bye when the bastard gets what's due to him."

I remembered now that Suzanne Epstein had been the mother of a ten-year-old boy.

"I'll be glad to pass on that message," I said.

Art Epstein teared up and managed to utter a husky "Good." Then he took my right hand and squeezed it between his hands before walking off.

Epstein had said that Haines's imprisonment had allowed him to start the healing process. It was clear he still had a ways to go.

From the front of the room, Walker began to speak. No one had to crane to hear him. "If everyone can take a chair or get as comfortable as possible, we'll begin."

He looked around. "We will start as we always do, with a few moments of silence remembering those who were taken from us."

Heads around the room bent, and eyes closed. After half a dozen seconds, Walker spoke again.

"As you know, we all come to this monthly meeting for different reasons. Many of us are still seeking justice for our loved ones. Getting that justice isn't easy. Sometimes it's impossible. As Justice Oliver Holmes once said to a lawyer speaking in his courtroom, 'This is a court of law, young man, not a court of justice.'"

A few people laughed; almost all nodded.

Walker continued. "Elisabeth Kübler-Ross was a Swiss psychiatrist who came up with the notion that there are five stages of grief. Those stages, she said, are denial, anger, depression, bargaining, and acceptance.

"Kübler-Ross and David Kessler wrote about these stages in their book, *On Grief and Grieving*. In it they said, and I quote, 'Those stages are part of a framework that makes up our learning to live with the one we lost.'

"These five stages, they wrote, 'are tools to help us identify and frame what we may be feeling. But they are not stops on some linear timeline in grief.'

"Let me repeat that: grief has no linear timeline. Maybe you've never gone beyond the grieving stage. Maybe that cloud of depression is still hanging over you. Maybe you thought you had come to terms with what happened to your loved one, but now you're angry again. There's no right or wrong way to deal with grief, but there are certainly healthier ways of coping. The loss we've all experienced is bad enough without compounding it through self-destruction.

"If you're wallowing in one of Dr. Kübler-Ross's stages, then maybe you should consider doing yourself a favor and calling someone on our friend line. Like I'm always saying, we're all in this together, even if it feels like we're all alone."

Voices called out, "That's right," and "Amen," and "Uh-huh." The fellowship of the 187 Club was trying to stand up to denial, anger, depression, bargaining, and acceptance. It seemed to me they were up against stiff competition.

"Tonight our guest speaker, or perhaps I should say, guest speakers, is Detective Michael Gideon and his partner, Sirius. This cop–K-9 team was responsible for bringing in a killer who murdered the wife of one of our members. Please welcome Detective Gideon and Sirius."

At the sound of applause, Sirius began wagging his tail. He's quite comfortable with people clapping for him. I'm not nearly as relaxed in public as he is. The one good thing about getting skin grafts over much of my body is that they don't sweat. I'm the picture of calm, cool, and collected, even when I'm not.

There was a small lectern at the front of the room. I was glad for it; I could hold on to it and hide behind it. My "speech"—such as it was—consisted of a cue card with a few notes jotted down. I put the card down on the lectern and studied it for a moment.

Usually when Sirius and I do appearances, I start with a joke. I wasn't sure whether humor had a place in the 187 Club, but I decided to take a chance.

"You know," I said, looking at my partner, "I don't know why people think Sirius is so smart, but they do."

My partner's ears perked up, and he looked at me. Everyone could see he was smiling, as if he was in on the joke.

"Yeah, yesterday the two of us were playing chess, and there must have been ten people who came by and said, 'That Sirius is so smart.' And I had to tell them, 'He's not really that smart. I'm the one who's won three out of five games.'"

Almost everyone in the crowd began to laugh. I pretended to take offense at the laughter. "You don't believe me, do you?"

Then I shook my head, gave Sirius a disdainful side glance, and said, "You were just lucky yesterday. *Usually* I do win."

The crowd laughed, and then laughed even more when Sirius chose to start licking himself. His targeted area seemed to be an editorial comment.

I decided not to tell them my joke about what Timmy had said after hearing that Lassie had been eaten by a bear ("Well, doggone"). There was no need. Sirius had already won over the crowd.

I took another look at the cue card. It hadn't magically filled up since I'd last studied it.

"I wish I had some great advice for everyone in this room," I said. "It would be nice if I could expound upon Kübler-Ross, but the truth is before today I'd never heard her name. And I wish I was as learned as Langston and could tell you what else Justice Oliver Holmes said, but I'd probably mix his words with those of Sherlock Holmes. Unfortunately, I'm a product of our times, and most of the quotes I know come from popular music and movies.

"But, like you, there have been times in my life when I've had to deal with those five stages of grief that Langston referred to. One time in particular it seemed as if my whole world was crumbling down around me. And that's when I got a call from a friend who said, 'Gideon, just remember this: *illegitimi non carborundum.*' And so I said to my friend, 'What the hell does that mean?' And he told me *illegitimi non carborundum* translates to, 'Don't let the bastards grind you down.'"

Most in the audience were smiling and nodding, which seemed a victory to me, as this was a group heavy with dark circles, haggard faces, and hunched shoulders.

"My friend's words made an impression on me. And so I wrote his phrase down in big bold letters and put that sheet of paper in a prominent place on my desk. And I referred to it when times were bad. This went on for a time, until I made the mistake of referencing my catchphrase to my oldest friend in the world, Father Patrick Garrity of the Church of the Blessed Sacrament on Sunset Avenue. And how did Father Pat respond? He chastised me, and not for using the word "bastards," but for my ignorance. Father Pat said that even I should have recognized pseudo-Latin for what it was. Did I mention that the Father is a classically trained Jesuit? Anyway, because of Father Pat, I can now properly curse in Latin. And now you can too. According to Father Pat, I should have said, *'Noli nothis permittere deterere.'* And that translates to, 'Do not allow the bastards to get you down.'

"Now that's not one of the Ten Commandments, I know, but when my world of terra firma became quicksand, I resolved that I wasn't going to let those bastards grind me down.

"We all have different bastards in our lives. Maybe you're trying to deal with an indifferent justice system. That can be a real bastard. Or you have a boss who doesn't understand what you're going through and won't cut you any slack. Or there's that lawyer who's making you jump through hoops. There could be bill collectors who keep calling with no regard for your situation. Yeah, there's no shortage of bastards trying to grind you down. I'm sure we can all compile quite a list.

"I can't claim to have experienced loss in the same way that all of you have. But I do know that when there's a hole in your heart, it's hard to get out of bed. You want to grieve, but you don't even feel like you have the energy to do that. You're at the end of your rope, and it feels like you're swinging from that rope. Maybe you're trying to keep the bastard that killed your loved one in a cage, while he's pulling every jailhouse-lawyer tactic at his disposal. I do know it's a fact that criminals know their rights better than their wrongs."

That line, which I'd stolen from somewhere, got a lot of people laughing and nodding.

"And I know it's hard not to let the bastards grind you down. You get tired and discouraged, and it seems like it doesn't matter, because even if you're doing the best you possibly can, that's still not going to bring your loved one back. And, of course, that's the only thing that would make you whole. But you can honor your loved one by not giving up. It doesn't matter how many times you've been knocked down as long as you're still getting up."

I looked over to Walker, my signal for a reprieve. I had covered all the points on my index card, and then some.

"Detective Gideon knows something about being knocked down," said Walker. "He lost his wife to illness not long before both he and Sirius were hurt in the line of duty and had to go through extensive physical therapy. But Detective Gideon didn't give up. He didn't let the bastards grind him down. What's that Latin phrase of yours, Gideon?"

"Noli nothis permittere deterere."

"Words to live by," said Walker. "And you know what I like about it? You can't help but sound smart when you go around speaking Latin.

"Now, I have plenty of questions I want to ask Detective Gideon, but I'm going to have the opportunity to do that later. So if you don't want me to hog the detective's time, this is your opportunity to ask your questions."

A dozen arms shot up. Usually people ask me about Ellis Haines or want details about the night we arrested him. For once, those questions didn't surface. The 187 Club wasn't interested in the voyeuristic aspects of that case; they had more pressing questions of their own.

I was asked how I handled stress and avoided being ground down by the bastards. I was put on the spot as to whether, as a matter of course, I offered loved ones of the victim advice as to where they could go for help. And then I was put on the spot again when I was asked what advice I gave to loved ones of victims. Two people asked variants of the same question: How could they make sure their cases didn't slide to the investigative back burner?

"As I'm sure Detective Walker has told you," I said, "if you want detectives to keep working the case, you might have to act as an advocate of the deceased. You should think about using social media and devote a website to the victim and what happened to him or her. I also would look into using Twitter or Instagram. The more outlets you have, the better your chance of getting someone to come forward who might know something about your case.

"Do whatever you can to get the fruit to fall from the tree. Someone out there knows something. It's possible you can prod the conscience of a reluctant witness. People might have heard something after the fact. Or they might remember an important fact. Keep posting reminders. Use whatever you can to keep the case alive, be it birthdays or memorial dates or any tie-in you can think of. And use LAPD social media if you can. In addition to our official website, there are plenty of departmental Twitter accounts you can follow. Don't hesitate to ask those accounts to reference your case."

I called out some of the Twitter accounts I knew offhand, such as @LAMurderCop and @77thHomicideCop, and saw some people writing them down.

"Two more questions," Walker announced.

I looked at the clock and was amazed to see it was already six forty-five.

"And one of them better not be where you can find the best doughnuts," I said.

It was the best comic relief I could come up with for what had been an intense evening.

The Hispanic woman who'd been helping Langston earlier raised her hand. She was an attractive woman, but her prominent frown lines and heavy dark circles bespoke a troubled life. I signaled her with my finger.

"I'm Catalina Ceballos," she said. "My husband was shot to death three years ago. According to LAPD, his case has been solved, and yet his murderers have never been convicted. When I tell people this, no one seems to understand how that could be. There was never even an arrest. On the books, LAPD says they solved this case. They call it a 'cleared other.' Because of that I'm in limbo. The police say they know who killed my husband, but the district attorney said there wasn't enough evidence to make a case. How is this possible?"

"I am sorry for your loss," I said. "Unfortunately, there are certain homicides that don't lead to an arrest but are sometimes still designated as 'cleared other.' For example, murder/suicides are almost always categorized as 'cleared others.'"

"My situation wasn't like that," Catalina said, her voice cracking slightly. "And there are others here"—she glanced at a white man sitting next to her—"whose cases LAPD also solved with an eraser."

Her voice had grown huskier, but she fought off tears and tried to continue speaking.

"The men that murdered my husband have never spent a day in jail. And when I try to get the detectives to do something, the only thing that happens is that I get threatened by the gang that murdered my husband!"

Catalina stopped speaking, her emotions silencing her. The man sitting next to her offered his hand and then stood up. He had long brown hair and appeared to be in his early thirties.

"I'm James," he said. "Catalina's situation is Kafkaesque. LAPD is cooking the books to improve its homicide clearance rate and not giving us any answers."

"While I sympathize with what Catalina has had to go through," I said mildly, "I wouldn't call it cooking the books."

"Then why does the *L.A. Times* continue to run stories saying the department's homicide solve rates are bogus?"

I had read those stories, and also the department's rebuttal. "LAPD admitted that in 2014 and 2015 there were some clerical errors, but subsequently the solve rates turned out to be actually better than first reported."

From her seat, Catalina found her voice: "Did you know that more than ten percent of LAPD's homicide solve rate over the last few years have been 'cleared others'?"

"No, I didn't know that," I said. "But sometimes there are reasons that are out of the hands of LAPD as to why charges weren't filed or arrests weren't made. As a cop, I can tell you we like putting away the bad guys."

"When a case is officially closed," said Catalina, "detectives no longer have any reason to gather evidence."

"Is there a question there?" I asked.

She shook her head, and it was clear I hadn't won her over. "I'm not sure if there is. I just thank God that Langston is trying to help reopen my husband's case."

Langston decided I'd been on the hot seat for long enough. "Ronaldo, last question," he said.

A Hispanic man who looked to be about forty stood up. He was wearing a soccer shirt in the colors of one of the Premier club teams, but I didn't know which one. I wondered if Ronaldo was his real name or if it was a nickname inspired by the soccer player.

"So, what do you do when your homicide dick retires," he asked, "and the new dick refuses to do jack about your case?"

"I'm sorry if that's what you're experiencing," I said. "Obviously I don't know the particulars of your situation, but sometimes perception isn't the reality. Some detectives communicate better than others. It's possible the new detective has been working the case but hasn't kept you in the loop. So what you need to do is schedule a meeting with him, and then you should document everything that's said. Insist that you be kept up to date. If nothing changes to your satisfaction, you can ask that the case be reassigned to another detective. But again, the more documentation you do, the better your argument will be."

A few more people in the audience tried to sneak in a last question, but Walker said, "No, no, and no. Rest assured, I will prevail upon Detective Gideon to come back in the future so that you can ask him more questions, but right now all I want to hear is some applause."

The clapping sounded generous to my ears, and I nodded in appreciation.

"I look forward to seeing everyone next month," said Walker. "I'll probably need that long to recover from my annual Cactus to Clouds trek."

Most in the audience seemed to know about Walker's walk, but he explained for those who didn't.

"Every year on the anniversary of my son's death, I hike from the Skyline Trail in Palm Springs to the Mountain Station in Mount San Jacinto. It's my way of making the worst day on the calendar one of the best. Like I'm always saying, we need to find ways to take the sting out of death.

"As we do every meeting, I close with the poetry of Langston Hughes, who I was named for. Tonight, as I often do, I'll recite his poem 'Dreams.'"

Langston the poet, and Langston the cop, urged everyone to hold fast to their dreams lest they become a broken-winged bird incapable of flight. It was a very short poem; it reminded everyone that despite what had happened, they still needed to dream.

We were the living, but many in the room needed to be reminded of that.

CHAPTER 2

THE LAST SUPPER

Walker gave me the name and address of where we would be eating and said he'd meet me there. The restaurant was located in the Baldwin Hills Mall, which was only about two miles from the park.

As Sirius and I settled into the car, I said, "Given the meeting we attended, I think we need some appropriate music for the drive. What do you say we go *really* old school with Bach's *Toccata and Fugue in D Minor*?"

Sirius didn't respond one way or another.

"Maybe organ music is a bit much," I conceded. "But in that case we should probably rule out hard rock as well. So let's eliminate Metallica's 'Fade to Black' and 'For Whom the Bell Tolls.' And I think we also need to rule out Queen's 'The Show Must Go On.'"

I chewed on my lip and deliberated. "Let's not go the ballad route either. No Elton John's 'Candle in the Wind.' But I'm thinking we can choose from three golden oldies: A, Bob Dylan's 'Knockin' on Heaven's Door'; B, Elton John's 'Funeral for a Friend'; or C, Blue Oyster Cult's 'Don't Fear the Reaper.'"

Sirius wagged his tail for both B and C, but C got it by a hair—or hairs. "Tough choice," I agreed, "but what's life without more cowbells?"

In my T-shirt collection I have one with a picture of Christopher Walken and the words *I Got a Fever, and the Only Prescription Is More Cowbell*. It references one of my favorite *Saturday Night Live* skits.

I found the selection on my phone, which synced with the car's sound system, and the music started. It was the right background for me to contemplate our time with the 187 Club. It's one thing to offer up metaphysical musings about death, but it's an entirely different experience when a loved one's life is violently wrested away.

John Donne wrote the sonnet "Death, Be Not Proud." It's an oft-repeated line. I tweaked it a little and said, "Murderers, be not proud."

Sirius offered up a chuff. Great minds think alike.

The restaurant Walker had chosen was called Post and Beam. I didn't know much about it other than that I'd seen celebrity Chef Govind Armstrong's picture with his smiling face and long dreadlocks featured in several publications.

Sirius and I waited for Walker at the outside entrance to the restaurant. The upscale bistro seemed a little out of place at a mall that housed a Walmart, a Taco Bell, and a Fatburger. The vast majority of the mall's patrons were black, just as the surrounding community was predominantly African American.

For a Monday night, it looked like the restaurant had a good crowd. I detected a few side glances thrown my way, which wasn't surprising. I was a north-of-forty white dude with a German shepherd, standing on a sidewalk, which meant I might as well have been screaming, "Cop." People wondered what I was doing there.

After half an hour of waiting and my almost giving up on him, Walker finally appeared. "I'm so sorry," he said. "I had to put out a fire or two. Normally I would have told you to be waiting inside for me with a drink in hand, but I wanted to be here to make sure there was no problem with getting Sirius inside."

"You needn't have worried about that. All police dogs are allowed to dine in restaurants. It's the law in California."

"There are laws and there are laws," said Walker. "When they got rid of Jim Crow laws, people of color could supposedly dine in any restaurant in the land, but that doesn't mean there haven't been occasions when I've run into inexplicably long wait times to get seated."

He led us inside, where the attractive hostess greeted him with a big smile. "It's so nice to see you, Detective Walker," she said. "We have your table on the patio waiting for you and your guests."

Her smile extended to Sirius and to me. "Please follow me."

We were seated on the patio and handed menus. Before the hostess took her leave, I said, "I'd appreciate it if someone could bring my friend a bowl of water."

"Certainly," she said.

I opened the menu and started scanning the offerings. It was an eclectic menu, fusion with a southern soul-food bent.

"I've had everything and everything is good," Walker said. "You shouldn't leave without having the cornbread, and I usually have two or three sides. My favorites are the mac and cheese, the cooked greens, and the black-eyed peas."

"I'm trying to find an accord between my stomach and my mind," I said. "My girlfriend has been trying to get me to eat sensibly. She's even taken to making my lunch lately."

"How's that working for you?"

"Sirius has been eating a lot healthier."

Walker nodded and offered a low laugh.

"Anything you particularly recommend?" I asked.

"I'm a sucker for the cornmeal-crusted catfish or the short ribs."

I consulted with Sirius. "Ribs?" He wagged his tail and I closed the menu.

"We can get him a burger if you want."

I shook my head. "He's a cheap date. Give him a few handouts and he's a happy camper."

A server appeared at our table, a midtwenties African American woman. She put the water bowl in front of Walker, and the two of them began laughing.

"I assumed you were the friend," she said.

"I'll take a water back," Walker said, "not a water bowl."

"Don't worry, Langston, you'll get your Hennessys in a minute."

"You better not serve my Hennessys to that dog," he said. "Leticia, meet Detective Gideon."

We exchanged nods and smiles.

"Before too long I'm going to have to call Leticia *Dr.* Leticia," he said. "She's at USC studying health behavior research."

We put in our orders. After Leticia left us, Walker said, "She knew my son Isaiah. He was her same age."

Walker offered the background as an explanation, not as a solicitation for sympathy. "You got kids, Gideon?"

I shook my head. "My wife and I were planning on having them." My sentence ended with a shrug, which saved me from having to say anything else.

"We had three, two boys and a girl. I remember two years after having our first son, Savannah told me she was pregnant, and all I could think was there was no way we could love our second child as much as we did our first. And then the third time came around when she was pregnant with Isaiah, and I thought, 'Well, there's no way we can love this child as much as the other two.'

"I think people have this mistaken notion that if you have a couple of kids, it's not quite as terrible losing one of them because you still have the others. But love is unique, just as loss is."

I wasn't sure where the conversation was going. Walker didn't strike me as someone looking for commiseration, and I wasn't sure what to say.

He looked up at me and smiled. "In the aftermath of the club's meetings, I tend to get philosophical," he explained.

"You did a good thing starting up the club."

"I'm glad you think so," he said, "especially after the grilling Catalina gave you tonight."

"I can understand her frustration," I said.

"She wasn't kidding about the death threats coming her way. The gangbangers think they can intimidate her. They don't know Catalina."

"What happened to her husband?"

"The Spook Town Compton Crips took exception to where her husband was dealing drugs. They said he was taking business that was theirs."

I nodded. The gang had been active in East Compton for as long as I could remember.

"Crazy world, isn't it, Gideon? You wear red or blue in the wrong neighborhood, and you pay with your life."

"The ultimate fashion statement," I said.

"Catalina says her husband wasn't a dealer. Both of them were enrolled in community college. She thinks his death was a case of mistaken identity, but then she was a newlywed and probably not privy to his secrets."

I thought about Jennifer. I don't suppose anyone thought of us as newlyweds when she died, but in my mind that's how it seemed to me.

"Has Catalina found love in the ashes?" I asked.

Langston didn't seem to understand my reference at first, but then he realized I meant her and James. "I think that hand-holding was more a case of how misery loves company," he said.

"Relationships have been built on a lot less. What does the department think of your trying to have the Ceballos homicide changed from a 'cleared other' to an unsolved homicide?"

Langston shrugged. "The brass is a lot more concerned about the clearance rate than the detectives working the cases. You know how the higher-ups love their good numbers. Something's wrong when top cops care more about appearances than finding killers."

"Victims need an advocate," I said. "It's a good thing they've got the club."

"I wish it wasn't as needed as it is, especially in the black community. I knew when Isaiah was murdered that I had to do something or go crazy."

"Was his killer caught?"

He nodded. "There were three of them in a car. Gangbangers who thought they were evening some score. In their defense they said it was a case of mistaken identity. They thought Isaiah was someone else, as if that should make any difference. Seeing them put away didn't make me feel any better. It was just three more black lives that were lost."

Leticia came up with a tray. She handed Walker his glass of Hennessey and then gave me my Jack Daniel's on the rocks. A basket of cornbread was dropped off between us.

"Would you like a refill, sir?" she asked Sirius.

"Better not," I said. "He's driving."

The two of us started in on the cornbread. I could feel eyes boring into me, and I tore off a piece and tossed it in the air. Sirius made the catch and swallowed it down. Mine disappeared almost as fast. It was delicious.

"Where do you live, Gideon?"

"Sherman Oaks," I said.

"Nice neighborhood for a cop."

"My wife was smart enough to have us buy what was supposed to be our starter home there."

Walker nodded. "We didn't give you a chance to talk much about your work tonight. I hear you and your pooch are pretty much your own bosses."

"Don't tell the COP that," I said, referring to the Chief of Police. "It was his idea to form the Special Cases Unit. I think he did it partly because of need, and partly because he wanted Sirius and me on retainer for the occasional PR appearance. By the way, I'll be counting tonight as one of those PR efforts."

"In that case we'll split the bill."

I wasn't sure whether Walker was kidding. His face was deadpan, his demeanor serious.

"Three ways," he added, with a head bob aimed at Sirius.

I opened my mouth to object, which is when he showed his smile. "Taking the hook was bad enough," he said, "without your also swallowing the line and sinker."

"Now you know why I don't play cards."

"That shows uncommon good sense for a cop. The old rule of thumb is that if you sit down at a poker table and can't identify the sucker in the first half hour, then *you* are the sucker."

We stopped talking when Leticia appeared with our entrees. "The chef had a ham hock he'd finished with," she said. "I had him cut it up, thinking your dog might like that."

"Him?" I said. "What about me?"

Our table quickly filled with the side orders, along with Walker's catfish and my ribs. I started with the mac and cheese; it was love at first bite.

"This ought to be against the law," I said. "It's that good."

"You should bring your girlfriend here."

"I'm not sure if that's a good idea. Lisbet might not let me order the mac and cheese. But I know she'd love the food."

"You know the food has to be good to get white people to come to a black part of L.A."

Walker made his observation with a smile, but it was clear he wasn't joking.

"I don't have to tell you that cops eat at notorious holes-in-the-wall," I said.

He nodded, but qualified it. "Then again, cops aren't your average people."

"True," I agreed, "but you can't blame people for not wanting to eat where they feel scared."

Walker nodded. "That's not only a white thing. I live in the middle of Ladera Heights. Do you know it?"

I shrugged and said, "Not really."

"The residents of Ladera Heights like to keep our three square miles a secret," said Walker. "We're afraid if white people find out about it, they'll start moving in."

"I won't tell any white people about it. I promise."

"The neighborhood's nickname is 'Black Beverly Hills.' I always thought that sounded silly. Ladera Heights doesn't have nearly the wealth, the mansions, or the pretense of Beverly Hills."

"I tried to call the Beverly Hills Police Department last week," I said, "but then I found out they had an unlisted phone number."

Walker laughed. Hearing his deep, throaty amusement made it feel like I was being rewarded.

It was an unhurried dinner, something that I needed to have more of in my life. Walker and I told old cop stories, and I got to hear about the goings-on at the 187 Club. He mentioned his imminent walk and elaborated on the "cactus to clouds" aspect.

"Isaiah and I had talked about doing it," Walker said. "When he was gone, that was one of my regrets. I wished I had just spent more time enjoying his company. To be honest, I don't know if we ever would have done the walk had he lived. I'm no daredevil, and when I see people climbing mountains, running a marathon, or doing extreme sports, I wonder what the hell is motivating them. Let's face it, they always look like they're in agony, which they probably are.

"If I had known what I do now about the walk, I probably would have told Isaiah 'no way.' I just remember him saying, 'Dad, what do you think about the two of us doing the Cactus to Clouds walk?' When you hear it that way, it doesn't sound so bad, does it? Isaiah didn't tell me the details. He just said something about how we'd start in Palm Springs and end up near Idyllwild.

"I didn't know it meant climbing up more than eight Empire State Buildings. I didn't know I'd be looking at having to walk more than ten miles. I didn't know about all the people who'd died during the hike. And we're not just talking about weekend warriors who keeled over from heatstroke and dehydration. There was one professional outdoor guide who bought the farm when he slipped down an ice chute.

"Isaiah had the cactus part right and the cloud part right, but he didn't tell me about what came between them. In order to beat the heat, you need to start before dawn. No water fountains along the way, so you better be hauling lots of liquids. In fact, you better start hydrating the day before the hike, like I'll be doing all of tomorrow. And I'm not sure whether it's harder to deal with the heat or the cold. When you start off in the heat of the valley, it's hard to imagine that you'll be fighting ice by the afternoon. You might even need crampons to keep your footing."

"All of that sounds pretty awful," I said.

"And it feels pretty awful. I'm no spring chicken. And I'm carrying at least twenty-five, hell, thirty-five more pounds than I should be."

"But you've still done it for the last three years?"

"I've made an anniversary of it. At the 187 Club we like to stress the importance of setting aside time for special remembrances of the dead. Isaiah and I make that walk together every year on the anniversary of his death. It's my way of spending time with my son and putting a positive spin on a terrible day. Crazy, right?"

"Not so crazy," I said. "I assume you take the tram back down?"

"You're damn right I do. I'm only half-crazy. The worst thing about that ride is that it only takes about ten minutes to go from Mountain Station to Base Station. It goes too fast."

"My wife and I took that tram years ago," I said. "We swore the next time we did it, we'd dine at that restaurant they've got up at the top."

"Peaks Restaurant," said Walker. "It's supposed to be pretty good, but everyone goes there for the view more than the food. Every year Isaiah and I have a long drink there before I take the tram back down.

You can't imagine the view. You feel like you're on top of the world. I suppose I remember that more than all the aches and pains that come with the hike."

"Memory is a crazy woman that hoards colored rags and throws away food."

Walker wrinkled his brow. "Say what?"

"My shaman next-door neighbor is fond of quoting that."

"One more time," said Walker.

"The shaman part or the quote?"

"The quote."

"Memory is a crazy woman that hoards colored rags and throws away food." Then I remembered the name of the writer. Seth was fond of several of his sayings: "Austin O'Malley."

"I like that. Instead of remembering the real substance, we're more likely to remember the pretty trappings."

"It certainly puts a perspective on what we choose to remember and what we don't."

"And you say your neighbor is a shaman?"

"He is."

"Only in L.A.," said Walker.

I qualified my head-nodding with an explanation: "I actually have a lot of respect for Seth. That's his name. He doesn't go by Soaring Cloud or Deep Waters or anything like that. Seth is one of those people who seem to know just about everything. When Jenny died, he helped guide me through some very difficult times. He did it because I'm a friend, but it's also one of the things he does professionally."

"And he's really an honest-to-goodness shaman?"

"I don't know if you need a license to practice being a shaman in California, but that's his job."

"So he's like a medicine man?"

"I've heard him describe his work as 'spirit healing.'"

"What the hell does that mean?"

"He offers healing tools to those who are sick in spirit. Seth is often a featured speaker in grief workshops."

"If that's the case, why don't you ask him if he'd like to be next month's speaker?"

"I'll do that," I promised.

"I like to get a mix of speakers. Most of the club members are still actively grieving, and they need to hear from someone other than a detective from Robbery-Homicide."

I nodded. "There was a time when I wanted nothing more than working RHD, but working Special Cases meant I could keep Sirius as my partner."

"It took me a lot of years in the field before I finally got to Robbery-Homicide," said Walker. "I'm not sure it was the best match for me. You know that Peter Principle thing about rising to the level of your incompetence? Now I'm not saying I was a bad detective. And I know no one outworked me. But some detectives seem to have this sixth sense. They intuit what's happened. I was always more plodding. I would work the evidence like a dog chewing his bone. I'd work it every which way, but the problem is sometimes you don't have the luxury of time to do that. You get assigned another case, and then another. When I look back at my years in Robbery-Homicide, it's the unsolved cases that gnaw at me."

"All of us have cases we haven't made."

"There's a difference between haven't made and should have made."

"You don't sound very retired to me."

"There's a *ghost* that's been haunting me," he said. "I'm working to put it to bed."

His affable expression hardened, as did his tone. The cold case was clearly important to him. Before I had a chance to ask him about it, Leticia approached our table, and his scowl turned to a smile.

"I heard your sweet tooth calling," she said, and we never did get back around to the ghost.

CHAPTER 3

A LONG WAY FROM HOME

Despite Walker's threat about splitting the check, he must have slipped Leticia his credit card when I wasn't looking, thwarting any chance for me to pay.

"Let's not be strangers," he said, and then he bent down and scratched Sirius's ear and told him, "Give my best to Little Red Riding Hood."

Walker stayed behind to give his regards to several of the staff while Sirius and I made our way out to the car. Because Sirius hadn't gotten enough in the way of handouts, I pulled out a dog protein bar from the food stock I keep for him. According to the ingredients on the label, his protein bar contained beef, bison, peas, flaxseed, carrots, broccoli, and blueberries.

"Good, huh?" I asked.

Sirius gave a few weak wags of his tail and began eating his bar, although it was clear he was a lot less interested in it than he had been in the pecan praline sweet potato pie Leticia had dropped off for dessert. I really couldn't blame him.

* * *

Our Sherman Oaks home is about a twenty-mile drive from the restaurant, but in its own way it could have been another world. I was going from a black and urban neighborhood to one that was white and suburban. As ethnically diverse as L.A. is by the numbers, neighborhoods still tend to divide along racial and ethnic lines. Within L.A.'s borders are Koreatown, Chinatown, Little Tokyo, Little Salvador, Little Osaka, and Little Armenia. The Fairfax District is sometimes called Little Israel. Much of Westwood has a large Persian population and is referred to as Tehrangeles.

Before we began our drive home, I lined up the musical selections. Peter Gabriel and Biko would lead off, followed by Joan Baez's dulcet tones singing about a terrible bombing in "Birmingham Sunday." Bob Marley's "War" seemed like a good choice, as did Neil Young's "Southern Man." My personal concert would conclude with the gospel singing of Odetta and "Motherless Child." Her version was a favorite of mine, although I had three or four covers of it.

The musical selections combined to give off the feeling of a long, thoughtful aperitif. Odetta started singing just as we entered the borders of Sherman Oaks. Even though I like to pretend that being abandoned as a baby doesn't play on my psyche, because I was adopted there's a part of me that feels like a motherless child. Of course when the song was written more than a century ago, it spoke to slave children being sold and taken away from their parents. Modern listeners take away their own notions of being a long way from home. Some of us measure it by the absence of a mother's arms; others look at it as separation from a place; many think about a bygone time. The universal pull and pall is an absence and a yearning.

"Such a long, long way from home," I sang.

Sirius nudged me. I think it was more a case of my sounding sad than my butchering a song, or at least that's what I wanted to believe. My partner doesn't like it when I sing the blues, even when I do a passable job.

"You're right," I said. "Home is where the dog is."

* * *

After we parked in our driveway, I took Sirius for a long walk. Dogs have a nose for news, because they have 220 million olfactory receptors, compared to humans' five million. With a good sniff, Sirius knew who and what had passed by that day.

There are dogs trained to detect medical conditions, bedbugs, termites, explosives, and drugs. Rescue dogs find the living under piles of snow; cadaver dogs locate the dead.

No wonder we humans put our nose to the grindstone. It's not good for much else.

"I'm still waiting for you to find me a truffle," I said.

Sirius wagged his tail and did a little more sniffing. No truffle was forthcoming.

It was a pleasant night. The temperature was in the low sixties, and there wasn't any wind. Sirius was transfixed by a scent he'd picked up. I didn't hurry him along even though I was ready to hit the sack.

If I was lucky, I would sleep without interruption. My fire dreams are more infrequent now, although they still occur more than I like. I hope one day they'll disappear altogether, but that's wishful thinking, which I know is no way to overcome my PTSD. I've known too many guys like me. We behave like the Black Knight in *Monty Python and the Holy Grail.* We lose an arm and insist, "It's only a scratch." We're bleeding out and proclaim, "It's just a flesh wound."

"It's just a dream," I tell Lisbet and Seth.

Of course when I tell that to Sirius, he knows what a liar I am.

CHAPTER 4

A SHAGGY DOG STORY

In police work you're never between cases. There's always overdue paperwork to catch up with, witnesses to interview, and depositions that need to be scheduled. All detectives have unsolved cases. There are crime scenes that need to be recanvassed and subpoenas that need to be served.

With all that said, though, there are periods of feast and famine, times when there aren't enough hours in the day, and times when you can catch your breath and even smell the roses. I was in one of those not-so-pressing periods. While I had plenty of work to catch up on, at the moment it didn't feel as if I was being squeezed by a vise. That was a good thing, because it was April 14, and like most red-blooded procrastinating Americans, I hadn't turned in my taxes. Still, I was rather proud of myself; there have been years when I haven't gotten around to doing my taxes until April 15.

"You'd think I could write off all the Frisbees and balls you've chewed up," I told Sirius, "not to mention your flea medication."

Maybe because I wasn't overly preoccupied, I found myself thinking about the talk I'd given the night before to the 187 Club and my evening with Langston Walker. The night had been much less difficult than I'd expected. Walker had put me at ease, and for the most part the club members had been respectful, especially given their circumstances. Only those who've experienced the homicide of a loved one can understand its engulfing anguish. Often it's a pain that keeps on giving.

Later in the week I'd call up Walker and thank him for dinner. I knew that today he was hydrating and preparing for his hike, and that tomorrow he'd be on the trail before the sun was up. He'd travel from the cacti to the clouds, walking with the memory of his son Isaiah.

"Death and taxes," I told Sirius, "death and taxes."

* * *

We made it to the post office before it closed. As a reward, I went to bed at ten thirty. Sirius settled on the carpet right next to the bed. When I have my fire dreams, Sirius is always there to wake me up.

"I suppose you didn't brush your teeth or say your prayers," I said.

The pot was calling the kettle black, but that wasn't something I mentioned.

"How about I offer up a short poem to the universe?"

I cleared my throat and quoted from Anna Hempstead Branch: "If there is no God for thee, then there is no God for me."

It was easy to remember Branch's poem because of its brevity. Elizabeth Barrett Browning wrote a poem for her dog Flush that goes on for about a hundred lines. That's why I don't remember any of it. Of course I'm not convinced Browning's Sonnet 43 wasn't written for Flush as well.

How do I love thee? Let me count the filets.

Sleep came on quickly and thoroughly. That's why it was so difficult emerging from my deep slumber. I awakened to Sirius's insistent pawing and whimpering. Usually that's how he awakens me from my fire nightmare, but since I wasn't sweating, hyperventilating, or going up in flames, it was clear something else was causing his alarm.

"What is it?" I asked.

Sirius offered a single, excited bark. I knew it wasn't the call of nature; he has a dog door that leads out to the porch.

My partner nudged me, insisting I get up. "Okay, okay," I said.

He ran to the bedroom door and then back to me. It was his way of telling me to get a move on.

"Yes, boss," I said, looking for my slippers and the one old robe I own.

While dressing I heard the nearby yipping of coyotes. "It better not be those coyotes that have you riled up," I said.

Hearing coyotes in our neighborhood wasn't uncommon, and I knew of several cat owners along the block who'd lost their pets to the predators. One neighbor with a home-surveillance system said he regularly recorded a pack of coyotes using our street as a throughway. We weren't far from an urban canyon, the pack's likely home.

Sirius had never been bothered by the coyote yips and howls before. This time, though, something was different.

"Has Timmy fallen down the well again, Lassie?" I asked.

Sirius barked at me, not hiding his impatience. It was clear he wanted me moving at warp speed. I didn't stop to get a leash, confident that Sirius would stay at my side as he always does, but as soon as I opened the door, he voiced a sound new to me, a growl that carried as if it had been snarled out of a bullhorn. It was an announcement and a call of the wild.

Then he raced off. Usually he runs silently. Not this time. He was announcing himself like an oncoming locomotive.

His roar caused a stir among the coyotes. Their alarmed cries filled the air. I did some calling of my own.

"Sirius! Sirius!"

I ran in the direction where I'd seen my partner race off. Sirius is much bigger than a coyote, but it sounded as if he was ready to take on the whole pack. I cursed myself for not having brought a bat, and stopped long enough to grab a few cobblestones out of the dry creek that runs through Seth's front yard.

The stones proved unnecessary. Judging by the retreating yips, the coyote pack was in full retreat.

"Sirius!" I called again.

Fifteen seconds passed and I shouted his name once more. This time he reappeared. His posture was a combination of triumph—"Look! I dispatched the enemy!"—and guilt. Sirius knew he'd run off without my leave.

"*Hier!*" I commanded.

His posture lowered near to the ground, his skulking body language asking my forgiveness.

"*Was ist los?*"

The German translation is: What is going on? Sirius knew what I was really saying was, "What the hell were you up to?"

He pressed himself against my side, and his eyes went from the ground up to mine and then back to the ground. He whined, a short little note. Imagine a child trying to say there's a good reason he shouldn't be punished for violating some rule. It was almost as if Sirius was saying, "There's a very good explanation for what I did."

"*Sitz,*" I said, and he immediately sat.

His obedience didn't come without offering up a plaintive note, though. His head kept moving, this time looking from me off into the distance. Something was out there, he was telling me. His body was tensed. He didn't want to stay put; the only reason he was at my side and doing what I was asking of him was to make me happy.

"Okay," I said. "*Voraus!*"

I gave him leave to "go out." He sprinted away, but before he was out of sight, he stopped to turn around and bark at me. I was being told to follow. Then Sirius continued running down the road. Before I lost sight of him, he stopped long enough to turn around and bark at me once more. It didn't take a dog whisperer to understand he was telling me, "Hurry up, Jack."

"Yeah, yeah," I said.

Slippers aren't very good for jogging, but I made do. By that time Sirius had turned the corner and come to a stop. In the darkness I could just make out a shadowed form that Sirius was hovering over. As I drew closer, I could see movement. A dog was struggling to rise to its feet. Quivering limbs spoke to its will, but the effort was too much and the dog collapsed in a heap.

As I approached, the dog offered up a deep growl. Sirius responded by gently licking one of the dog's wounds. If I was being anthropomorphic, I would have said he was telling the dog, "There, there."

I heeded the growl and stayed my distance. The dog was medium-size, a mixed breed with spotting on the chest, and looked to be mostly hound. I was pretty sure the dog was female based on how Sirius was treating her. Generally he gets along better with females.

There wasn't enough light for me to see very well, but it was clear the dog was hurt. I wondered if the coyotes had gotten to her. She was panting, and her coat was dirty.

"It's okay," I said, speaking in my most calming voice.

The dog growled, but this time without as much throat. Sirius redoubled his licking, vouching for me.

"I'm not going to hurt you," I said, and moved a little closer.

Maybe the dog believed me. Maybe Sirius had sold me as one of the good ones. She watched me closely, but stopped growling. I noticed she turned her head to follow my movements. The reason for that could be seen in the milky patch of her left eye, an indication she was probably blind in that one. Sirius seemed to know that already. He'd positioned himself on the side of her bad eye.

"How are you, girl?" I asked.

Even in the dim light I could see she wasn't doing well. The pads of her feet were worn and bloody, and she continued to pant. Everything was telling me the dog was dehydrated.

"Sirius, stay," I said.

The command was probably unnecessary. It looked like he wasn't about to leave his companion.

I turned around and began jogging home. The neighborhood was quiet, and there was no traffic. As I ran, I considered my options. No one was on duty at animal control; personnel wouldn't come on until the morning. That meant it was up to me until then. I thought about covering the dog with a blanket and making sure she had plenty of fluids. But what if the coyotes returned? I couldn't leave an injured animal to that fate. That meant I had to find a way to bring the dog home with us. Luckily I had some specialized equipment that might help me transport her without getting bitten.

Once home, I raced around and gathered everything. Instead of taking the time to put on a full bite suit, I just put on an arm sleeve. Then I grabbed a gallon of water, a bowl, a blanket, a glove, and some dog treats. Everything got tossed into a garden cart, which I pulled along behind me. I was halfway down the front pathway when I heard a familiar voice in the darkness.

"Are you running away to join the circus?"

I suppose I did resemble a runaway. "You seem to have forgotten I already work there."

Seth Mann joined me. Though he must have been awakened by the noise, he was still smiling like the Happy Buddha he physically resembled. "So, where are we headed to at two thirty in the morning?"

"Sirius is standing guard over a dog that looks like she's been through the wringer. He ran off a pack of coyotes that I suspect had the intention of making a meal of her."

"That explains the roar I heard, followed by the annoyed sounds of you calling Sirius's name."

"He tends to be hard of hearing when there's a damsel in distress."

"Is that an ongoing problem?"

"I would categorize it more as a display of testosterone than I would a problem."

"There are always neuticles," he said.

"New to what?"

"Neuticles," he said. "Fake balls for male dogs that get neutered."

"You're kidding. Or should I say, 'Are you *nuts*?'"

"One of my clients swears by them. He says his dog's behavior is much improved since he was neutered. The only reason he hesitated having the procedure done was that he didn't want his dog's appearance altered."

"Your client is crazy."

"He says half a million dogs are walking around with neuticles."

"The thought of that gives me the *willies*."

"I blame myself for initiating this line of conversation."

"You should. And you should also know K-9 dogs are purposely left intact. There are situations that call for ample aggression, and that means balls to the wall and no neuticles need apply."

"Say no more. The topic is now closed."

"You don't need to be *testes*."

Seth sighed. I was at least hoping for a groan. The appearance of Sirius, who came bounding over to see one of his favorite people in the world, spared Seth from more puns.

Sirius led us back to his friend, who growled at our approach. Seth pulled up short and gave me a look.

"I'm pretty sure her bark is worse than her bite," I said. "Everything I've seen suggests she's doing it more out of habit than intent."

Sirius played the role of ambassador, moving back and forth between his friend and the two of us, assuring everyone that all was well with the wagging of his tail.

"I think she's blind in her left eye," I said. "I'm favoring her good eye so as not to spook her."

I filled a bowl with water, and then slowly, carefully, drew close to the wounded dog.

"How about some water?" I asked. My voice was high and unthreatening.

I placed the bowl on the ground. She tried to stand and drink, but her legs were too wobbly, prompting me to reposition the bowl so she didn't have to get up. She immediately started drinking and didn't stop until the bowl was empty. With measured, deliberate movements I retrieved the bowl, filled it once more, and again placed it within reach of her muzzle. She quickly finished most of what was there.

Seth asked, "How do you say, 'I come in peace?' in caninese?"

"I am a firm believer in the time-honored method of bribery."

I gave Sirius a sweet potato-and-duck strip, and then offered one to his friend. She seemed shy about taking it from my hand, but when I put it on the ground, she made quick work of it.

Each of the dogs was given another strip. Bit by bit I narrowed the distance between me and the wounded dog. She was mindful of my proximity, but no longer looked threatened by it.

Speaking in a calm, happy tone, I said to Seth, "You can see by her pads they're almost worn away. There's a lot of cracking and bleeding on them. She's traveled a long way and gotten a few wounds along the way. I'm not sure if those coyotes took a few bites out of her, or whether it was dog versus car, with the car winning.

"She's not wearing a collar. My idea is to drape the blanket over her body. If I can get her comfortable, I'll try and lift her into the wagon. I'm going to take it slow, reading her body language every step of the way."

"What do you want me to do?" Seth asked.

"As wobbly as she is, she still might think about making a run for it. I want you standing between her and the open road. I also want you monitoring her and looking for the same things that I am. I'll be listening to the seriousness of her growling and watching for any sign of her hackles rising. You see how she's looking at me? That's a good thing. If she begins averting her gaze, that could signal trouble. One of the big telltale signs in a spooked dog is whale eyes. That's where you see the whites of a dog's eyes in the corners and rims. Dogs bite when they feel threatened. Of course I'm going to do my best to present my padded arm as the only potential target."

"Is your Last Will and Testament in order?"

"I'm more worried about the possibility of needing to order my own set of neuticles."

"You're lucky dogs pick up on tone and vibes more than what's being said," said Seth, referring to how we'd been doing all of our talking in overly polite tones. "You sound as slick as a used-car salesman."

"Thanks so much for that comparison," I said.

"Unctuous becomes you."

"Fuck you very much," I said, sounding like I was offering him the greatest of compliments.

I offered another treat to Sirius and his friend. As they were eating, I gently spread the blanket over her body.

"So far so good. Now's the tough part."

I talked to the dog all the while I repositioned myself: "That's a good girl. You're a very good girl. Does that blanket feel nice?"

When I squatted down next to her, Sirius came over to my side. Most of the time when I get down low, he thinks we're playing a game. He wagged his tail while I worked my hands through his mane. His friend was watching us. I felt emboldened enough to reach a tentative hand out to her. She sniffed my hand for a few seconds and seemed to be reassured by whatever she smelled.

"That's a good girl," I said, gently stroking her.

I wanted her to get used to my touch. At first she didn't feel or look relaxed, but she didn't growl, raise her hackles, or offer up whale eyes.

"That's right," I said. "You're doing so well. You're a good girl."

I continued with the platitudes, and the petting, until her posture grew less rigid. Sirius helped the effort by doing his version of a licking massage.

"It's showtime," I said to Seth. "I'm going to lift her now."

I put a padded glove on my hand and then draped my arm with the bite sleeve around her midsection. She growled, and I said in my most soothing voice, "It's all right."

Her growls grew increasingly louder as I lifted her up. The cart was only two steps away. Over her growls, Sirius and I both spoke; he offered encouraging sounds while I said, "That's a good girl." I think she was more swayed by Sirius's reassurances than mine. With great care I deposited her into the wagon. I took a step back and let out half a minute's worth of pent-up air.

"I think you've earned yourself a drink," said Seth.

"Just so long as it's not the hair of the dog that bit me."

CHAPTER 5

LITTLE ORPHAN ANNIE

After converting the laundry room into what felt like a miniature M*A*S*H unit, we began working on the patient. Sirius played the role of mother hen. It quickly became apparent I wasn't the best Florence Nightingale. My shaman friend proved a much better nurse, and he was the one who applied the Betadine solution to the dog's wounds, as well as the Neosporin to her paw pads.

"Dogs sweat from their paw pads," I said, offering up a tidbit of information learned during my time with Metropolitan K-9, but really just pretending to be useful while Seth did his careful work. "I'm thinking we should leave the pads exposed."

"Normally I'd opt for booties to stop her from licking at the Neosporin," he said, "but I think she's at her limit now, and I don't want to push her any further than we already have."

He stepped back from his work and gestured to his patient. "What do you think?"

The question wasn't directed to me, but to Sirius, who'd been at his side assisting the entire time. Sirius began sniffing at the shaman's handiwork.

"Maybe it's the patient you should be asking," I said. "What kind of job did he do, Little Orphan Annie?"

The dog surprised me by turning her head toward me. She was responding to some cue, some familiar word. I thought about what I might have said and ventured a guess.

"Does that feel better, *Annie?*" I asked, emphasizing the name.

If I hadn't been looking, I wouldn't have seen the small movement of her tail.

"I think our patient's name is *Annie*," I told Seth.

Once more there was an almost imperceptible movement of her tail.

"Good girl, *Annie*," said Seth.

Annie wasn't the only one exhibiting approval. Sirius finished with his examination of Seth's work and began wagging his tail.

"You approve, Dr. Sirius?" asked Seth.

"Wasn't it you who lectured me about the perils of giving Sirius human titles?"

"It's not like I'm claiming Sirius is a board-certified surgeon. His doctorate is honorary."

"What in?"

"Canine Studies, with a minor in Interspecies Relationships with Difficult Humans."

"Really?"

"The important word is 'honorary.'"

"His degree should be in Thinkology."

"What is Thinkology?"

"That's what was written on the diploma Ray Bolger received in *The Wizard of Oz*."

"Fine, Sirius's *honorary* degree is in Thinkology."

"On second thought, I don't think his degree should be in Thinkology."

"Why not?"

"Because after the Scarecrow was given his diploma, he immediately demonstrated flawed thinking by citing the Pythagorean Theorem and stating, 'The sum of the square roots of any two sides of an isosceles triangle is equal to the square root of the remaining side.'"

"And what's wrong with that?"

"Pythagoras really said that the square of the hypotenuse, which is the side opposite the right angle, is equal to the sum of the squares of the other two sides."

"I am impressed by your knowledge of mathematics."

"Don't be. I memorized the facts in order to support the movie trivia."

While the two of us had been discussing Dr. Sirius's credentials, the good doctor had taken it upon himself to sidle in next to Annie. She seemed a lot more comforted by his contact than she had been by our doctoring.

Both dogs settled into the blankets that had been laid down on the floor. I filled up a water bowl, and next to it placed a bowl of kibble. The dogs already looked as if they were asleep.

"I think his honorary degree should be in comforting," said Seth.

I nodded. "A few years ago I saw this video on YouTube where this dog went to try and help another dog that had been hit by a car. It was a busy highway with lots of traffic. But that didn't stop our four-legged hero. He managed to get to the dog that had been hit and began dragging him to the side of the road. You can't teach that kind of behavior. I know it's what Sirius would have done, and I'm pretty sure I'm not being anthropomorphic. He always wants to help those in need. It's part of him."

"What happened to the dog hit by the car?"

I shook my head. "He was already dead. All those cars kept speeding by his body."

"What about the rescue dog?"

"It was believed to be homeless. Lots of people wanted to adopt that brave dog, but it couldn't be found."

I turned out the laundry-room light, but not before saying, "Good night, Sirius, good night, Annie."

* * *

Seth and I settled in the living room, where I played host. We both decided on the need for caffeine, and I made each of us a Kahlúa and coffee.

"To being up with the owls," was Seth's toast.

We clicked coffee mugs. "Owl you need is love," I added.

Midswallow, Seth's expression soured. "That answers that question."

"What question was that?"

"Whether you make bad puns while you sleep."

I wasn't quite asleep, but I was comfortable. The coffee and alcohol and sugar and late hour somehow combined for a calming effect, and both of us sipped contentedly.

"So what are you going to do with Annie?" he asked.

"I'll see if anyone is looking for their lost dog, even if I'm not hopeful of finding the owner. I always think it's a bad sign when I see a dog not wearing a collar. At best it speaks to an irresponsible owner."

"It's possible she just lost her collar. That could have happened during her journey. It's clear she's traveled a long way. Something was pushing her to keep going."

"Male dogs, especially unneutered male dogs, have the reputation of wandering much more than females."

"So what was driving our Little Orphan Annie?"

I did a Winston Churchill bulldog face and said, "She's a riddle, wrapped in a mystery, inside an enigma."

"I thought you were supposed to be the dog whisperer," said Seth.

"Tomorrow morning I'm taking her to the real dog whisperer, which is Sirius's vet. I'll see what she can tell me about Annie. Afterward I'll do my Sherlock Bones thing and see if I can track down her owners.

I hope to hell she wasn't abandoned. On the asshole scale, people who abandon their dogs are right up there near the top."

"One day I should write a paper on Michael Gideon's Asshole Scale and determine if there is a correlation with Dante's Circles of Hell."

"The world could only benefit from such a study. But of course Dante had it much easier than I did. Back when he was writing, there were a relatively small number of people in hell. While he was dealing with millions, I'm working with billions."

"But not everyone is an asshole, correct?"

"That's true. Maybe we need to explore a formula that you could expand upon in your paper, something like AH equals some constant percentage of the population."

"I'd need more specific parameters for your AH scale. For example, I've heard you refer to some individuals as major-league assholes, whereas others have been categorized as buttholes, anuses, anal orifices, dinguses, and the like."

"It's a sliding scale," I admitted, "but at the top are pedophiles and those who physically abuse, as well as those who abandon their animals. Those would be the major-league assholes."

It was a ridiculous conversation, of course, but it was the middle of the night and the two of us were both punch drunk. We were good friends making silly conversation, as only good friends can do.

"Can I get you a refill?"

Seth contemplated his empty glass and said, "How about half a drink?"

"That sounds about right to me."

I went and poured us half a drink each. When I handed Seth his libation, he raised his mug and said, "To Aristotle, who said the antidote to fifty enemies was one friend."

It was the middle of the night, and we were toasting a philosopher who'd been dead for more than two thousand years. Somehow it all made sense.

CHAPTER 6

ALONE IN THE DARKNESS

Heather awakened with a splitting headache. Her mouth felt gummy and dry, and her throat was sore. She was dehydrated, and in her fog she found herself reaching over to where she expected to find her water glass. Every night she placed it on the nightstand next to her bed. It wasn't there, though. That was strange. She always kept her water glass handy. And what were those clanking sounds accompanying the movements of her arm?

She opened her eyes. Even though it was dark, she could see that she wasn't in her room. She could also see the reason for the clanking noises. Her arms and legs were chained to the wall.

Her sharp intake of breath gave her the moment's reprieve needed to not start screaming. As she fought off panic, she tried to remember what had happened to her. She recalled how Angie had alerted her to the presence of an intruder, and how she'd barely gotten Angie out the window when her door crashed open. The home invasion had occurred on the heels of Emilio's threat to make her "pay."

Heather remembered thrashing around on the floor. One moment she'd been in her bed, and the next she was convulsing. She'd been on the wrong end of a Taser, or stun gun, or something that made her flop around out of control. The attack had left her helpless and incapacitated; she hadn't even been able to scream. She had some slight recollection of a foul-smelling rag being forced up against her nose and mouth. Probably chloroform or ether—wasn't that what kidnappers always used? Whatever it was, she'd blacked out without even being able to say a word.

How long had she been out of it? The memory of nightmares kept intruding into her thoughts. Or were they nightmares? She had this bad feeling about what had gone on, even if specifics eluded her. She seemed to remember having awakened a few times, but only for a matter of seconds. Her grogginess, and her thirst, made her suspect she'd been drugged multiple times during her captivity.

She took stock of her surroundings. The chains weren't the only things holding her. She was confined to the inside of a small jail cell. The cell had been built into a square room with thick concrete walls. It looked like a bunker of some kind, with ceilings that appeared to have been lined with acoustical soundproofing panels.

She tested out the soundproofing of the room by screaming, "Help! Help!"

Her plea was swallowed up. Heather took in as much air as she could so as to give it her all: "Help!"

She tried to shake the walls and did her best to make her voice a trumpet, but the soundproofing and the concrete muted her cries. The room gave up only the slightest echo; it was as if the cavern had absorbed her scream and spat back a disdainful whisper.

Heather began shaking her chains. Forgotten was her promise not to panic. She fought her iron bonds with all her strength, but succeeded only in slicing her skin. Her screams started up again, but there was a difference this time. She wasn't testing the acoustics. She was voicing her terror.

CHAPTER 7

A CHIP OFF THE OLD DOC

Before Seth left, I told him about my meeting with the 187 Club, and Langston Walker's interest in having him as their next month's speaker. Seth promised that he'd call Walker, and said that as far as he knew, he was available.

"Murder is not an easy subject to deal with," he said, speaking like a shaman.

"You're telling me," I said, speaking like a cop.

"With such a traumatic ending of life, the soul often needs assistance in settling. The survivor also needs assistance so as to not be stuck in grief. Healing is needed on many levels."

Being a skeptic, I said nothing. Seth doesn't mind my being a Doubting Thomas. He believes that's part of my journey.

"I'll see if my friend Rose is also available to attend," Seth said. "She has a way with click sticks that seems to resonate with all."

Seth's ceremonies often involve native instruments from around the world. Sometimes he brings his work home, and his backyard sounds like the soundtrack to a Peter Weir film, complete with didgeridoos, drumming, bells, birdcalls, jaw harps, and rattles.

"I'm sure that would be appreciated," I said.

I refrained from asking if there would also be cowbells.

* * *

When I awoke it felt strange to not have Sirius by my side, but I knew my partner was where he needed to be.

I found Sirius and Annie in the living room. Sirius had led her to where the first light of the morning showed itself, and both of them were sunbathing.

"Good morning," I said.

Sirius bounded over and gave me the kind of greeting that humans would only give if you hit a walk-off homer or game-winning shot. Annie stood up and slowly approached. I didn't expect a hero's welcome from her, and didn't get one. Still, it was good seeing her moving around. She sniffed my hand by way of greeting. Sleep, hydrating, and eating had her looking much better.

I decided we could all do with breakfast. After putting some olive oil in a frying pan, I made sunny-side up eggs. In the same pan I heated up leftover spinach and cut-up apple. The dogs didn't get salt and pepper on their eggs; I did. I also sprinkled some sugar and cinnamon on my apples. They went without.

While the dogs ate in the kitchen, I sat at the counter. I'm not sure who finished first, but in short order there were three clean plates, and I picked up the phone.

Sirius's vet is Dr. Emma Wolf. Instead of harboring resentment at her parents for giving her such a name, Dr. Wolf is actually grateful to them. She's convinced her vocation was preordained and claims that from the time she was a girl she knew she would be a vet.

During our last office visit, I'd noticed that Dr. Wolf was wearing an engagement ring. She told me her fiancé was named Andrew Fox, and her dilemma was whether to hyphenate her married name or change it from Wolf to Fox. Their union, Dr. Wolf was sure, had also been fated because of their names. Of course she probably would have said the same thing if she was marrying a man with the last name of Boxer, Shepherd, Pointer, Basset, or Cocker.

We lucked into a late cancellation; Dr. Wolf had time for us that morning.

* * *

Annie didn't resist when I slipped one of Sirius's old collars around her neck, and when I walked her to the car it was clear she'd been taught the basic commands of heeling and sitting. She was also no stranger to traveling in a car. Instead of me having to lift her up to the seat, she followed Sirius's lead and jumped in. I secured the two dogs side by side, and during our drive I kept looking in the rearview mirror to observe how they were doing. Sirius's presence clearly comforted Annie, and she huddled close to him. I had the back windows cracked open, and a breeze circulated through the car. Annie kept sampling what the flowing air brought her.

Now that she was no longer dehydrated, I could see that Annie was a drool machine and clearly couldn't care less where her drool landed. When she shook her head, her long, droopy ears flapped back and forth. In fact, her entire face seemed to be in motion, with her jowls and wrinkles also flapping. Whenever she shook her head, there was no safe spot. Even sitting in the driver's seat, I couldn't escape being hosed down in drool.

Her constant sniffing reminded me of the way an oenophile takes stock of a wine's bouquet. She seemed to be searching for something, her head shifting from side to side. At one point she perked up, becoming alert and pulling at her restraints, but her excitement didn't last long. Whatever she was looking for proved elusive. When the scent disappeared, Annie acted listless and dispirited.

Dr. Wolf's practice was located off Ventura Boulevard. Whenever we go for a visit, I think of the group America and their song "Ventura Highway." It's a quintessential Southern California song, with a mellow vibe and beat. The song's refrain "in the air" seemed appropriate for Annie. She was looking for something in the air.

It was Dr. Wolf who'd helped with Sirius's recovery from our run-in with Ellis Haines. The caring way in which she tended to my partner left me forever in her debt. She and the other vets in her practice like to refer to themselves as "the love doctors." They are definitely the new age group in town, offering holistic medicine, acupuncture, chiropractic services, and nutritional programs that include raw foods, vegetarian and vegan diets, and natural supplements. I'm fond of telling everyone that Sirius has more healthful options than I do.

The three of us were shown into one of the waiting rooms. Annie was led to the walk-on scale and weighed in at sixty-two pounds. The receptionist asked me a number of questions about Annie, most of which I couldn't answer. She agreed with me that Annie was a "hound mix of the Heinz 57 varieties."

A minute later Dr. Wolf appeared. "Sirius!" she said.

That was all she had to say. My partner was immediately putty in her hands. It was only after she told Sirius what a handsome boy he was and scratched him in those places he liked most that she acknowledged me. I knew where I ranked.

"Good morning, Detective Gideon," she said, extending her hand.

"How are you, Dr. Wolf? Or is it Dr. Fox?"

"I'll be a lone wolf for the next two months," she said, smiling. "As for what happens after that, we're still working out the name logistics."

"Maybe the two of you should compromise and change both of your last names to Coyote."

Dr. Wolf had to think about that for a second before she started laughing. She had a good sense of humor, but it came with a slight time delay. It always seemed to take her a moment to realize I was joking.

Personally I hoped she'd keep her name. She struck me more as a wolf than a fox; maybe that's because her hair was dark and not red.

"Hi, sweetie," she said to Annie, beginning her examination by gently touching her. "What do we have here?"

I explained how Annie had come into my life the night before. While I talked, Dr. Wolf continued her teeth-to-tail evaluation.

"She was bleeding last night in a couple of places," I said, "and at first I thought her wounds might have been caused by coyotes. A friend helped me apply Betadine, but upon closer inspection, her wounds didn't look as if they were caused by bites. I'm thinking she might have been grazed by a car."

"Uh-huh," said the doctor, but I couldn't tell if she was agreeing or just showing that she was listening.

"I would be cautious when approaching her blind eye," she said. "I can see she's a little skittish."

"I've noticed she prefers Sirius on that side," I said.

"Smart dog," said Dr. Wolf. "I'd want Sirius protecting my blind spot as well."

Her attention moved to the pads of Annie's feet.

"When I found her, all her pads were worn and cracked and bleeding," I said. "They each got a coating of Neosporin."

Another "Uh-huh" was offered as Dr. Wolf intently searched the inside of Annie's ears.

"No tattoos," she announced.

"Why would there be tattoos?"

"Although it's not as common now, some dogs still get tattooed inside their ears with a number that links them to a national dog registry."

Dr. Wolf finished her examination of Annie, gave her a friendly pat, and said, "Good girl," and then turned to me.

"I think our Annie has been on quite a journey, but I don't think she's been a vagabond for more than two or three days. Despite the outward signs, everything else indicates she's been well cared for. Her wounds and the abrasions on her pads are all recent."

"I wonder what caused her to be a runaway."

She stroked the loose folds of skin beneath Annie's chin. "These dewlaps indicate the bloodhound in her. Her black spotting looks like what you'd find on a coonhound, but she's not as large as a purebred bloodhound or coonhound, so there are a few more mixes in her. Overall, though, I'd say bloodhound predominates. Her behavior says that as well.

"Bloodhounds are known to be quite independent. Detractors might say they're stubborn. Part of that has to do with their physiology. I've heard them referred to as 'noses with dogs attached.' They most definitely are scent-oriented. I think you're right about this one having been grazed by a car. That doesn't surprise me either. With her nose leading her, I'm sure she was taking no notice of cars or anything else. Her priority was following the scent wherever it took her."

"So you think Annie glommed onto something and just kept going until she dropped?"

Dr. Wolf nodded. "Tracking dogs have been known to follow a scent more than a hundred miles. And their olfactory senses are such that they've been able to track down a scent ten days old and more."

"How is it that they can pick out one scent among so many?"

"In general they're able to key onto a combination of things. They can be following an odor unique to an individual, or their breath, their sweat, the smell of their skin, or a combination of all those things. Annie has a sense of smell that's a thousand times better than yours. It's believed that certain hounds create an odor image that goes from their nose to their brain. We carry mental pictures of what people look like in our heads; Annie and her ilk have scent images."

"So in military terms, Annie gets a radar lock on her target?"

"I think that analogy is more apt than not."

"Remind me not to get in your crosshairs," I told Annie.

She shook her head and sent slobber everywhere. "Don't tell me her drooling also helps with her sense of smell."

"Not exactly," said Dr. Wolf, "but I have heard that bloodhound wrinkles catch scent particles that have been swept up by their ears. Most experts seem to think that their droopy ears sweeping along the ground stir up scents. So I guess in an indirect way, you can say the slobber is the price you pay for their having such a marvelous nose."

Even though I made it clear to Dr. Wolf that I had no intention of keeping Annie, she warned me that hounds were susceptible to GDV—gastric dilation-volvulus—and what to watch out for. I was also warned to keep water out of her long ears, as the breed was prone to ear infections. Her final piece of advice was to not leave Annie alone in my house unless I wanted to return to a scene of devastation. Hounds needed lots of exercise and definitely didn't take to being cooped up, she said.

"I've set aside the day to find the owner," I told her, "and if that doesn't work, I'm afraid I'll have to take her to the shelter. I've heard most dogs are found within four blocks of their home, but I'm guessing Annie traveled a lot of miles, which is going to make finding her owner harder. Of course I'm going to put posters up in the neighborhood and call the local shelter and—"

"Before you go to the trouble of putting up posters," said Dr. Wolf, "I'm hoping Annie has a microchip in her."

I had put that possibility out of my mind when I hadn't found a collar on her, but that was before hearing about hound behavior. From the first, I'd assumed the worst about Annie's human, but Dr. Wolf seemed to think Annie had been well taken care of until recently. Sirius had a microchip embedded between his shoulders; maybe Annie did as well.

"This is a universal scanner," Dr. Wolf said, showing me a handheld device. "If Annie's carrying a chip, the scanner will reveal it."

As she turned on the scanner, I was reminded of the way Dr. McCoy scanned patients on the original *Star Trek* series. Dr. Wolf ran the scanner between Annie's shoulders, holding it about an inch above her fur. It took her only a few seconds to find pay dirt.

"Eureka!" she exclaimed.

"As in the California city?" I asked.

"That remains to be determined. The microchip isn't a transmitter. It's a transponder that emits a radio frequency signal. The scanner picked up that signal, and what I now have is a unique identification number provided by the chip's manufacturer. All I have to do now is call the microchip company and give them that number, and they'll consult a national pet-recovery database. Let's hope our luck continues and that the owner is up to date with contact information."

"You ever hear of Murphy's Law?" I asked.

"Don't be such a pessimist," she chided.

Dr. Wolf had her cell phone in hand and was already making the call. She put her phone on speaker. After providing the identification number and satisfying the service of her status as a pet professional, she began jotting down the information given to her. I listened to the owner's name, the dog's name, two telephone numbers, and an address.

When I heard the location of *Angie's* home, I softly whistled. She lived in Burbank, a city that was about a ten-mile drive from Sherman Oaks; that is, if you traveled along the Ventura Freeway. Angie wouldn't have been able to do that, of course. I tried to imagine all the side streets that she would have needed to walk along in order to make it to my neighborhood. At a minimum, I imagined she must have walked twenty miles, but it was more likely she'd traveled thirty or forty miles. Making it through that urban jungle couldn't have been an easy journey for her.

Dr. Wolf finished her conversation. The microchip service said they would also be contacting Angie's owner with Dr. Wolf's information.

Annie was no longer an orphan; she was also no longer Annie. *Angie*, I said to myself. I wondered if it was short for Angela. In the City of Angels, an angel had come to me.

Dr. Wolf handed me the owner's contact information. In a much-too-sweet tone, she asked, "Would you also like a half-empty glass of water with that, Detective?"

"Being a vet's office," I said, "I would have thought you'd want me to eat crow."

CHAPTER 8

MY LITTLE RUNAWAY

From Dr. Wolf's office I called the first of the two telephone numbers that the microchip service had provided. I even gave Dr. Wolf the opportunity for another "I told you so" by making the call on my speakerphone. Unfortunately, we got the home answering machine and not a live person, denying us the happy ending we both wanted.

A pleasant-sounding female voice said, "Hi, this is Heather. And this is Angie."

On the recording, Angie barked.

"Please leave a message at the beep. Or at the bark."

The recording concluded with another of Angie's barks.

Dr. Wolf and I watched Angie's response to the sound of Heather's voice. Her head swiveled around and her tail wagged. I felt bad for inadvertently making her think her beloved human might be nearby.

"This is Detective Michael Gideon of the Los Angeles Police Department," I said. "I have Angie in my possession, and she's doing just fine. Please call me on my cell so that we can make arrangements to hand her off."

I provided my number and then tried Heather Moreland's cell phone. Once again I reached a recording. This one wasn't cute like the other, but businesslike. I didn't put this call on speakerphone; it wouldn't have been fair to Angie.

For the second time I provided my name and number. I could tell the outcome was anticlimactic for both Dr. Wolf and me, but it was even worse for Angie. It was almost as if we'd offered her a treat and then pulled it back from her.

"I guess this will be a case of delayed gratification," said Dr. Wolf. "That's supposed to be one of the things that separate *Homo sapiens* from other animals."

"I can resist everything except temptation," I said, not crediting Oscar Wilde.

It took Dr. Wolf a second to realize I was joking, and then she laughed.

* * *

I promised to call Dr. Wolf as soon as Heather Moreland contacted me. Both of us hoped that would be sooner rather than later. That's why I was slow to pull out of my parking space; I kept expecting, or at least kept hoping, that my cell phone would ring. I knew if Sirius was missing, I would have been sitting on the edge of my seat hoping for a call telling me he'd been found. Even without knowing Heather Moreland, I was sure she was the same way. So why wasn't she calling me back?

My impulse was to drive directly to Heather Moreland's house. After all, I did have her address. But seeing as it was a weekday, the odds were that even though her dog was missing, Heather was at work. It was certainly possible the demands of her workplace had kept her from picking up my messages.

Since my phone stubbornly refused to ring, I decided to follow through on my promise to contribute clothing and household goods for an upcoming rummage sale at the Blessed Sacrament Church. Most of the clothing wasn't mine. I'd been a widower for more than four years now, but I was just getting around to parting with Jenny's clothing.

I opened the windows several inches for the drive, and that perked Angie up. She immediately began testing the air. I wondered if she was looking for one scent in particular, or if she was just seeing what was out there.

"This one's for you, Angie," I said, synching my phone to the car's sound system and making my selection.

The notes from Max Crook's so-called musitron filled the car. Crook's musitron was an early version of a synthesizer; to build it, I had read, he cannibalized parts from televisions, stereos, and early electronic equipment. Then Del Shannon began singing "Runaway," one of the all-time classic heartbreak songs. It was no wonder that groups like the Beatles credited Shannon with helping them find their sound.

If Sirius hadn't been there, I'm sure I would have joined in Shannon's falsetto chorus. Each time he sang *why*, it sounded like a sad cry of "wah." He was a grown man coming as close to crying in a song as a grown man could.

Like too many great musicians, Shannon had taken his own life, putting a bullet in his head.

"Why?" I asked.

And, like Shannon, I wondered about my own little runaway. Why had Angie run away? Or what was she running to?

I'm nosy. That's why I'm a cop. I like getting to the bottom of things. I had the who, what, when, and where, but I still didn't have the why, and that made me wonder. I why, why, why, why, wondered.

* * *

I drove to the place of my birth, the Blessed Sacrament Church on Sunset Boulevard. More than forty years ago, Father Patrick Garrity had heard the cries of a newborn coming from the church's parking lot. It was a good thing Father Pat had such acute hearing back in those days.

In the years since, I'd never tried to track down the identity of my birth mother. It wouldn't surprise me if she'd delivered me while strung out on drugs. I knew nothing of my ancestry, so I'd taken on the ways of my adoptive parents. The woman I considered my mother was still alive, and for that I was grateful. Sirius and I had visited with her before my talk the day before. We hadn't been able to leave without taking home three containers of food she'd made specifically for me. Mom still seems to harbor doubts as to whether I'm capable of looking after myself. She couldn't understand why I hadn't already married Lisbet, and why the two of us weren't providing her with grandchildren.

Even though I'm adopted, I have unfortunately absorbed the trait of Catholic guilt.

Although the church doesn't allow dogs on its premises, I like to say Sirius has a papal dispensation. Father Pat skirts the issue by saying Sirius is my service dog. He's probably right about that. Today, though, I had two dogs. I hadn't wanted to leave Angie alone in my car.

"Mikey, Mikey." Father Pat greeted me in his office with open arms. He's the only person who calls me "Mikey." The name sounds right coming out of his lips.

Sirius also got an enthusiastic greeting. As for the third in our party, Father Pat took a good look at Angie and then gave me a questioning look. "What are you doing with a bloodhound?" he asked.

"A madman escaped from the local mental institution," I said. "Angie led me to this office."

Father Pat smiled. "Thank you for your donation to the education fund being supported by this weekend's rummage sale."

I could only blame myself for that hundred-dollar fine. Father Pat always keeps my irreverent comments in check by imposing "donations" of one hundred dollars whenever I cross the line, of which he is the arbiter.

I'd tell him the real story of how Angie had come into my life when there was more time.

"I just dropped off my donations for the rummage sale," I said. "Or maybe I should say Jenny did. Most of the items were hers."

"I imagine that it wasn't easy for you to give them up."

"It wasn't," I admitted, "but it was time. Sirius did a lot of sniffing of the clothing I brought out. The two of them only had a few months together, but he grieved when she was lost to us. Jenny actually named him. She couldn't abide his German name of *Serle*, so she renamed him Sirius."

Father Pat smiled. Like Sirius and me, he had loved Jenny, although he always called her Jennifer. Father Pat had officiated at our wedding. He'd even surprised us and everyone in attendance by singing "Ave Maria." No one had ever suspected what a good voice he had. Of all the presents we'd received at our wedding, Jenny and I agreed that was the best.

I didn't tell Father Pat that I'd contributed a number of our wedding gifts to the rummage sale as well.

My phone still hadn't rung. Heather Moreland hadn't called. Rather than wait any longer, I decided to go and visit her home in Burbank.

"I have to go look for Angie's owner," I said, rising from my chair.

Father Pat stood up and gave me a hug. "Seek and you will find," he whispered.

I wished it was that easy.

CHAPTER 9

LOST HUMAN

Heather Moreland's home was located in the central part of Burbank. The city is probably best known for the forty years it was home to the *Tonight Show*, when it was hosted by Johnny Carson and then Jay Leno. Carson especially made Burbank a nationwide punch line, including it in many of his monologues. Now that the *Tonight Show* is filmed in New York, Conan O'Brien is the sole Burbank talk-show host.

As I drove along the Burbank streets, I couldn't help but wonder how Angie had survived her journey to my neighborhood. Most of Burbank is paved with busy residential streets. Angie's home was just a block away from Burbank Boulevard, one of the most active corridors in the city.

Still, nature has a way of surfacing even in urban jungles. The most famous resident of Griffith Park, home of the Hollywood sign, is P22, a mountain lion believed to have somehow survived crossing the 101 and 405 freeways before he took up home in and around the park's six square miles. In 2015, P22 was discovered in the crawl space of a residential house nearby. In the dark of the night, the six-foot, 130-pound lion made his escape from the home. Although P22 is the undisputed king of the Griffith Park jungle, his is a lonely kingdom. There are no female mountain lions anywhere nearby. And though he survived one encounter with L.A.'s freeways, it is doubtful he could survive another. Even humans in big cars are grateful whenever they make it through L.A.'s freeway gauntlet.

As we drew closer to Angie's house, it was clear she knew exactly where we were. I could see her trembling with anticipation in the backseat. Her enthusiasm could also be heard in the sounds she was making—little woofs followed by the unmistakable baying of a hound.

The entire neighborhood, and the surrounding blocks, consisted of tract homes built in the forties during the World War II housing boom. Most had originally been two bedrooms with one bathroom, constructed on a little more than an eighth of an acre. In the years since, many of the homes had seen the addition of a third bedroom. Heather Moreland had made sure her home had high gates on all sides. Somehow even those hadn't kept Angie in.

Sirius made it clear he didn't want to be left behind. I put a leash on him, even though that wasn't necessary. On Angie it was absolutely necessary, but it didn't exactly rein her in. Even though I kept a tight grip on her leash, she all but dragged me to the front door. My commands to "Heel" worked on Sirius; they had absolutely no effect on Angie.

I rang the doorbell; it was a signal to Angie to start barking. When no one answered, I knocked. Apparently Angie thought no one could possibly hear my knocking; she began loudly baying.

"No," I told her.

She wasn't deterred. German shepherds want to please their handlers. It's in their DNA. Angie didn't feel that need. Maybe she was considering the source, deciding she didn't have to answer to me.

"Shush," I said, tugging on her leash. She didn't completely stop barking, but she did humor me by taking it down a few notches.

As I stood waiting on the porch, I took in the eye-level motion detector to the side of the front door. There was something about the two spotlights that didn't look right. The lights had been unscrewed to the point where their threads were showing. In fact, they looked as if they were almost ready to fall out of the sockets. I doubted whether the lights were operable and suspected they'd been tampered with. Out of habit I pulled out my cell phone and began taking pictures.

I opened the mailbox; it was half-full. As I started examining the postmarks on the letters, an older man emerged from the neighboring house to the west and stared me down from his front pathway, glowering eyes, arms folded across his chest, his expression sour. It was a shame I didn't have a copy of *The Watchtower* to wave his way. Instead, I decided to annoy him by smiling and waving.

"Beautiful day, isn't it?" I said.

He grunted, and looked that much more annoyed.

"Do you know when Heather will be back?" I asked.

"Do I look like I'm her secretary?"

"I came here hoping to drop off Angie," I said.

He didn't look thrilled by that prospect, nor did he seem pleased to see Angie. She didn't appear any happier seeing him. Both of them were exchanging glances bordering on the baleful.

"I'm not about to take her into my home, if that's what you're asking," he said. "I have nice, quiet cats. That dog is a nuisance."

His arms remained folded; his expression still looked as if he was getting by on a diet of lemons. I pulled out my wallet badge and flashed it.

"I'm Detective Gideon," I said. "I wonder if I might ask you a few questions."

He sighed loudly, and with undisguised reluctance took a roundabout route over to me. Instead of cutting through his neatly trimmed front lawn and following a dry creek bed that ran along Heather's xeriscaped front yard, he went down his walkway and then up hers. The man struck me as someone who didn't like thinking outside the box, or walking outside it.

The neighbor stopped about five feet from me, keeping his distance from the dogs. That gave both of us an excuse not to shake hands. Between holding both dogs' leashes, I managed to pull out a notepad and pen. "What's your name?" I asked.

"*Commander* Reinhard Becker. Retired, US Navy."

At least he didn't give me his serial number. Becker seemed to want to establish that he outranked me.

"And you live next door, Mr. Becker?"

"*Commander* Becker," he said, correcting me before he offered a nod.

"I assume you're acquainted with this dog," I said, jiggling Angie's leash.

"Unfortunately," he said.

"Has the mail come today?"

He seemed surprised by my question, but it did give him a chance to provide another sour editorial. "We're lucky to get our mail by four o'clock," he said. "I've complained to the postal service. They say their studies have established the most efficient routes. What should I expect from an inefficient bureaucracy that's losing millions and millions of dollars every year?"

"When was the last time you saw Heather Moreland?"

Becker shrugged. "I'm not sure."

"Did you see her over the weekend?"

"Do you think I keep tabs on my neighbors?"

It wouldn't have surprised me if he did, but I didn't say so. Becker thought a moment and said, "I don't believe I have seen or talked to her for several days."

"You're sure about that?"

"I am not a person who makes up stories. I did try calling her very early on Monday morning. In fact, I left several messages."

He wagged a finger in Angie's direction. "That bothersome dog was making enough noise to wake the dead a few nights ago. I would have called Burbank PD to lodge a noise complaint, but I know your department would have just given me the runaround."

I didn't bother to tell him I was with LAPD. "So, what did you do after calling Miss Moreland's number and leaving messages?"

"I came over to see what was causing her dog to make such a racket."

"And did you notice anything out of the ordinary?"

He shook his head. "The dog was making a ruckus for no good reason."

"What happened then?"

He averted his gaze. "I'm not sure I understand your question." His voice had lost its challenging edge.

I was sure he did understand my question. "A six-foot fence surrounds the sides of the house and the backyard. How is it that Angie got out?"

"What you need to understand is that this dog was barking pretty much nonstop from two in the morning until around three thirty or four. All that noise made me sleep deprived."

"I understand," I said. I understood he was establishing an excuse.

"I didn't think to bring a flashlight," he said. "And the dog was yammering, so I tried to quiet her down, but like I said, she was riled up. Since I couldn't see what was bothering her, I opened up the gate just a crack. She pushed by me and took off."

He still wasn't meeting my eyes. I wasn't sure whether he was embarrassed at being the cause of Angie's escape, or whether he'd opened the gate wide enough for her to "accidentally" run off.

I pretended not to be judgmental. "And that occurred Monday morning at around four?"

Becker nodded. I thought about the time frame. Angie had turned up in my neighborhood less than forty-eight hours later.

"Was it usual for Angie to be home by herself?"

"No," he admitted.

"I'm assuming Ms. Moreland works?"

He nodded.

"So what does she do with Angie on those days she works?"

"I think she drops the dog off at some kind of kennel. But two or three days every week, she works from home."

"Do you know where Ms. Moreland works?"

"At the Mickey Mouse building downtown," he said.

He meant Disney Studios, which was located in Burbank. "Do you know what she does there?"

"I think it has something to do with accounting or finances."

"Do you happen to have her work number?"

Becker was quickly returning to acting put upon. "It's over at my house."

"I'd appreciate your getting it for me."

While Becker went off sighing, I tested the front door and found it unlocked. From the stoop I looked inside; nothing appeared out of place. Still, I wasn't reassured. Too many alarms were going off in my head.

I decided not to go inside the house, knowing Burbank PD would probably look unfavorably upon my tampering with a potential crime scene. That didn't prevent me from asking Becker more questions when he returned, though.

"How long have you known Ms. Moreland?" I asked.

"She bought the house a little more than a year ago."

"Do you know where she moved from?"

"I don't know, but I don't think it was very far. My wife said she was in the process of getting a divorce from her husband."

I was jotting down notes when Becker added, "She was the perfect neighbor at first. But that was before she brought home that damn dog."

Not for the first time, I thought about how lucky I was to have Seth for a neighbor. Becker was no Fred Rogers.

I took down his phone number and thanked him for his help. He was grumbling when he left, so he didn't hear the singsong under my breath: "Won't you be my neighbor?"

* * *

I decided to take a look at the backyard prior to calling Burbank's finest. Before opening the side gate, I told Sirius to sit and stay. Angie was enough of a handful. She pulled me into the backyard and came to a stop at a bedroom window. On the ground beneath the window lay its screen. I moved my face close to the glass so that I could better see inside. The bedroom was in disarray: the bedspread and pillows were strewn about, and there was an overturned lamp on the floor. I couldn't spot any blood, but it appeared a struggle had taken place in the room.

While I did my eyeballing and snapped pictures with my cell-phone camera, Angie did her sniffing. Neither one of us looked satisfied with what our senses were telling us.

I decided not to call the Burbank police until I made sure Heather Moreland wasn't at work. My call went to her voice mail, where a pleasant and professional voice said, "This is Heather Moreland, assistant director of corporate accounts. I'm sorry I am unable to take your call, but please leave your name and number, and I will get back to you as soon as possible."

I didn't leave my name and number. Instead, I used my phone to look up the number for Disney's corporate and shared services section in Burbank. When the company operator answered, I offered up my name and title and said that I needed to be directed to one of Heather Moreland's coworkers.

Thirty seconds later an anxious-sounding woman came on the line. "Is Heather all right?"

"That's what I am trying to determine," I said. "Who am I talking to?"

"Katie Rivera," she said. "I work with Heather."

"You sound concerned about her well-being. Why is that?"

"Heather didn't come into work yesterday. That's not surprising; she telecommutes. But it was strange not hearing from her. And when she didn't come in today, I got worried. Between yesterday and this morning, I must have left half a dozen messages for her."

"I have Heather's dog, Angie," I said. "I believe she's been on the loose for the last two days."

"That bastard," whispered Katie. "Heather said he was all talk. I told her not to discount his threats."

"Who was making threats?"

"Her soon-to-be ex," she said. "Emilio Cruz. If you found Angie wandering the streets, then I know something is wrong with Heather. She loves that dog more than anything."

"Is there any chance we can meet away from your workplace? I'd like to ask you some questions without unnecessarily alarming your coworkers. I don't want everyone jumping to conclusions about Heather's absence from work."

"I can meet you during my lunch break in about an hour if that works for you."

I told her it did. "Do you happen to know any dog-friendly restaurants in town?"

"Heather is one of my best friends," she said. "That means I probably know *every* dog-friendly place in town."

Love me, love my dog. I was getting to know that about Heather.

"Are you going to bring Angie Arrow?" Katie asked.

"I'm going to bring my K-9 partner, as well as Angie. Did you call her Angie Arrow?"

"Heather sometimes called her that. I think she got the name Arrow from some dog in an old movie."

"*The Point*," I said.

"That's it. She was always humming a song from that movie. Heather said it was a favorite of hers."

"Me and My Arrow," I said.

"Yes! She loves that song."

Harry Nilsson sang it, but I didn't tell her that, nor did I offer up its refrain. Katie gave me the name of the restaurant and its address. It was only after we said our good-byes that I found myself humming Heather's favorite song. *The Point* is a short, cute animated film. Its hero is Oblio, the only roundheaded person in the land. Oblio's faithful companion is his dog, Arrow. I didn't really know Heather Moreland, but what I did know about her I liked.

Angie and I made our way back to the front of the house. I closed the gate behind us while Sirius made a fuss about our return. I added some music to our celebration.

Sirius and I were like Heather Moreland and Angie. We both had our Arrow.

Judging by Angie's perked-up interest, she knew the song. I wasn't Oblio or Heather, but she still rewarded me with some tail wagging.

CHAPTER 10

LOST DOG ANSWERS TO NAME OF LUCKY

Sergeant Sergio Reyes arrived at Heather's home twenty minutes after I put the call in to Burbank PD. He was wearing a uniform that made him look doughy, but no one looks svelte wearing a Kevlar vest. Reyes limped up to the porch where I was waiting.

"Gout," he said by way of explanation. "It's a bitch."

"The disease of kings," I said.

"Maybe there's something to that," he said, "seeing as my last name is Reyes."

I knew enough Spanish to know his surname translated to "kings."

"The doctor says my uric acid is sky-high. He recommends I lose twenty-five pounds and drink less. I asked if he could give me a prescription for a new job."

"If he's handing out those kinds of prescriptions, there will be a long line of cops waiting for them."

Reyes leaned against the wall, putting his weight on his good foot. I had told him Heather's story over the phone, or at least given him the bullet points.

"Where's the dog?" he asked.

"She's with my K-9 partner in the car."

My vehicle is equipped with a special AC system to keep Sirius cool in the car even on very hot days. It also has what's referred to as a *Hot-N-Pop*, which is a system that sets off an alarm if it gets too hot in the car. And if for some reason I can't respond to that alarm, a door automatically pops open.

"So you say this woman"—he looked at his notes to get her name—"this Heather Moreland didn't show up for work the last two days, and her neighbor said he hasn't seen her for a few days?"

I nodded, and then did my Vanna White imitation, pointing to the mailbox and then the motion detector. "The mail hasn't been collected. And if you look at the motion detector, you can see it appears to have been purposely disabled. I was told Ms. Moreland was finalizing her divorce and the ex wasn't happy about that and supposedly was making threats."

Reyes winced, but not from what I'd told him. He was still trying to get comfortable. "So did you enter the house?" he asked.

I shook my head.

He stared at me. "I'd hate to find out otherwise and have that come back and bite me in the butt if I find anything that makes this look like a crime scene. You sure about that?"

"I'm sure. I did go in the backyard, but I didn't touch anything. Angie—that's the dog—was anxious to get back there."

That information didn't sit well with Reyes. "You'd think an LAPD detective would know better than to potentially dirty the waters, but you just couldn't wait to snoop around, could you?"

Little brother had a chip on his shoulder. "I could wait, and I did. I had cause to go inside the house, but I didn't."

"This is Burbank, not L.A., just in case you might have forgotten that."

"And just in case you forgot, I came here to return a dog."

"Uh-huh," he said, not even making a pretense of hiding his doubts.

It was probably his gout talking, or at least I hoped it was. I handed him my business card and said, "If you don't need me for anything else, I'll be taking off."

It would be up to him to canvass the neighborhood, see if he could locate any surveillance cameras at nearby homes, check on the status of Heather's credit-card purchases, and start a missing-person search. I would gladly leave that to him.

"Where's the neighbor you talked to?" he asked.

I pointed to Becker's house.

"And where did you say this woman works?"

"The happiest place on Earth," I said.

At his blank expression, I added, "Disney Studios Burbank."

"What are you planning to do with her dog?" he asked.

I shrugged. "Right now that's still giving me paws for thought."

He didn't get the pun, which was just as well. My escape was delayed another ten minutes when Sergeant Reyes asked me to wait while he did a quick inspection outside and then inside the house. When Reyes returned, he wasn't as convinced as I was that a struggle had taken place.

"No blood," he said. "And the master bedroom is kind of a mess, but I've seen worse. It could have been she was just entertaining someone."

I decided not to argue.

"Here," he said, handing me a blue dog collar with tags. "You can use this more than I can."

He'd evidently found Angie's collar in the house. I did a quick inspection. One of the tags was a record of rabies vaccination; the other identified Angie by name and supplied two telephone numbers.

"Where did you find this?" I asked.

"It was on the floor next to her bed. I wouldn't be surprised if Ms. Moreland just took off for a long weekend, and the dog got out without her knowing it. Nine out of ten times these kinds of situations turn out to be big fuckups. But I'll do whatever needs to be done to locate her."

"Keep me in the loop," I said.

"I'll do that."

I didn't believe him, and he didn't believe me. And I didn't mention that I was leaving to have lunch with Heather's friend and coworker Katie Rivera.

I arrived at Moore's Delicatessen on Orange Grove Avenue right at the agreed-upon time. With two dogs in tow, I headed toward the deli's patio area. Angie identified Katie Rivera before I did and started yanking hard on the leash and pulling me toward her.

"Heel!" I said.

Sirius immediately responded; Angie kept tugging until she was greeted by an attractive dark-haired and -complexioned woman who looked to be about thirty. Until now Angie hadn't expressed much enthusiasm for anything or anyone, but she was excited to see Katie. The woman bent down and hugged her, and appeared unmindful of Angie's slobbering.

When she finished with their reunion, Katie extended a hand my way, and with a lilting Latina accent said, "Katrina Rivera." Then she sounded like an Anglo when she added, "But everyone except my parents calls me Katie."

As we shook hands, I said, "Michael Gideon and Sirius. I'm Michael. He's Sirius."

"Thanks for clarifying that," she said.

We took our seats; Sirius settled next to me while Angie leaned next to Katie.

"At the onset I should say that I'm here more in an unofficial capacity than not," I said. "The Burbank Police Department is now looking into Heather Moreland as a potential missing person. It's their jurisdiction and their case. I'm with LAPD."

She frowned. "I thought you wanted to ask me questions about Heather."

"I do, but officially I'm only working the Angie angle. I'm not going to let jurisdictional restraints stop me from looking for Heather."

"I called the Burbank Police yesterday afternoon," said Katie, "and told them I was worried about Heather because she hadn't come in to work. When I admitted she sometimes telecommutes, they said I'd need to wait another day before they could take a report. I guess you need to be missing for a certain number of hours before you can officially become a missing person. But I still knew something was wrong. Heather is hyper-responsible. At a minimum, she would have called me with some explanation. And as soon as you told me Angie was wandering the streets, I began fearing the worst. I'm praying Emilio hasn't killed her."

"He's your prime suspect in this?"

"I don't know anyone else who could possibly wish Heather ill. She acts like a saint in a nonpious kind of way."

Heather's life story was interrupted by a server who took our orders: Katie went with the Cuban sandwich; I had the meatloaf sandwich. While I ordered, I couldn't help but notice Katie staring at the keloid scarring on my face. I try to not be self-conscious about it even though I know it's the first thing people notice about me. My scars also seemed to jar her memory.

"Do I know you?" asked Katie. "You look familiar."

I shook my head and said, "I would have remembered you."

It was both flattery and fact, not to mention evasion. Sirius and I had gained unwanted notoriety when we brought Ellis Haines in, and were still remembered for that by lots of Angelenos. I never help people make that connection; to my thinking it's better to keep the Haines genie bottled up rather than let him spill out.

"You were telling me about Emilio Cruz," I said.

"I think he was the first male to pay attention to Heather. I suspect she was vulnerable to someone like Emilio, especially given her life history. I knew Heather for years before she finally opened up to me. I always assumed she led a charmed life because of her upbeat and happy personality. That's why I could barely believe it when she told me she spent her teen years in foster care. As bad as that was, Heather said her home life before foster care was much worse. Her father was abusive; when Heather was twelve, she saw him beat her mother to death."

My profession brings me in contact with the worst stories of humanity. Cops get desensitized because we hear too many bad things. But we're still human.

"God," I said, shaking my head. It was half curse for what had occurred; half sanction asking for providential blessing.

"Heather told me she wanted to work at Disney more than anywhere else because as a child Disney films gave her hope when her own life didn't. That's what drew her to Disney Studios."

"The House That Snow White Built," I said.

"That's us," said Katie.

More than a half century ago, Walt Disney had used the profits from his animated blockbuster *Snow White* to buy acreage for his studio in Burbank.

"I wonder why it is in that house-building description there's no mention of the seven dwarfs," I said. "It seems as if they got shortchanged."

"I am sure there were plenty of jokes back then," she said, "just as there are now. I know it sounds awful, but some employees like to say they work for Mauschwitz or Mickey Mauschwitz."

I nodded; most in L.A. had heard that job description.

"Heather wasn't that way, though. She loved her job. In real life she was sort of like the Hayley Mills character in *Pollyanna*. You ever see that film?"

"My dog Sirius loves sappy films," I said, giving him a head rub. "He's made me watch it more than once."

"I imagine *your dog*," she said, "would like Heather." Katie reached down and stroked Angie. "Do you know one of the main reasons for her picking out Angie at the shelter when no one else would?"

I shook my head.

"Heather said Angie reminded her of Pluto. But I know it was more than that. Angie was on death row. She'd been returned a few times, and her number was almost up. I think Angie's life reminded Heather of her own. The two of them were abused and unloved. Heather found a way to a better life, and she was determined to give Angie that same chance. It was a real challenge for her. I don't think Heather could have picked a more difficult dog. Anyone besides Heather would have given up on Angie Arrow."

"She should have named her Angie Lucky," I said.

"Lucky?" asked Katie.

"It's an old joke. There's an advertisement for a Lost Dog. Under the description it says: *Blind in one eye, mange-ridden, only has three legs, recently neutered, has a mean disposition, answers to the name of 'Lucky.'*"

Katie started laughing. "That pretty much describes how Angie was at first. But Heather turned her around. I'm not sure which of them loves the other more."

"How long have you known Heather?"

"About five years. She joined Disney about six months after I did."

"How old is she?"

"I think she's twenty-nine. She got an entry-level position right out of college."

"How long has she been married?"

"Six years, I think, although she's been separated for most of the last two years."

"What does Emilio do?"

"When he's not drinking, hitting Heather, or chasing other women, he works in an auto-body shop."

"Do you happen to remember the name of his employer?"

Katie gave me a name and location, which I wrote down, and then the two of us talked more about Heather. From what Katie said, she was too good to be true. It wasn't until the age of seventeen that Heather was diagnosed with dyslexia. And then beginning at age eighteen she was all alone in the world. Somehow she managed to work her way through college while still getting perfect grades. With each achievement, she got a little more self-esteem, even though her boyfriend and then husband, Emilio, had been anything but helpful in that regard.

"The unbelievable thing is that Emilio is now acting like he's the victim," said Katie. "It wasn't until Heather left him that the idiot realized what a gem he'd had. He even tried to win her back by agreeing to take anger-management courses, but Heather knew better than to trust him. It was too little and too late."

Our sandwiches arrived. Both of us conceded half of our meals to the hairy muzzles begging under the table.

"Lucky," said Katie, remembering the punch line to my joke and laughing once more.

She scratched at Angie's ear.

"I really don't know how Heather was able to have such a good attitude after all she went through. She was like a real-life ugly duckling. She told me that growing up she had bad teeth and was afraid to talk to people. And she was anything but a natural student because of her dyslexia. But her circumstances never stopped her. And despite everything, she thought of herself as lucky. That's why people always like being around her. In her presence you feel better. All morning I've been praying that she's all right."

"Keep praying," I said, "and I'll keep looking."

CHAPTER 11

THE RED EYE

When Heather came to, she tried not to panic. If Emilio was holding her here, she was sure he would listen to reason.

Still, if it was Emilio, how had he managed to secure this space? Of the two of them, Heather had always been the saver. That's how they'd been able to buy their condo, and that was how she'd bought her house.

I'm alive, Heather thought. That's what convinced her Emilio was behind this. If she'd been taken by a serial murderer or some crazed abductor, she'd already be dead, wouldn't she?

Nearby Heather could see a bucket and a pitcher of water. Suddenly she realized how thirsty she was and reached for the pitcher, forgetting her shackles; her chains were just long enough for her to grasp it. She took several long gulps, came up for air, and then drank more. The movements made her feel lightheaded, and she carefully placed the pitcher on the cement floor. It wouldn't do to drink all the water, so she left some for later.

She sat down with her back to the dank concrete wall and took deep breaths to try and clear her head. The room looked like some kind of torture chamber, but she knew there were couples who engaged in bondage. In fact, on one or two occasions, Emilio had suggested they try it. When he'd shown her what he wanted her to wear, Heather had been unable to hide her distaste. He'd wanted to bind her with wrist-and-ankle restraints and a spiked dog collar. The idea of a dog having to wear such a collar seemed horrific enough. And what she would never put around a dog's neck, she would never put around her own.

"What about a chastity belt?" he'd asked her.

"I am not your property," she had told him. "I am no one's property."

Emilio had sulked. He'd told Heather she was no fun. He'd tried to make her feel guilty, saying he was only trying to add some spice to their marriage. There had been a time when she might have agreed to some of his demands, but she'd matured. There had been a time when she hadn't believed she was worthy of being loved.

She shifted against the wall, and the movement drew her eyes to a red light on the far wall. She moved her head again; no, she wasn't imagining it. The light was mostly hidden within a recess, but in the darkness its glow stood out. Demons supposedly had eyes that color. But Heather was convinced the unblinking red light came from another source. She was being recorded.

Goddamn Emilio, she thought. That was another thing he'd wanted to do. He'd pestered her about filming their lovemaking. Thank heavens she'd had the sense to tell him no. But was he filming her now?

She reached out and felt her chains, confirming the substance of the metal links. It was important to be sure her observations were grounded in reality. One of her greatest fears was that she might end up like her mother, bedeviled by demons, imagined and real. Heather's father had been demon enough without the other creatures her mother only imagined she saw.

After she survived foster care, Heather had lived with the worry that one day she too might end up as a schizophrenic. The fear was still there, even though she was almost thirty, and statistically, the disease usually struck by now.

As dire as her condition appeared, she felt relieved that she wasn't imagining her imprisonment. Her captivity was real, and she would have to deal with that, but at least she'd do so with her faculties intact.

She thought of Angie, and remembered hearing her howling just as she was attacked. What had her dog thought? Her third-chance dog had already gone through so much pain and abandonment.

"I didn't abandon you," Heather whispered, softly enough so the camera couldn't pick up her words. "I tried to save you. I hope you're all right."

And then she remembered one of the last things she'd done just before being attacked. She'd taken the tracker from Angie's collar and clipped it beneath her nightgown. She wanted to check and see if the tracker was still there, but she was afraid the camera might pick up her inspection. The tracker was designed to work with the GPS on her cell phone—insurance, in addition to Angie's microchip. There had been a few close calls, but Angie had never escaped, and because of that, Heather had never needed to locate her with the tracker.

She tried to think back to when she'd last charged the tracker. At a minimum, it had been several days, but it might have been as much as a week. The device would do her no good if it ran out of juice.

Of course it was a long shot that anyone would even realize she'd taken the tracker from Angie's collar. Even more unlikely was the possibility of anyone noticing the tracking app on her phone.

Heather suspected she'd have to rely upon herself to find a way out of this mess. But that wasn't anything new.

CHAPTER 12

A SNAKE IN THE GAS

There are certain neighborhoods around L.A. that don't stand out. Most people describe Van Nuys as being in the middle of the San Fernando Valley, and then are hard-pressed to say anything else about it other than that it has more than its share of gangbangers. Gertrude Stein once said of Oakland, "There is no there there." If Stein had lived in Van Nuys, she might have said the same thing. The area does have a nice Japanese garden, and you could do a lot worse than sitting down to a serene cup of tea in its teahouse. Like all scenic locations around L.A., the Japanese garden has been featured as a setting in film and television. It was the location of Starfleet Academy in several episodes of *Star Trek: The Next Generation.*

Of course, there's a *Star Trek* bumper sticker that essentially takes Stein's observation and applies it to our entire planet: "Beam Me Up, Scotty: There's No Intelligent Life on This Planet."

Emilio Cruz's employer had carved out a busy business along Sepulveda Boulevard, but I've always thought any car-repair shop operating in the L.A. area is bound to succeed. With so many cars and so many accidents, it seems like shooting fish in a barrel.

The shop's lobby belied the nature of its business. You couldn't hear the banging and clanging going on in the repair lot, and the music was classical and calming. The customer-service manager greeted me with a smile and "May I help you, sir?"

It seemed almost rude to flash my badge, so I merely said, "I'm Michael Gideon, and I need to talk to Emilio."

I would have bet the manager knew the general nature of my business and that I wasn't with the Welcome Wagon. Nodding, he spoke into an intercom, asking Emilio to come to the front desk. The extensive soundproofing spared waiting customers from hearing his voice broadcasting out to the lot.

I took a seat in a comfortable padded chair. Half a dozen people were seated in the lobby awaiting their restored vehicles. Most of them were working on their laptops, tablets, or phones. There was a mixture of ethnicities similar to what I'd seen at the 187 Club, and I realized I'd found something other than homicides that brought L.A. together: car crashes.

A medium-size thirtyish male appeared behind the desk. With a little costuming he could have been an Elvis impersonator. He had the slicked dark hair and the muttonchops. There was also that curl on the left side of his lip that wasn't quite a smirk. His shirtsleeves were rolled up, revealing a coiled rattlesnake tattoo on his right arm. The rattlesnake's fangs were bared. Along with the snake I could make out the words, "Don't tread on me."

I wasn't sure what I disliked more: the inked snake or the threat that came with it. During the Revolutionary War, the so-called Gadsden flag had been an American banner warning the British. Since that time the Tea Party has adopted a once-great historical symbol for its own devices.

As Emilio wiped his hands with a rag, the service manager pointed me out with a tilt of his head. When Emilio looked my way and saw what was awaiting him, he rolled his eyes. He knew I wasn't there to present him with a check from Publisher's Clearinghouse.

With his finger, he pointed to the door. I stood up and followed him out. He led me around the corner out of potential earshot of those in the lobby.

"What now?" he asked.

I showed him my wallet badge and offered my name. "When was the last time you saw Heather?" I asked.

"Why do you want to know?" he said.

"I'm the one asking questions."

"What's she claiming now?"

"When?" I repeated.

I was guessing Emilio was a second- or third-generation American. He spoke without an accent and sounded like just another millennial. Of course in L.A., more than half the millennials are bilingual.

"It was maybe a month ago. She came here and had me sign some papers."

"What kind of papers?"

"Why don't you ask her?"

I let the silence build until he said, "They were real estate papers. We sold our condo. Of course she wanted me to believe that one day we would be cohabitating in the Burbank home."

"And that was the last time you communicated with her?"

He shook his head. "She called a few days ago."

"What day?"

"Friday morning. That was when she announced it was fucking D-Day, as in divorce."

"You sound surprised. Weren't the two of you separated for some time?"

"News flash, dude: being separated isn't the same thing as being divorced. The bitch pulled a bait and switch on me. She said the only way we'd get back together was if I changed my ways. And that meant jumping through all her hoops. But even after doing everything she asked of me, that wasn't enough. She told me she was going through with the divorce."

"And how did you respond to that?"

He clenched his fists as he spoke. "How do you think I responded? For the last eighteen months I've done every goddamn thing she wanted, and then I'm told that's the way the fucking cookie crumbles."

From what I'd observed, he would have been justified in asking for a refund from his anger-management sessions.

"Did you threaten Heather during that conversation?"

He studied my expression, and appeared to catch on that there was an underlying reason for our chat. Of course he might have been acting as well.

"Did something happen?" he asked.

I shrugged. "When the two of you talked on the phone, did you say anything that might have upset Heather?"

"I already told you I got hit with her D-bomb. So whatever I said wasn't exactly pleasantries. Heather knew I didn't want a divorce, so I doubt she was shocked."

"Where were you on Sunday night?"

"In my crappy studio apartment on Vanowen in Lake Balboa."

"Any witnesses to your being there?"

"Do cockroaches count? The apartment has plenty of those."

He challenged me with his look. I tried waiting him out again, but he wasn't going to volunteer anything else without my revealing the purpose of my visit.

"From what I've been able to determine," I said, "Heather has been missing since Sunday night."

Emilio's surprise looked real. As he took in the implications of Heather's disappearance, he began nodding.

"I left a lot of messages for her over the past few days," he said, "but I suppose you already know that."

I didn't comment. It was possible he'd made the calls to establish an alibi.

He seemed to consider those phone calls. "I guess I said a few things to her that don't sound very nice. Like anyone in my position wouldn't be pissed, though. All this time she had me believing we were getting back together."

I pretended to be privy to the messages he'd left. "Those calls sounded like threats."

"Like I said, she provoked me."

"I thought part of anger management was taking responsibility for what you say and do, instead of pointing the finger at someone else."

"You do the drill I did for eighteen months and then get told to go eat shit, and let's see if you're smiling."

"They say a leopard can't change its spots."

"I'm glad I'm not a leopard, then. Like my doctor says, 'We know what we are, but not what we may be.' I've been working on that 'may be' part."

"Who's your therapist?"

"Why? You need help with anger management?"

I didn't say anything, but let my clicking pen speak for me.

"Dr. Alec Barron," he said.

"Do you have his telephone number?"

Emilio sighed and then reluctantly pulled out his cell phone, looked through his contacts, and gave me the number.

"I'm going to be contacting Dr. Barron today," I said. "If you've been working through your issues like you say you have and if you're the poster child for good patients, then I would suggest you call Dr. Barron and give him permission to discuss your particulars with me. If you don't do that, he won't be able to vouch for you. Doctor/patient privilege. You can certainly go that route, but I wouldn't, because right now you're the number one suspect in your wife's disappearance."

"How do you know Heather just didn't go off on some getaway?"

"I found her dog on the streets more than ten miles from where she lives."

"You found Angie?"

I nodded.

"Good luck," he said. "That dog is a nutcase."

"She doesn't like you?"

"She doesn't like men. Maybe that's Heather's problem as well."

"Yeah, that must be it," I said.

He reddened at my sarcasm. Why is it that every insecure man who's been dumped by a woman goes around questioning her sexual orientation?

"When Heather turns up from wherever she is, are you going to come back here and apologize for hassling me?" he asked.

"Yeah, I'll do that. Maybe I'll even bring flowers. But first let's deal with her being a missing person. From what I could determine, Heather's been away from her house for the last two days. And she hasn't shown up to work this week, or called to explain her absence. I'm told that's not like her."

Emilio reluctantly agreed. "She's a workaholic. We had fights over that. She put her job ahead of our relationship."

"You have any idea what could have happened to her?"

"Maybe she has the flu or something. Maybe she went to the hospital."

"I'll look into that. Any other ideas where she might have gone?"

He thought about it, then shook his head. "She's usually doing something with that stupid dog of hers."

I asked him a few more questions and took down some personal information. He said that he would call Dr. Barron as soon as we were done and give him permission to talk freely with me. While we spoke, Emilio ran a finger along his tattoo. I wondered if it was a habit, or a nervous gesture.

And I wondered if he was telling me the truth about not knowing anything about Heather's disappearance, or whether he was a snake-oil salesman.

CHAPTER 13

FELIZ IF YOU PLEASE, FELIZ IF YOU DON'T PLEASE

When I called Dr. Alec Barron, I was told he was with a patient, so I left a message asking him to call me back as soon as possible regarding Emilio Cruz. After that I called Sergeant Reyes to see if he had any updates on Heather's disappearance. His voice mail suggested I leave a message, and I did.

From the car I worked on my case notes. It was midafternoon when Dr. Barron's receptionist called me back. She said the doctor could see me at six o'clock after he finished with his last patient, and provided me with the address.

I'd had my fill of paperwork, so I announced to the dogs, "We've got about two hours to *play*."

Sirius wagged his tail. He was well acquainted with the word "play."

"How about we all go for a *walk*?"

I got a bingo out of Angie as well. Suddenly my passengers perked up.

Dr. Barron's office was in Los Feliz, so I thought about dog-friendly spots nearby. I decided on the Bronson Canyon Trail in Griffith Park. I always think of Griffith Park as the lungs of Los Angeles, with its more than four thousand acres of greenery and green spaces providing oxygen support to a city that needs it. Griffith Park is an oxygen canister tied to a patient with chronic emphysema.

The back windows were open enough for both dogs to stick their muzzles out. I think dogs believe cars were invented for just that purpose. After driving into the park, I lucked into a parking space not far from the trailhead. Then it was a matter of hitching up the team and taking to the trail. Normally taking Sirius on a walk is a straightforward enterprise, but entering Angie into the equation threw my partner and me off our stride. The two of us had worked together for so long we were attuned as to what to expect from the other. Angie was captive to her nose, which meant we were as well. She liked to abruptly stop and start, as well as meander at will. Sirius understood that you keep to the trail. Angie didn't feel bound to the confines of the trail. She wanted to go where her nose told her, and that meant my partner and I felt like we were in a tag-team wrestling match.

We weren't alone walking the Griffith Observatory Loop. Most of those we met up with appeared to be tourists intent upon getting the best possible photo of the Hollywood sign. Lots of selfies were being taken with the sign as a backdrop. Nothing had changed. Everyone wanted to be in pictures.

The farther we walked, the more the dogs and I had the trail to ourselves. I kept taking deep breaths, enjoying the aroma of the coastal sage. Walking the park allows you to get a glimpse of what the L.A. area looked like a century ago. There were shrub oaks and coast live oaks, as well as toyon with its red berries, which early settlers mistook for holly. Hollywood owes its name to toyon.

I was mindful to take it easy with Angie. Her recovery from the night before was nothing short of amazing, but I didn't want to put any more wear on her pads. That didn't seem to be Angie's concern. She acted as if she was on a mission, taking in smells as if cataloging them. Occasionally she came to a full stop to see what the breeze was bringing to her. It might have been my imagination, but it looked as if she was intent on finding one particular scent.

"You are a rather single-minded sort," I told her during one of her sniff stops.

But what was it, I thought, that she was so single-minded about?

Sirius and I usually made it around the entire trail, but because of Angie we took it easy. A half hour into our walk, we took a water break. The dogs lapped away while I took a few long pulls from my insulated water flask. I wiped the sweat from my face and then gave the dogs a little love. Angie tolerated my attention but remained independent. She'd given her heart to another, and I respected that. As I was thinking about Heather Moreland, my phone rang. The display told me the caller was Sergeant Reyes. I was glad there were no walkers in the area; I always hate it when others carry on phone conversations in spots where silence should be the rule.

"Gideon," I said.

"This is Reyes," he said. "I thought we'd agreed Heather Moreland was Burbank PD's case, and not LAPD's."

"You'll get no argument from me. But there's still the matter of Heather's dog."

"If that's the case, why is it that you talked with Heather's coworkers?"

"I talked with one coworker hoping she would take Heather's dog."

"I suppose that's the same reason you talked to Heather's husband?"

Sergeant Reyes had been busy.

"As a matter of fact, it is. He said the dog was crazy, and wanted nothing to do with her. So far no one wants to take her. What about you?"

"You can keep your dog, and your dogshit."

"Some days you're the dog," I mused, "and some days you're the hydrant."

"Hey, if I toss a stick, will you go away?"

"No, but if you tell me what's going on with Heather's disappearance, I might."

"The operative word regarding her disappearance is that it's 'suspicious.' She's been categorized as a missing person."

"Has there been any credit-card activity on her accounts?"

"Nothing since last Saturday," he said.

"Have you narrowed down a time frame for her disappearance based on messages left on her home phone and cell phone?"

"What's this got to do with finding a home for her dog?" he asked.

"Throw a bone to this dog," I said.

"I'll tell you what Old Mother Hubbard told her dog, 'Tough shit.'"

"That's not how I remember the poem."

"The end result is that the dog didn't get no effen bone."

I let him get the last word in, which might be why he opened up. "Messages were left beginning Monday morning. As for phone activity, her last outgoing calls were on early Sunday evening."

"Was Heather's purse inside her house? And did it look undisturbed?"

"Yes and yes," he said. "Now if you'll excuse me, I wouldn't want to keep you from finding a home for that dog."

He clicked off, and the dogs and I continued with our walk. By the time we made it back to the car, I figured we'd gone about two miles, which was as far as I wanted to push Angie. The three of us took another long water break. Angie seemed less restive than she had before the walk, but still didn't look like she was ready to circle around three times and drop down for a long nap. I watched her sampling the air and wondered what it would be like to have her sense of smell. I thought of my favorite scents, and a memory stream came wafting my way: the aroma of brewing coffee, the ozone announcement of an impending desert rain, jasmine, a balsam pillow, buttered popcorn, a baby's head, a McIntosh apple, the brine of the ocean, coastal sagebrush, a freshly peeled orange, honeysuckle, the temptations of cinnamon rolls, a pine forest. Nothing transports us like certain aromas. With the right bouquet, you travel through time and space.

"Come on, Snuffles," I said, lightly tugging on Angie's leash.

I must have found that portal to travel through time and space, because my reference was to one of my favorite childhood cartoon characters. Snuffles was a bloodhound who appeared with Quick Draw McGraw. He would do anything for a dog biscuit. After eating one, he would hug himself, and then float rapturously in the air to the sounds of "Um, um, um." There was something about seeing that floating dog that always made me laugh. Whoever created Snuffles knew about dogs and how they happily get lost in the moment.

My own version of Snuffles was still searching for a scent. I bribed her away from her vigil with a dog treat, and she settled next to Sirius in the car.

* * *

I've always liked Los Feliz, probably because my favorite movie theater in the world is located there. The Vista is one of the oldest theaters in Los Angeles. It has a Spanish Colonial exterior, but its interior is pure Egyptian kitsch. When the theater was being built in the early 1920s, the King Tut craze was sweeping the country. That national mania was put on exhibit inside the building. Everywhere you see hieroglyphics, faux gold, pyramids, mummies, camels, and Old World décor. And unlike modern movie theaters, the Vista offers plenty of legroom.

While growing up, I always heard Los Feliz pronounced either *Lohs-Fee-Liz* or *Loss Fee-lus*. Neither of those names took into account the Spanish pronunciation of *Los Fay-lease*. You say toe-may-toe, I say tah-mah-toe.

A Disney song from *Lady and the Tramp* took hold in my brain: Peggy Lee singing "The Siamese Cat Song." Today many consider the lyrics racist. They don't like the singsong cadence of the two cats singing about being Siamese, whether you please or whether you don't please. The word "please" was pronounced *pleez*, which rhymed with Los Feliz depending on how you said it. I suppose I was thinking about Disney because of Heather Moreland, or maybe it was because Walt Disney's first studio was in Los Feliz. The space is now a copy shop.

All around L.A. you'll find Spanish names that have been Anglicized, or more accurately, that took on a definite Midwestern form of speech because of all the heartland transplants that came to the area in the twentieth century. While the Midwest intonations of Los Feliz still hold sway for the most part, it's only a matter of time before its Spanish roots take hold. One thing is for sure: in Spanish, *feliz* means "happy."

Our destination was on North Vermont. I'd been told to look for an office building down the street from the Hollywood Presbyterian Medical Center. As we neared the building, Angie sat up. I drove down into the subterranean parking and stopped to collect a ticket at the garage entry dispenser. Angie raised herself up and stood with straight legs and a vigilant posture. The hackles on her back rose, and a growl came to her throat.

"It's all right, Angie," I said.

She wasn't at all sure about that. There was something about our being in the garage she didn't like. There was something I didn't like either: the price of parking. Angie continued growling.

"Does something wicked this way come?" I asked. She seemed to think so.

We made a few loops, and by the time I found a parking space, Angie had settled down. My partner had a lot to do with that. He rested his head on Angie's chest, acting as a reassuring presence and clearly putting her more at ease. It always worked on me as well.

I offered the dogs water again, but only got a polite lick or two from each of them. After making sure the air-conditioning and the *Hot-N-Pop* were working, I set out in search of Dr. Barron's office.

In the building's lobby, an office directory told me he was located on the third floor. I punched a button and waited for an elevator. Only a few days ago, I'd read a magazine article on ways to achieve "easy fitness." The writer had said it was a no-brainer to always walk up and down the stairs if your destination was five floors or fewer. Feeling virtuous after my walk with the dogs, I made a promise to myself that if the elevator didn't appear in the next ten seconds, I would take the stairs.

As it turned out, the elevator car opened on my count of nine. Of course I chose not to count "One Mississippi, two Mississippi," nor did I do as the Brits did and count with "One Piccadilly, two Piccadilly." I went with another word count, namely "One pneumonoultramicroscopicsilicovolcanokoniosis, two pneumonoultramicroscopicsilicovolcanokoniosis." It was pure happenstance that I chose to count with the longest word in the English language.

Like at the offices of most shrinks, I found that Dr. Barron's patients were afforded separate entrances and exits. Mental-health professionals say this is for the privacy of patients. I think it might be that therapists are afraid of what kind of conversations their patients might have with one another.

I approached a bored-looking dyed-blonde receptionist who was fighting back a yawn. She was sitting behind a plexiglass window with an opening in the bottom, much like a teller in a security-minded bank. The setup didn't make for a very welcoming office. It wasn't too removed from prison décor; all it lacked was a phone on each side of the plexiglass.

"Detective Michael Gideon here to see Dr. Barron."

I could tell by her voice she was the one I'd spoken to on the phone. "He shouldn't be very long," she said.

As I took a seat, my hope was that the doctor didn't count by pneumonoultramicroscopicsilicovolcanokoniosis.

Most of the office walls were taken up by poster boards displaying affirmations and quotations. After being burned in the fire set by Ellis Haines, I'd gone through physical and mental therapy. My therapists also believed in offering up positive, pithy statements. Clever phrases, I knew, were shorthand for their longer sermons. Still, I found all the poster boards overkill. I guess I'm too much of a skeptic to accept easy bromides.

With nothing else to do, I studied Ben Franklin's picture and words: *Anger is never without reason, but seldom with a good one.*

Ben had never driven in L.A.'s rush-hour traffic, I thought.

The music coming out over the office intercom was Karen Carpenter's "Top of the World." I wondered if that was a coincidence.

I took in another wall, and another poster, and whispered what I read: "Holding on to anger is like drinking poison and expecting the other person to die."

The words seemed deeper than the others I'd read, almost Zen. I thought about which quotation I'd want up on the wall if I had an office, and decided on Mark Twain's words: *Be careful about reading health books. You may die of a misprint.*

"Detective Gideon?"

I turned my head toward the receptionist's voice, and she pointed to the entry door. "The doctor will see you now."

"Thank you," I said.

The buzz of a security door allowed me access to the inner sanctum. The hallway led to an office with an open door. Dr. Barron was talking on the phone, and I hesitated at the doorway. He motioned for me to sit in a chair. I was glad he didn't direct me to a couch, but then I saw there wasn't one.

He quickly finished up his conversation. At its conclusion I stood up and extended my hand.

"Michael Gideon," I said.

He made it about halfway up, and we shook. "Dr. Barron," he said.

"Emilio Cruz promised me he would contact you today," I said.

"He *did*," said Dr. Barron, drawing out the word and then making a little grimace.

"Is there a problem?"

He did some finger tapping as if to show me his dilemma. The doctor looked to be in his midthirties, but tried to assume the gravitas of someone much older. He wore glasses, but they looked more like a hipster's eyewear than Sigmund Freud's. His frames were rose-colored, and his curly dark hair fell in ringlets toward his lenses. You don't see perfectly disheveled hair like his except on shows like *Game of Thrones*. He wore his professional credentials in the form of a stylish linen sports coat and a yellow oxford shirt with blue stripes, but showed his supposed rebel side with a one-day stubble look and 501s.

"Mr. Cruz did call me and tell me I was free to discuss him with you," he said. "I said I didn't think that was a good idea. He didn't seem inclined to listen, so I said that I would need him to sign a release giving me permission."

Dr. Barron looked at the screen of his new iPhone and read the text that was there: *You have my consent to talk with Detective Gideon and answer any of his questions about me.*

He looked up at me and said, "That text was sent by Mr. Cruz."

"So what's the problem?"

"It feels wrong. It feels like I'm violating my professional ethics."

"I'll note your qualms," I said. "As you probably heard, Emilio's wife, Heather Moreland, is missing. Have you ever met her?"

He nodded and said, "She came in on one occasion. Unfortunately, Ms. Moreland wasn't receptive to reconciliation."

"When did this session take place?"

"Several months ago. If you need an exact date, I can look it up."

"Maybe later," I said. "Right now I'd like to hear about their session together."

Barron made a small grimace. "You put me in a difficult position. Ms. Moreland might not approve."

"Emilio is your client, not Ms. Moreland."

He moved his head to the right and left as if to show his inner debate, then conceded, "I suppose you're right. Besides, there's not that much to tell. Emilio apologized and promised that he would never again be physically or verbally abusive. Ms. Moreland said she accepted his apology."

By his tone, it was clear he didn't believe that.

"You don't think she was sincere?"

"I think she had already decided to go through with the divorce no matter what Emilio did."

"What were your impressions of Ms. Moreland?"

"I was in her presence for less than an hour. That really isn't even enough time for a thumbnail sketch."

"I'll take that digit anyway. Was she likable? Did she have much to say, or was she closemouthed? Was she guarded? Did you get a favorable impression of her?"

"It's likely my opinion was colored by what Emilio has long been telling me."

"And what's that?"

"Behind a warm and caring veneer, he said his wife was very manipulative. Of course given her circumstances, that's not surprising."

"What circumstances are those?"

"When she was a girl, Ms. Moreland watched her father murder her mother; the rest of her childhood was spent in foster care, an environment that certainly took its toll on her psyche."

"In what way?"

"It would stand to reason that she has a desperate need to be loved. However, because of childhood issues, she would doubt whether she is worthy of being loved. In most cases someone like that is never going to be settled, or happy. She will sabotage her relationships in the self-fulfilling prophecy that she can't be loved."

"That's quite a thumbnail sketch."

He shrugged, but looked pleased with himself.

"So you're saying Heather Moreland is quite needy, but hides that from others?"

Barron nodded.

"And she wants love, but is incapable of receiving it."

"Yes," he said.

"Why would someone like that adopt a dog that by all accounts was next to impossible to live with?"

"Dog?" Barron's face contorted, as if he didn't understand the question.

"If Heather Moreland was as needy as you believe, I don't understand why she would put herself in a position where she had to provide almost unconditional love to an animal."

"I deal in *human* relationships, Detective Gideon, and the *human* psyche. I can't conjecture about interspecies relationships."

I nodded. But I was glad I *could* conjecture about interspecies relationships, and the way Heather had tended to a third-chance dog told me a lot.

"How long have you been seeing Emilio?"

"Almost a year now."

"How did he become your patient?"

"My client," he corrected.

I thought about asking him how he pronounced Los Feliz, but instead waited for his answer.

"Mr. Cruz told both the court and his wife that he wanted to change. In order to try and save his marriage, he agreed to anger-management therapy. He did this at his own cost without insurance. Because of that, I agreed to work with him at a much reduced rate. I have three other clients with similar circumstances. The reason I have taken on these individuals is that I am a great believer in the efficacy of anger management. I do my best to teach coping skills, and offer alternatives to anger and violence. If these individuals can be freed from their vicious cycles—'vicious' being the operative word—their lives can change for the better."

"Are you following any program or guidelines in your treatment?"

"You have to manage each case on an individual basis."

"So you're saying there are no standards and no testing of results?"

Barron looked amused. "It's rather difficult to quantify teaching someone how to keep their emotions in check."

"Emilio Cruz was arrested for domestic violence, wasn't he?"

"Those charges were reduced."

"But you're not denying that he beat Heather Moreland on multiple occasions?"

"My client admitted that he did so, and that he deeply regretted his actions. You need to remember that he came to me on his own volition and that he wanted to change his ways in order to save his marriage."

"Do you think your treatment of Emilio is working?"

"I believe he's much improved from when we first started."

"When I talked to him today, it seemed to me that he had a short fuse."

"I wasn't there. I can't comment."

"Can you comment about whether Emilio has made statements that he'd like to commit violence against Heather?"

"I could comment, but I won't."

"And why is that?"

"I stand by what I said before: Mr. Cruz has been making progress."

Barron's smug expression and self-satisfied way of speaking showed how he was enjoying controlling our session.

"Do you think Emilio is capable of abducting his wife and/or potentially committing violence against her?"

"The human species is capable of anything. It would be disingenuous of me to say otherwise."

"That doesn't sound like a ringing endorsement."

"That's your interpretation."

"I noticed Heather Moreland didn't take his last name. Do you know if that was a point of dissension between them?"

"Apparently Ms. Moreland had already changed her name once and was reluctant to do so a second time."

That was news to me. "Why did she change her name?"

"Emilio said that while she was still in foster care, she petitioned the court to lose her father's name. When they became engaged, she told him she was deeply attached to the name of Moreland because she had selected it for herself."

"Earlier you intimated that Heather had a public face and a private face."

"That's what Mr. Cruz believed. He says Ms. Moreland likes to cry wolf."

"What did he mean by that?"

"He said she liked to act like a vestal virgin in public, but was the opposite in private. He said in their love life she liked it rough and enjoyed being debased. She asked for it that way. And then afterward, he said, her guilt would kick in and she would act like the aggrieved party."

I had dealt with enough abusers to be skeptical. To them, it was always the victim's fault. I didn't hide my doubts; the doctor responded to them.

"It was Freud who first wrote of the Madonna–whore complex," he said. "Since his time the meaning has evolved and expanded. In the private lives of Ms. Moreland and Mr. Cruz, both of them navigated the boundaries of the Madonna and the whore. Ms. Moreland's public persona was the Madonna. In private she was the whore."

"I'd consider the source," I said. "It's Cruz who is the convicted abuser."

"I will be the first to say that Mr. Cruz has anger issues. But I would venture to say that Ms. Moreland would certainly have benefited from therapy also."

"Last Friday Heather told Emilio that she wanted to proceed with a divorce. Other than today, have you talked with him since that time?"

"We briefly chatted on Friday."

"What did Emilio tell you?"

"He said that Ms. Moreland was going to proceed with the divorce."

"And what did he say about that?"

"He was upset, naturally."

"Did he say he was going to do anything to Heather?"

Barron hesitated before saying, "No comment."

"Emilio gave his permission for you to talk freely to me."

"I am aware of that. But I am still allowed discretion in the matter."

"It sounds like you're hiding something."

He smiled. It wasn't a friendly expression, but a display of superiority. "Is that your best attempt at reverse psychology?"

"Your Jedi mind tricks won't work on me," I said.

Dr. Barron looked like he was smelling gas. I tried again. "You know what they say—a Freudian slip is when you say one thing but mean your mother."

CHAPTER 14

IS THAT ALL THERE IS?

As I opened the door to my car, I saw that Angie had been busy chewing up the backseat upholstery during my absence.

I made an exasperated sound but then corralled my temper. Having a fit might make me feel better, but I knew the guilty party wouldn't understand. As it was, Angie was oblivious to my displeasure, whereas my glowering caused Sirius to shrink into the seat and lower his head. No one wants to please me as much as my partner does, and I felt bad for causing his discomfort.

"It's all right, Sirius," I said. "You're a good boy."

He immediately brightened.

I was probably lucky Angie hadn't done other damage before this. Dr. Wolf had warned me about bloodhounds being active dogs. I knew that posed a problem for tonight's docket. Lisbet's apartment was about seven hundred square feet and full of her artistic expressions. Angie, I suspected, would think those were chew toys.

As I thought about what to do with her, Angie suddenly decided I was the most interesting man on the planet. I had to keep her from crawling over the seat in order to sniff me down. From head to toe I was suddenly fascinating. It wasn't a lovefest, though. She wasn't wagging her tail or acting like we were best friends. There was something about me that had all her attention.

As Angie continued to probe me with her nose, I told her, "I'm wearing Ralph Lauren's latest, *Eau de Roadkill.* You like?"

At least she was distracted from chewing apart more upholstery. As Angie continued her nasal invasion, I thought about where I might house her for the next night or two. There were kennels at my old stomping grounds of Metropolitan K-9, but I wasn't sure if I could get her placed there. It wasn't only that I'd have to do some groveling to get permission, but more that Angie needed an on-call human to potentially reassure her at all hours. She'd been through a lot. Both Angie and I were lucky that a healer by the name of Sirius had been helping her.

A potential solution occurred to me. With Bluetooth in operation, I said, "Call Lisbet."

Caller ID gave me away, because when Lisbet answered she said, "You had better not be canceling. Dinner is going to be ready in about fifteen minutes."

Angie's probing nose was suddenly tickling me. Stifling a laugh, I said, "I am not canceling. But I will be a *little* late."

"What's a little?"

Because of my past tardiness, Lisbet had every right to sound suspicious. "That depends. Didn't you say you had a friend in Los Feliz Hills who takes in dogs?"

I pronounced it *Lohs-Fee-Liz.* Naturally, when Lisbet answered that she did have a friend with a large estate who took in dogs in need, she pronounced it Los Fay-Lease. After I explained Angie's situation, Lisbet volunteered to call her friend to make arrangements.

My girlfriend has one of the biggest hearts of anyone I know. The two of us first met through the tragedy of a baby who was abandoned and died. For years Lisbet's been tending to throwaway babies who've died in the L.A. area. Her big heart seems to attract those with the same in all walks of life. Good people and kindred spirits gravitate to Lisbet. She's not fond of her sometimes nickname of "the Saint," but there's a reason people call her that. I wish I had her Rolodex of good people, but it's something she's earned by being who she is.

On the drive over to Los Feliz Hills, I played a Peggy Lee tune quite different from "The Siamese Cat Song." There's something disquieting about Lee's anthem to nihilism, "Is That All There Is?" I listened to Peggy talk about the world going up in flames, and remembered how that had felt. And then she spoke about her disillusionment with the greatest show on earth, and love, and life itself. It's a song as compelling as it is depressing. There had been a time Lee's lyrics could have been mine. Life was better now.

The GPS directed us deep into Los Feliz Hills. The area has some of the nicest houses in L.A., and when the female voice of the directional muse told me we'd arrived at our destination, I could see that Angie had lucked into some splendid digs. The house was set back from the street, and behind it was a huge lot that extended into the foothills. We walked up a flagstone pathway, making our way past huge birds-of-paradise and trellised stands of flowering Mandevillas of pink, white, and red.

"You've hit the jackpot," I told Angie. "Don't blow it."

I rang the doorbell. Sirius sat down and comported himself like a gentleman. Angie was more interested in sniffing the doormat than she was in making a good first impression. The door opened, and luckily for Angie, her slobber and appearance didn't put off the hostess one iota.

"Oh, you poor dear," she said, immediately taking Angie's leash into her hand.

"And aren't you handsome?" she said to Sirius.

He wagged his tail, his way of saying, "Tell me more."

"As you can see," I said, "Angie is blind in her left eye. My vet cautioned me to approach from her good side. I've forgotten that advice all day and didn't suffer any consequences, but it's probably better to be safe than sorry."

"I'll look before I leap," she promised, outdoing me in the cliché department.

I talked for a minute with "Doggy Doreen," as she called herself. In appearance Doreen reminded me of a sheepdog, with her long salt-and-pepper bangs almost covering her eyes. She was on the heavy side and wore a man's large dress shirt. Her drawstring pants advertised her true love: it was a print with silhouettes of dog breeds showcased up and down her pant legs.

"Welcome to our menagerie," Doreen said to Angie.

From the backyard I could hear a chorus of dogs; their range of sounds could only come from a variety of dog sizes and shapes.

"I'm currently looking for Angie's mom," I explained, "but at this time she's a missing person."

From Doreen's nods, I could tell that Lisbet had already filled her in. "I hope you find her soon," she said. "But like I told Lisbet, I'm happy to accommodate Angie for as long as it takes."

I thought I should also mention Angie's chewing, which I did in a roundabout way. "Angie doesn't seem to like being confined," I said.

"The dogs are free to come and go," she said. "We have more than an acre here. Seven-foot wrought iron fencing surrounds the property. We've taken in several so-called escape artists, but so far not one of our charges has broken out."

"That's probably because none of them have wanted to."

Doreen laughed. "The dogs do seem to enjoy their vacation here," she said.

"Sorry," I told Sirius.

Doreen scratched his ear. "Maybe Daddy will let you visit another time."

CHAPTER 15

CACTUS TO CLOUDS TO SHROUDS

I wasn't far from Lisbet's when my cell phone began ringing. My car's display showed Seth Mann was calling. I accepted the call hands-free and began talking.

"Good timing for your call," I said. "I was just wondering with the amphibian die-off if there was an acceptable substitution for eye of newt and toe of frog."

I expected my shaman friend to have fun with my politically incorrect cauldron ingredients, but instead he said, "I expect you haven't heard the news, Michael."

The tone of his voice bespoke his seriousness. "What news is that?"

"I called the number you gave me for Langston Walker. A woman answered, and I said that I was calling about Walker and the 187 Club. She apparently thought I was identifying myself as a member of that club, and told me the funeral would be taking place on Saturday."

"I'm not following what you're saying."

"I am afraid Detective Walker died, Michael."

I made some incoherent sounds; Seth correctly interpreted my attempt at speaking as incredulity.

"I took down the funeral information," he said, "and afterward I went online. According to the reports I read, the detective was found dead near the top of the Skyline Trail. It's believed he slipped and hit his head, but as I understand it, they're also conducting an autopsy to see if he had a heart attack. He was less than a thousand feet from the top of the trail when it happened."

I was still lacking the words to respond. I'd broken bread with the man only days before, and found it difficult to get my mind around the fact that he was gone.

Seth didn't intrude on my silence. If he was waiting for me to come up with something profound, that didn't happen. Finally I said, "Shit."

"Do you and Sirius want to stop by?" he asked.

"Lisbet's expecting us," I said.

"Maybe tomorrow night," he said.

"That would be good."

* * *

I decided not to tell Lisbet about Langston Walker or Heather Moreland. My good intentions didn't even last five seconds. When Lisbet greeted me at the door to her apartment, she took one look at my face and asked, "What's wrong?"

The divorce rate among law enforcement officers is said to be seventy to eighty percent. I'm not sure if that divorce rate is a result of cops sharing what's going on in their workplace, or not sharing. I'm hoping it's the latter, as Lisbet has proved to be a great sounding board.

When I said I wasn't yet ready to eat, Lisbet fed Sirius, and then we both sat down to a glass of wine. I told her about Langston, and it was almost like I was telling the same news to myself. It's always a shock when someone dies unexpectedly; I had trouble getting my mind around the detective being gone. I rehashed some of what we'd talked about at dinner, and I told her about the 187 Club.

"He was a godsend to so many people," I said, shaking my head.

And then I did a lot more shaking of my head when I told her about Heather's disappearance.

"As bad as I feel about Langston's death," I said, "I'm feeling worse about Heather. Langston died on the trail doing something he wanted to do; I don't know what happened to Heather."

"Then why are you assuming the worst?" asked Lisbet. "It would be hard to imagine someone growing up in Heather's situation that wasn't—*damaged*." It took Lisbet a moment to find the right word.

"I'm sure she is damaged," I said. "But that's what makes me admire her. She overcame her circumstances."

"Maybe the prospect of divorce brought up those circumstances. She must have been bottling up a lot. Is it possible she harmed herself?"

I shook my head with a vehemence that seemed to surprise her. But I had a one-word answer for my certainty, one that had me convinced Heather hadn't gone off and committed suicide: "Angie."

Lisbet understood my shorthand and nodded.

"Heather's coworker told me that she saved Angie from certain death. She said Heather didn't give up on Angie when just about anyone else would have. I can't see Heather killing herself without first making arrangements for Angie."

"You think she was abducted?"

"So far nothing else adds up. And not only that, I'm pretty sure Heather's last act was to protect Angie. Her coworker said Angie always slept in the same room with Heather. When I went into the backyard, I found a popped screen, but the bedroom window was closed."

"You'd think she would have kept Angie close to her for protection."

"I suspect Heather was afraid of Angie's getting hurt. Her own protection was secondary to the safety of her charge."

"You think she was acting like a protective mother?"

"I do."

I thought about those occasions when I'd had to send Sirius into danger. It was something I always hated doing. Luckily, Sirius had only been badly hurt one time. That had been the second worst day of my life.

"I wonder what that psychologist would say about your theory," Lisbet said.

"In the words of Freud, he'd probably say, 'Yo mama,' and maybe he'd be right."

"It sounds like he believes Heather was leading some kind of double life."

"Shrinks love familial dynamics," I said.

"But he believed that when it came to her relationship, she was crying wolf, right?"

"Emilio supposedly told him Heather liked to overreact after the fact, but I'm not sure I'm buying that. That's the same argument defense attorneys and their clients use when they try and put rape victims on trial."

"You think Emilio is a liar?"

"All of us practice revisionist history. But if you've admitted to domestic abuse, no matter how much perfume you spray, you still end up smelling like a skunk."

"He probably snapped when Heather told him she was going to proceed with the divorce."

"He did admit to going ballistic."

"But he claims to know nothing about her disappearance?"

I nodded.

"Do you think he's guilty?"

"I know he's guilty of having been abusive," I said. "I don't know if he's guilty of having abducted his ex. To his credit, Emilio willingly entered a certified Batterer Intervention Program, what's known as a BIP. He agreed to pay for the fifty-two weeks of courses in an attempt to win his wife back. Maybe he snapped because he spent all that time and money for nothing."

"What's your gut telling you?"

I shook my head. "I'm not sure. I think he tried to underplay the extent of his anger. And I don't believe he's the reformed innocent he'd have me believe. I couldn't help but feel his shrink was damning him with faint praise. In fact, he was careful to withhold comment on several of my questions."

I sighed, which somehow turned into a yawn. "Excuse me," I said. "It was a long night."

"And an even longer day," said Lisbet. "Are you ready for dinner?"

I nodded and said, "Thanks." Surprisingly, I was actually feeling hungry. Maybe getting things off my chest had opened up room in my stomach.

Once a week Lisbet cooks for me, and once a week I cook for her. We also usually get takeout one or two nights a week, which means on average we spend half our evenings together. For the time being that seems perfect. I'm not sure if that's because we are both used to our own space or whether neither one of us is willing to fully commit to our relationship. If there's a problem, I suspect it's with me. My wife's death, coupled with my burns and PTSD, changed me. I kept pretending to be who I was until it got to the point where I had trouble remembering who that person was. I was an actor who'd forgotten his old lines. Lisbet kept me from going down the drain.

She served both of us. What I saw on my plate looked familiar. "Isn't that what you just gave Sirius?"

Lisbet nodded and smiled. "I was looking for a dinner that I could serve all of us. It was simple: whole-wheat penne pasta, along with broccoli and turkey sausage sautéed in a little olive oil. And then at the end I added some cut-up grape tomatoes and basil."

"Five ingredients and delicious," I said, finishing a big mouthful.

"Sirius had five ingredients," she said. "You added a lot of parmesan cheese that he didn't."

"Try sharing a car with a lactose-intolerant partner."

"You're lucky Sirius is too polite to complain about you."

"Isn't that the truth?"

* * *

After dinner I fought off another yawn. Eagle eyes noticed and said, "You need to go to bed."

"In a few minutes I'll get my second wind."

She shook her head. "It's time for you to go to sleep."

Lisbet is a graphic artist who works for herself. As I've told her too many times, she has a real SOB for a boss.

"Let me do the dishes at least."

"Do not do the dishes. Do not pass go. Do not collect two hundred dollars."

"How about collecting a kiss?"

"Later," she said. "And I might throw in some interest. But for now, go and count sheep."

Even though I've been dating Lisbet for more than a year, I still have trouble sleeping over at her place. The thought of my fire dream is always hanging over me. When it occurs, I get swept back to the night of the fire and find myself once more immersed in flames. Every time, my journey back is so realistic, and so *personal*. And in its aftermath I feel exposed. I hate being that vulnerable.

But I was too tired to worry about a fire dream. As I pulled back the bedcovers, I thought about wolves and sheep, and about crying and counting.

I didn't have to count many sheep. I think I was even asleep before one pneumonoultramicroscopicsilicovolcanokoniosis.

CHAPTER 16

THE NOT-SO FUNHOUSE

Heather opened her eyes and saw the squinting, leering face winking at her. Screaming, she pushed herself up.

In front of her eyes, the horrible figure transformed itself into a grimacing dwarf who was shaking her chains at her and screaming.

Just like I'm screaming, Heather thought. And there was something about the misshapen face that looked familiar . . .

It was a distortion of her face, she realized, with her eyes scrunched and her forehead distended. Her arms and legs were truncated. Heather took a step to her right, and then a step to her left. Her tiny legs mimicked her movements.

It's a funhouse mirror, she realized.

The notes from a calliope started up. It sounded like circus music, but with a twist. There was a nightmarish quality to the tune, with harsh notes and discordant syncopation, and that was even before sinister laughter joined in.

A nearby wall suddenly became illuminated. Heather followed the trail of light and could make out the lens of a projector. The music changed, but there was little improvement. "Send in the Clowns" played, not as sung by Barbra Streisand or Cher, but more like Jim Morrison on acid.

Clown images showed themselves, each one creepier than the last. They were clowns with claws, fangs, dripping blood, and animal eyes; their makeup was running so that they resembled Heath Ledger's Joker. The last featured clown looked more normal than the others; he was holding a bouquet of balloons and waving. He was identified by name, and Heather thought the name was familiar: John Wayne Gacy.

And then her memory was jarred: pictures of Gacy's victims appeared. Heather turned away and covered her mouth, fighting off sickness.

"Stop it!" she cried. "Stop it!"

The music stopped, and so did the projection.

"Hello!" Heather cried. "Is anyone there?"

No one answered her cries.

"Hello!" she called again. "Hello!"

She tried to sound controlled, to keep her panic in check. Someone had to be observing her, or at least hearing her.

She took a few deep breaths. *This is real,* she told herself. I am not imagining this. I am a prisoner, and I must not submit to fear. I have to think.

Soft music came from the hidden speakers. This time it wasn't scary. In fact, it was familiar to her. It was music she'd asked to be played at her wedding. Etta James was singing "At Last."

She and Emilio had danced to this song.

"Emilio, are you out there?"

No one answered her question.

The light came on again, but what was being played was out of focus, and at first Heather had no idea what she was seeing. One moment she could almost make out what was there, and then everything became blurry.

The picture became more distinct as James sang of "a thrill to press my cheek to." But it wasn't a cheek that was being pressed. A naked female form took shape, images shown in bits and pieces. Heather saw toes and fingers, and lips and hips. The arch of a foot turned into a backside curve. At first the shots were fast and didn't linger. The model's face remained hidden. Her body appeared unmoving until the camera lingered for long enough to show a chest rising and falling.

Heather grew uneasy when a hand with a surgical glove appeared and began cavalierly tracing its way along the woman's body, the sheathed fingers displaying a familiarity and contempt with the flesh upon which it was probing and prying. The hand slapped the buttocks once, twice, and then a third time. Flesh reddened, but the woman didn't respond.

"No," said Heather. Her throat was dry.

The gloved index finger and thumb came together, pinching down hard on a pink nipple.

That was why she'd awakened to her chest and different parts of her body hurting. It was her own body she was looking at. She was witness to her own violation.

Heather didn't want to scream, but she couldn't help herself.

While Etta James called out, "At last," the gloved hand continued its assault.

CHAPTER 17

MAKING A COLLAR

Sleeping through the night is something I rarely do. In the words of Rodney Dangerfield, "I don't know how to sleep. I know how to pass out." Exhaustion had made me pass out.

Lisbet had left me a note on the kitchen table saying she had an appointment and would talk to me later in the day. She signed it XXOO but didn't stop there. The impression of her lipstick brightened the stationery, and my day. Next to her note, a bowl of her healthy cereal sat alongside a bran muffin. As I took a seat, Sirius joined me.

"Nice try," I told him. "Lisbet wrote that she fed you and took you out for a little walk."

I took a bite of the bran muffin. Lisbet was always extolling its virtues, talking about how her favorite local bakery sweetened its muffins with applesauce. After what felt like a few minutes of chewing, I was able to swallow.

Sirius was still waiting me out, so I gave him half the bran muffin. It took him a second to inhale it.

"Lisbet says that these muffins are low in fat and cholesterol, and high in fiber, magnesium, phosphorus, and manganese."

What she hadn't said was that they tasted like cardboard. Sirius finished the rest of the muffin. As he ate I thought back to how I'd told Langston Walker that Lisbet was doing her best to make me eat healthier. It still seemed almost incomprehensible to me that he was gone.

Out of respect to Lisbet, I made it halfway through my bowl of puffed whole-grain cereal before disposing of the evidence.

"Don't tell," I said to Sirius.

As early as it was in the day, I was already feeling the weight of the Heather Moreland case. That's how it is when I'm working on something that matters to me. I get obsessive, and I want answers. The weight of a case is something I can't shake. I feel it in my gut sitting there like an undigested meal. It's a pressure that keeps growing, and the only relief comes from getting answers. I was hoping Sergeant Reyes had some of those answers, or at least updates.

My call to Reyes went through to his voice mail, and I wondered if that was his way of reminding me that officially I was just a cop trying to reunite Heather with her dog.

There it was—that weight in the gut. And I couldn't even blame Lisbet's cereal or Langston's death.

I took a quick shower and put on fresh clothes. Lisbet allows me a drawer in her place, as well as some closet space. On my end she has pretty much taken over the guest room closet and drawers. When Lisbet does the laundry, she uses things like conditioner and dryer sheets. I sniffed approvingly; Sirius sniffed approvingly. I thought of Angie and wondered how she was doing; I thought of Angie's mom and wondered how I was doing making headway into her disappearance. That pressing weight I was feeling told me things could be going better.

"Office," I said to Sirius.

My partner eagerly followed me to the car. He knew "office" was Central Police Station in downtown Los Angeles, where I have my work cubicle. Officially, Sirius and I only report to the Chief of Police. At the time the Chief and I came to that understanding, I was offered an office in the Police Administration Building. In a rare show of wisdom, I knew it would be a smart career move to distance myself from the brass. Central is only a mile away if the Chief needs a face-to-face. Luckily, he doesn't feel the need to meet with me very often.

The drive was the usual stop-and-go, but I was glad on this commute there was more go than stop. It's not usually that way. As Sirius and I made our entrance into Central, Sergeant Perez decided to serenade us with the song "Puppy Love." There were two problems with his rendition: he only knew the first line, and he couldn't sing worth a damn. Perez is the watch commander of the station; his service stripes, or what cops call hash marks, put his long seniority at LAPD on display.

Sirius wagged his tail at the sergeant's musical greeting. My partner is fond of Perez. There's no accounting for taste.

Other than Perez, there were only a few cops at the station. Everyone was out in the field. Sirius and I offered up our greetings to those who were there, and then I settled into my cubicle. My wish for solitude wasn't granted. Perez came back and joined us, but luckily it wasn't to sing another verse of "Puppy Love."

"Too bad Captain Becker isn't here," he said. "I know she wanted to talk to you."

"About what?"

"One of our fair citizens had a complaint about you."

Perez's deadpan expression and delivery always makes it difficult to tell if he's on the level or if he's pulling your leg.

"What did I supposedly do?"

"It isn't what you did, but what you said. You remember a few weeks back when you ticketed some lady for talking on her cell phone while operating a vehicle?"

I did remember. If the woman hadn't been violating almost every law known, I would have ignored her. Detectives don't like handing out tickets. That's the job of traffic cops.

"I could have written her up for speeding, texting while driving, talking on her phone while driving, and negligent driving," I said. "She was actually putting on lipstick while talking and texting. And get this: since her hands were occupied, she was controlling the steering wheel with her legs. Vishnu would have had trouble doing as many things as she was."

"That's what you remember?"

I shrugged. "That's about all there is to remember. As I recall, she tried to talk her way out of the ticket and act all flirty, until I made it clear that wasn't going to work."

"Now you're getting warm. This lady even tacitly admitted to Captain Becker that she was playing up to you. But she said that still didn't give you the right to say what you did."

"Remind me what I said."

"Does this ring a bell? This lady is probably batting her eyelashes at you. One of her blouse buttons might have even magically disengaged itself, as they frequently do whenever there's a prospect of a ticket. And she says breathlessly, 'I didn't think L.A. cops gave pretty women tickets.' And you replied, 'We don't.' And that's when you handed her the ticket."

It had been a hot day, and I'd been provoked. I wished I hadn't said it, but now I remembered that I had. "She wasn't batting her eyelashes, but she was kind of lisping."

"We don't," said Perez, laughing.

He tried to give me a high five, but I ignored him. He tried the same tactic with my partner. Sirius is more polite than I am, and gave him five.

"We don't," said Perez again. "I think the captain was on that call for fifteen minutes. And when she hung up, she said something about having to deal with another Detective Sirius situation."

I had hoped the captain would have forgotten about that incident. A few months earlier, "Detective Sirius"—or someone writing a report using his name—had sent a letter to the public defender representing a lowlife I'd arrested. The lawyer had wanted "Officer Sirius's" account of the situation leading up to the arrest.

"Hey, Gideon," said Perez, "what do your dog and your phone have in common?"

I shook my head.

"They both have *collar* ID," he said. "Get it?"

"I wish I didn't," I said, and waved him away.

He didn't leave quietly. "We don't," Perez said again, and laughed all the way back to his desk.

After making quick work of messages, mail, and email, I began studying my case notes on Heather Moreland. Reyes still hadn't called me back; I hoped he had more on her disappearance than I did. Even though I'd never met Heather, I had this sense of knowing her and wanting the best for her. After everything she'd gone through while growing up, Heather deserved a happy ending, the kind reserved for old Disney movies.

Given my few options, I called up Katie Rivera.

"Any news?" she asked, sounding slightly breathless.

"That's what I was going to ask you."

I heard her let out some disappointed air. "Everyone around here is sort of in a state of shock."

"What are they saying?"

"They're hoping Heather's absence is some kind of misunderstanding," she said. "No one could imagine anyone wanting to hurt her."

"Not even Emilio?"

"Only a few of us are aware of what's going on in Heather's marriage, so it isn't like everyone is pointing a finger at him."

"Did Heather ever indicate to you she might be seeing someone else?"

"No, she didn't. And I'd be shocked if that was the case. She would have told me."

"Is it possible that Heather didn't confide in you about everything?"

"Let's just say I would be surprised if she kept any secrets from me."

"So you don't believe she had some kind of secret life?"

"If I wasn't so upset, I think I'd laugh at that," said Katie. "Like I already told you, Heather was Pollyanna, but in the best sense of that word. It's not that she didn't know there were bad things and bad people out there, because growing up she experienced both of those things, but she chose not to let any of that color her thinking."

"Emilio's therapist seemed to suggest that Heather was an enabler when it came to his behavior, and that she might even have initiated his physical and sexual abuse."

"The only person I know who would believe that is Emilio."

"The therapist indicated that since her father was an abuser, she might have been looking for the same in a husband."

"He doesn't seem to have factored in Heather's response to Emilio's controlling ways and his abuse. She ultimately decided she couldn't forgive him for what he had done."

"You don't think Heather could have liked bondage or engaged in sadomasochistic behavior?"

"That doesn't even remotely sound like her."

"What can you tell me about her sex life?"

"Heather wasn't a prude, if that's what you're asking. At first her relationship with Emilio was all that she could have wanted, but then he started trying to control her, and matters got worse from there."

"Was she afraid of Emilio?"

"I think it was more of a case of once burned, twice shy. She'd suffered enough abuse to not want any more. Imagine having her childhood. Heather was forced to be all grown up by the time she was eighteen. By then she'd seen her mother murdered, her father imprisoned, and her brother die of an overdose. After what she went through as a child, I don't think she was afraid of anything."

Katie took a moment to consider what she was saying, and then said, "Except one thing."

"What's that?"

"Heather's mother was mentally ill. From what Heather remembers, her mother's condition grew worse over the years. It scared her to think she could end up like her mother. Heather said her mother was probably schizophrenic and was always seeing and hearing things that weren't there."

I wrote down, *Depressive Disorder?* My bout with PTSD had acquainted me with phrases like that. If Heather had suffered some kind of breakdown, that might explain her absence. She could have gone off the deep end.

Katie told me she was late for a meeting but said I could call her later.

I made a second call. Emilio wasn't nearly as charitable as Katie and wasn't happy to hear from me.

"I'm on the job," he said. "You cops have already gotten me on my boss's shit list. Don't call me at work."

"Let's talk after work, then."

"Let's not. I've been advised not to talk to you. Hell, even that other cop who talked to me said I didn't have to talk to you."

He hung up on me before I even had a chance to say, "Temper, temper."

Other than Angie, Heather had no family. I decided to hold off interviewing Heather's friends and coworkers in lieu of organizing my case notes. Most young cops don't bother with paper, doing everything on their computers, but I'm a great believer in scribbling. Scratching and doodling has a way of clearing my mental logjams. I could use a little magic.

I wrote *Angie's trail* underneath my entry of *Depressive Disorder?* Then I drew a map from Burbank to Sherman Oaks, with some of the landmarks in between. What was it that had brought Angie to my neighborhood? Was it mere chance? And was it only self-preservation that kept her away from the freeways?

Google Street View took me in and around Burbank. From Heather's house I followed several street routes to my neighborhood. Even though I was using my fingers to travel the ten miles, it still seemed like a long way. The pads on Angie's worn paws told me she'd walked even farther than that. What had her nose been telling her? I suppose it was possible that fear had been driving her. Although thunderstorms are rare in Southern California, when they occur dogs frequently panic. During *Sturm und Drang* I've seen some dogs in panicked flight, fleeing with no regard as to where they were going. Over the last decade I've been involved in two rescues of soaked and shivering dogs trying to distance themselves from the roar of thunder.

Another entry: *Did something spook Angie?*

When I tired of navigating Google Street View, I decided to tap *Pluto the dog* into the search engine. The cartoon images of Pluto didn't look all that much like Angie. I read through Pluto's film biography; he'd been in more films than most A-list actors. His 1941 film, *Lend a Paw*, had Pluto saving the life of a kitten put into a bag and thrown into a river, and I was reminded of Sirius running to Angie's aid. *Lend a Paw* had been dedicated to the Tailwagger Foundation, a group that I knew was still providing treatment to sick and injured animals around the globe. It is mostly the fault of uncaring humans that dogs and cats end up in dire straits; luckily there are good humans who try to counterbalance the bad.

Every few minutes I found myself checking the time. Finally, I called Sergeant Reyes and again got his voice mail. I tried to take the high road, hoping that would help my chances of his calling back.

"This is Gideon," I said, "still waiting for your call. If your gout is bothering you, I'd be glad to help with any legwork you might have in the Moreland case. Call me."

I continued with my scribbling. For some reason I kept hearing Perez's punch line about what your dog and phone had in common: collar ID. I suppose it was better than hearing his version of "Puppy Love" polluting my thoughts.

Collar ID. The words seemed to write themselves on the paper in front of me. I underlined them a few times and then added some stars. Then I encapsulated the two words in a cube. I don't claim to be an artful scribbler, but I sensed something was there.

When I'd found Angie, she hadn't been wearing a collar, and I'd incorrectly assumed she was an abandoned dog. Reyes had given me her collar, not out of any goodwill, but to make it clear that he was in charge and I was merely the animal keeper.

I pulled out my cell phone and began looking at the pictures I'd taken at Heather Moreland's house. While it was clear I was no crime-scene photographer, thanks to technology my pictures were mostly legible. With my index finger I scrolled through the shots, stopping when I came to the pictures I'd taken through the master bedroom window that faced the backyard. Some of the pictures I'd lined up; others I had shot blind. Even though I'm six feet tall, I'd done most of my looking into the room on my tippy-toes because of the drop-off from the window to the ground below.

At the time I took the pictures, I had wanted to document what I thought looked like a struggle. I hadn't consciously noticed the dog collar, but now I saw it on the ground near the window.

It seemed like a strange place for a dog collar to be. It almost looked as if the collar had purposely been removed. But if I was right about Heather keeping Angie out of harm's way by putting her out the window, why would she have removed her collar? Angie's tags were on the collar; Heather's personal information was there.

Maybe the collar had fallen off while Heather was lifting Angie through the window. Or it was possible my initial supposition was wrong. Angie could have been in the backyard when the intruder broke into the house. There was a doggie door, after all.

I used my thumb and index finger to expand the image and give me a better look at the dog collar. There didn't seem to be anything special about what I was seeing. I'd handled many nylon collars just like it. The collar had a quick-release buckle and a snap hook for the leash. I could see the dog tags in the picture. The color of the collar was a robin's-egg blue, which was what made the vivid rectangular patch stand out. The discolored area looked to be about half the size of the soap cake they provide in discount motels. Something had shielded that section of the collar from the elements.

It was probably nothing, but Doggy Doreen was on my call list anyway. Now I had a reason to call her other than finding out how Angie was doing. Doreen picked up on the second ring.

"This is Detective Gideon," I said. "How's our friend?"

"Angie is a very sweet girl," Doreen said, "but it's clear she would rather be home with her parent."

"I hope she hasn't been too much trouble."

"No, it's not that. She was pacing the grounds last night, and she's been pacing them this morning. Dogs are pack animals," Doreen said, "and she wants her pack leader back."

"Still working on that," I said. "I hate to ask, but could you take her for another night or two?"

"It's not Angie's fault that she loves too much. As I told you, I'll be happy to keep her into the foreseeable future."

"I've got another favor to ask of you," I said.

"What's that?"

"I wonder if you could look at her collar. I want to see if there's a brand name inscribed on it."

"It will take me a minute to round Angie up," she said. "Do you want me to call you back, or do you want to hold on while I get her?"

"I'm happy to hold on," I said.

Doreen and her portable phone went in search of Angie. Along the way I heard her talking to other dogs. If I wasn't mistaken, it sounded like one of those took to sniffing the mouthpiece of the phone. I could hear Doreen calling to Angie. Most of the other dogs responded to her calling, but not Angie. Finally, she caught up to her, and was slightly breathless when she came back on the line.

"I have both Angie and her collar in hand," Doreen said. "And now I am looking at the collar."

I could hear the sounds of her examining it. After around ten seconds of silence she said, "There's no brand name visible."

I felt a twinge of disappointment, but not much. It had been a long shot anyway, and I wasn't even sure if knowing what kind of collar it was could have helped my investigation in any way.

"Thanks for looking."

"But I think the reason I don't see a brand name is that the tracker is missing," she said. "I'm fairly certain this is a Doghound collar."

"Tracker?" I asked. "Doghound?"

"I've seen collars that look just like this one before, except this collar is missing its GPS tracker."

"And you think it's a brand called Doghound?"

"Now that I think about it, maybe it's Dogfound. Or it could be Dogfind. It's something like that."

"And this collar comes with a GPS tracker?"

"I hear it's very effective. If your dog goes missing, you can track its movements."

"Doggone," I said, trying to control my growing excitement.

My bad pun found pay dirt. "Yes, that's it!" said Doreen. "That's the name of the collar! I'm sure of it."

CHAPTER 18

A PRAYER IN THE LAIR

Heather awoke to the world spinning around her. She shook her head and tried to orient herself, but it almost felt like she had water in her ears that was throwing off her equilibrium.

What time is it, she wondered, *and what day is it?* She couldn't even guess at how long she'd been held, and didn't know if it was day or night.

At least she could move more freely now. Her shackles had been removed, but the damage to her hands and legs had already been done. The cuts and scabs on her wrists and ankles were oozing and looked infected.

Still, that was the least of her worries. Her stomach churned. Her abductor had made a film showing his violation of her. He'd treated her like some kind of curiosity to be used and abused, like a sideshow in his circus. Heather had tried not to watch, and most of all not to react. A camera was filming her. Even if no one was watching at that moment, she had to assume she was being monitored at all times. It was even possible her jailer was watching her remotely. If so, she would offer him no satisfaction. She would deny him his live theater.

But what if it wasn't Emilio? What if she was the prisoner of a crazed killer? *Then I will have to deal with it,* she thought. *And wasting time thinking about it won't help me escape.*

During her drugged sleep, the dungeon had been rearranged. The funhouse mirror was gone. And her clothes had been removed and replaced by a robe. On the floor she saw what looked like an article of clothing, and she picked it up.

The burka had been designed to cover up her face. There was colored mesh that was designed to hide her eyes and mouth. Heather's first reaction was to throw the headdress to the ground, but then she decided the burka might prove useful. She could put it on at a time of her choosing and hide her face from him.

He had exposed her body and used it, and then had covered it up. Her captor was trying to exert control of her mind and body. She was in his cage, but there were ways out of cages. All of her life Heather had been finding those ways.

She thought of Angie's GPS tracker. It was possible her captor had overlooked the device attached to the strap of her nightgown.

At least she'd succeeded in preventing any harm from coming to Angie. Her drooling, snuffling Angie.

Heather prayed then, but not for herself. She asked God to deliver Angie into a good home.

After her prayers were finished, she began a painstaking search of her cell. She would go over every square inch again and again until she figured a way out.

CHAPTER 19

FALSE FRONTS AND DOUBLE MEANINGS

I was forced to listen to Sergeant Reyes's voice mail once again. This time I said, "I might have something on Heather Moreland's disappearance. If we're lucky, together we might even be able to pinpoint her location. I need you to call me back pronto."

While awaiting Reyes's call, I went to the Amazon website and acquainted myself with Doggone and similar tracking systems incorporated into dog collars. According to the device's description, Doggone offered real-time global positioning satellite readings that could be accessed through a web tracking platform used with either a GSM phone or a computer. What that translated to was you could supposedly get a bead on your missing Fido if he was wearing the tracking device. To use the system, you needed to have a SIM card.

Several potential pitfalls surfaced as I read about Doggone. The manufacturer said that the battery life of the product was "up to one week when fully charged." I suspected the real battery life would be less, and it was likely that Heather Moreland had already been missing for four days. That meant the battery could be dead. There was also the chance that Heather had decided Angie was no longer a runaway threat and let her SIM card lapse to avoid paying its monthly fee. My final worry was whether we could access the web tracking platform in a timely manner. I suspected Heather had downloaded the Doggone app to her cell phone, but even if that was the case, I didn't know if the program was password protected. I also wasn't sure if I'd be able to figure out how to use Doggone. The manufacturer's claim was that it was "easy to use." I was skeptical.

My phone rang, and the readout told me it was Reyes. I sure as hell wasn't going to tell him any of my doubts.

"I assume you have Heather Moreland's cell phone in your possession," I said.

"Your message said you had something. Was that just a fishing expedition?"

"Before we get into specifics, I need to know if you're currently able to access Heather's cell phone."

"In Burbank we actually have cell phones," he said. "And in case you're wondering, I've been studying her incoming and outgoing calls and text messages. I've even gone through her pictures and made a list of her contacts. And right now I'm trying to get in touch with every single one of her contacts, or I would be except I keep getting interrupted by your calls. So do you have something or not?"

"I *might* have something," I said, "but I'm trying not to get ahead of myself. Have you checked the phone's apps?"

"Yeah, that's been a priority of mine," Reyes said. "I've been sitting here alternating between Tinder and Angry Birds."

"I want you to look at her apps and see if she has one called Doggone. It has the image of a paw print."

I listened to Reyes's heavy breathing while he tapped the phone. The movements of his finger sounded like someone hitting a heavy bag with slow, hard punches. Reyes wasn't a technophobe, but like everyone over the age of forty, he hadn't been weaned on technology.

His grunt made it sound as if he'd landed a particularly solid blow. "I found it," he said.

"In that case I'm crossing my fingers that we've found her," I said.

* * *

Reyes wanted an explanation over the phone, but I insisted upon a face-to-face. He reluctantly agreed, but said I'd have to drive to Burbank. He said he'd be grabbing a quick bite at the deli across the street from the police station. Ironically, it turned out to be the same deli where Sirius, Angie, and I had met with Katie Rivera. That wasn't something I told Reyes.

It took me five minutes to print all the instructions I could find on Doggone's website, and another half hour to drive to Burbank. I found Reyes sitting in a booth finishing what looked like a meatloaf sandwich. As I made my approach, the same server who'd waited on me before asked, "Where are your dogs?"

"In the car," I said, hoping Reyes wasn't paying attention.

"They're cutie-pies," she said. "You want me to see if the kitchen has some extra bones for them?"

By now Reyes was listening closely.

"No, thanks," I said. "I'm just here for a quick meeting."

I joined Reyes in his booth. "Seems like you're a regular here, Gideon," he said.

"It *is* a dog-friendly restaurant."

"Why is it that you were dining at a dog-friendly restaurant in Burbank instead of one in your neck of the woods?"

"You want to talk about dogs, or see if Heather Moreland's cell phone holds a clue as to where she might be?"

He answered by pulling the phone out of his shirt pocket and sliding it across the table so that it rested between us.

"Talk," he said.

"Heather Moreland was worried about her dog running away. That's why she got a collar with a GPS tracker. The collar you gave me didn't have that tracker on it. I think there's a chance Heather unhooked it from the collar right before she was abducted. I'm hoping she still has it on her person and that the tracker will tell us where she is."

Reyes suddenly looked interested. "The stage is yours," he said, gesturing to the phone. "I'm hoping you can pull a rabbit out of the hat, Gideon."

My adrenaline was pumping as I turned on the phone and called up the Doggone app. Then I read the instructions aloud; everything on the phone seemed operational. From what I was seeing, the GPS function was installed, outfitted, and ready to go. According to the Doggone website, the readout would indicate within ten feet where the tracker currently was. I tapped the search function. Almost instantly a flashing red *X* marked a spot on a map.

"West L.A.," I said, and looked at the readout. "If this thing is accurate, our target is on West Pico Boulevard and the corner of South Genessee Avenue."

"You drive," said Reyes, "and I'll hold on to the phone."

* * *

"Geez," said Reyes, rolling down a window, "what'd you feed that dog?"

Maybe the bran muffin hadn't been such a good idea. Sirius could tell that Reyes was talking about him, and looked chastened.

"My partner's not the one with gout," I said.

"I think his gas is worse than my gout." Reyes shifted in his seat. The movement caused him to wince and mutter under his breath, *"Pinche madre."*

We had about a twenty-mile drive, but from Burbank there's no fast route to West L.A. Reyes kept watching the phone. The tracker didn't show any movement.

I kept racking my brain trying to remember what kind of businesses were operating along West Pico and South Genessee. As far as I recalled, there was the usual L.A. hodgepodge of fast food eateries, flooring stores, auto-repair shops, and strip malls. I remembered seeing some kind of new TV studio on West Pico at roughly that location, but there was no guarantee it was still in business. It's rare to find anyone in L.A. without a business card identifying them as a producer.

As we drew closer to the location, it felt increasingly wrong to me. I wanted to say that out loud, but I didn't, afraid of jinxing our operation. When we were right on top of where the tracker was broadcasting, I pulled up to the curb and cursed.

"What is it?" asked Reyes.

"The tracker must have been dumped."

Reyes looked at what he thought was an office building. "Maybe she's somewhere in that building," he said.

I shook my head and said, "There's no chance of that."

"Why?"

"For one, we're right on top of where the tracker says we should be, and it's supposed to be accurate within ten feet. But there's the other more pertinent reason. She's not inside the building because that isn't a building. It's a veneer. It's a fourteen-story facade that hides a working oil field with all sorts of derricks and pumps."

Reyes looked at me as if I was crazy.

Most L.A. natives aren't aware that much of the city is built atop scores of oil fields. Early pictures showed operating oil wells lining the streets—wells that at one time supplied half the world's oil. Those wells still exist, but many have gone underground. There are still more than thirty thousand active wells producing a couple hundred million barrels of oil a year, but a lot of those wells are hidden. The ritzy Beverly Center mall houses such stores as Bloomingdale's, Gucci, and Louis Vuitton; out of sight on the western periphery of the mall, you can find oil wells actively drilling.

Reyes, Sirius, and I got out of the car and approached the pale-yellow building. Up close you could see it was windowless; driving by you might never notice the building doesn't even have a roof.

The three of us approached a six-foot wrought iron fence. Sirius stopped to lift his leg while Reyes kept limping along the fence line. Behind the fence was a nicely landscaped area with trees, a lawn, and shrubbery. Anyone expecting fumes and noise had to be pleasantly surprised by very little of either.

Reyes looked at the building and shook his head, then went back to trying to locate the tracker through the readout on Heather's cell phone. He walked east along the fence, extending his phone like it was a Geiger counter. "It should be right here," he said.

We both started searching around the area. I wondered whether I would have to jump the fence to see if the tracker had been thrown inside the enclosure. It was something I would have to do gingerly; the pickets came with points. Then I noticed something that looked a little off. A growth of sorts rested between a picket and the top rail. Closer inspection showed that what I was seeing was a swatch of black duct tape that blended in with the wrought iron.

I pulled out my phone and snapped some shots. Reyes thought that was a good idea and did the same thing. Then I slipped on latex gloves and carefully removed the duct tape. Inside was the Doggone tracker.

"I'll take that," said Reyes.

I shook my head and said, "We're not in Burbank." Then I pulled an evidence bag from my pocket and dropped the tracker and duct tape inside.

Reyes's face reddened. "What happened to me having the missing-person case, and you having the lost-dog case?"

"It's hard to tell where the lost-dog case ends and where the lost-human case begins."

Reyes wasn't pleased. Under his breath I heard him muttering *culero* and *pendejo*. You don't need to work as a cop in Los Angeles for very long to know that both were Spanish variants for asshole. Reyes's temper didn't improve when I called SID and asked them to join us. It was probably overkill bringing in the Scientific Investigations Division, but I wanted them to make sure there were no fingerprints or trace evidence.

While we waited I looked around for security cameras, but didn't see any. Management probably didn't care what went on outside a fake building. They would be more concerned about all those oil wells operating inside the four faux walls. Still, in the hopes that there were hidden cameras, I found an informational number for the Packard Well Site and wrote it down.

Reyes was chafing at the wait for SID. It was no cakewalk for him with his gout. *"Estába picándo los ojos,"* he muttered.

It must have been apparent that I was struggling to figure out the meaning. Reyes decided to give me a Spanish lesson, or at least a Mexican-Spanish lesson. "It's a way of saying we're wasting time," he said. "What it translates to is 'I'm poking my eyes.'"

"You're probably right," I admitted. "But this is as close as we've been to Heather Moreland's abductor. I'm guessing he found the tracker on her and this is where he decided to dispose of it."

"He played us. And the longer we stay here, the longer he keeps playing us."

"If SID isn't here in the next half an hour, we'll take off."

The offer seemed to mollify him. He looked at his watch, noted the time, and then nodded.

"I'm hoping this tracker has some kind of memory," I said. "I doubt whether Heather's kidnapper discovered it right away. Maybe the tracker can tell us where it's been before it was brought here. I'll call the manufacturer and check on that."

"We could use a break," he said.

I nodded.

"If you're right about our lady's pulling the tracking device off of the collar," Reyes said, "that was fast thinking on her part."

"She's always refused to be a victim."

He nodded. One thing we could agree upon was that Heather Moreland had always shown lots of guts. I hoped she was still alive.

CHAPTER 20

AULD LANG SYNE

While waiting for SID to show up, I was able to contact technical support for Doggone. My hopes that the tracker had a memory were quickly dashed. A man who identified himself as "Roger" told me with a pronounced Indian accent, "The tracker can only tell you where it is now, not where it has been."

It was a disappointment, but at the same time, Reyes and I were now that much more convinced Heather had been abducted. This wasn't depressive disorder, or someone running away from her problems.

SID showed up right after I got off the phone with Roger. I didn't know the tech, a young woman who identified herself as Linda Handler. She was new to LAPD, she told me. Her enthusiasm was refreshing, and she didn't make me feel as if I was wasting her time.

"You can always tell the new hires," said Reyes on our drive back to Burbank. "They're so damn rude."

"What are you talking about?"

"She kept saying, 'Yes, sir,' and 'No, sir,' to me. It made me feel damn old."

"I'm sure her politeness won't last."

"That will be a relief."

The two of us began discussing what we had, or what we didn't have.

"Why didn't he just smash the tracker to pieces?" said Reyes.

I shrugged. "Maybe he planted it for misdirection. It's probably nowhere near his home or business."

"Or maybe he just wanted to send us on a wild-goose chase."

No one likes to be played for a fool, but . . . "That's possible. If so, the spot he picked makes for a good commentary."

"What do you mean?"

"He left his tracker at the site of the city's biggest false front. Maybe he was saying welcome to my hidden world."

"You think he was sending us a message?"

"I hope not. If he's gaming us, he's probably gaming Heather. My hope is that Emilio has locked Heather in a shed somewhere. This year a woman in Missouri was imprisoned in a wooden box for four months. Her boyfriend put her there after she threatened to break up with him. Luckily for her, she was able to free herself. That's our best-case scenario. "

"What's the worst-case scenario?"

"I've crossed paths with one serial murderer," I said. "I'm hoping that this isn't a case of encountering a second."

"Why would you even think that's a possibility?"

"For the last two years, I've been working with the FBI's Behavioral Science Unit, and one of the profilers there told me that at any given time, there are upward of forty active serial murderers doing their stalking around the country."

"That's not something I've been looking at."

"I think we're going to have to take a hard look at break-ins in the Southland. Serial murderers usually don't begin by going all-in. Their fantasies set them on a slippery slope. It's a learning curve for killers. We need to look at women who were threatened in their homes or apartments, and red-flag anything that resembles a potential abduction."

"What kind of time frame?"

"Let's narrow it to the last year. And while we're at it, let's also look at recent crime scenes that were staged so as to thumb their nose at law enforcement."

"You think that's what this is?"

I shrugged. "It's more likely I'm grasping at straws."

"Maybe the tracker was just left where it was for the sake of convenience," said Reyes. "Like my old man used to say, 'Location, location, location.'"

"Was your father a real estate agent?"

Reyes shook his head. "Septic tank cleaner. He liked to say he knew his shit."

* * *

The one good thing about spending time with Reyes was that the two of us had come to a better working arrangement. Our border wars felt like a thing of the past, put aside for the greater good of finding Heather Moreland.

"Another suck day," said Reyes as he exited my car.

"Another suck day," I agreed.

It was already getting dark, and I decided to give up for the day. Sirius and I drove home in silence. My partner didn't like that and gave me a nudge with his muzzle.

"I shouldn't have gotten my hopes up," I said. "It was a long shot to begin with."

Heather Moreland was still out there—I hoped.

Sirius nudged me again. "No, we're not stopping at a restaurant," I said. "You're getting too used to eating out. Uncle Seth said he'd be making you a nice meal tonight."

Only a few nights before, Sirius had been getting handouts from both me and Langston Walker. Thinking about Walker, I asked the car system synced to my cell to dial up Dave Holt, a detective in Robbery-Homicide.

"Make it fast, Gideon," he said. "It's almost time for the Final Jeopardy question."

"I'm calling about Langston Walker's death," I said. "Did you know him, and what can you tell me about what happened?"

"I knew him, but not all that well. And I don't know much about his death other than that he died like Jack."

"Jack who?"

"Jack fell down and broke his crown."

"I take it you're not reading the eulogy, or that poem, at his funeral?"

"Like I said, I didn't know him very well. But every year I pay close attention to the Darwin Awards. What's a sixtysomething guy doing climbing a mountain?"

"If you really want to know, he was keeping a promise to his murdered son. The two of them had planned on doing the Cactus to Clouds Trail together four years ago. So every year since, Walker has remembered him by doing a hike on the anniversary of his death."

"I didn't know that." Holt sounded a little chastened, but his conscience didn't trouble him for long.

"Hold on," he said. "Here's the Final Jeopardy question: 'He was prime minister of the UK from 1945 to 1951.'"

I didn't say anything.

"The category is World Leaders," Holt said, apparently thinking he was helping me to the answer.

"That stands to reason, but I still can't help you."

"A lot of good you are, Gideon. I think it's a trick question. Everyone is going to say it was Winston Churchill. But I happen to know that right after World War II, the Brits showed their gratitude to Winnie by booting him out of office. I can't remember who the hell replaced him, though, so I'm going to be forced to look at Trebek preening. He thinks he's so goddamn smart. Of course you're smart if you've got the answers written down in front of you. You know what I'd do if I didn't know the answer? I'd write down: *Who is Jack Mehoff?* And I'd be the one smiling when that smug prick Trebek read what I wrote."

Before I could comment, Holt said, "Neville Chamberlain? What's that lady thinking? What an idiot. Neville was the PM who bent over for Hitler and dropped trou. She might as well have guessed 'Wilt the Stilt' Chamberlain. Churchill replaced Chamberlain as PM. Everyone knows that."

I tried to get back to the subject of Langston Walker. "Who's still working in RHD who'd know Walker best?"

"Clement Attlee," said Holt.

I was trying to think if I knew a detective named Clement Attlee when Holt said, "Who the hell is Clement Attlee? And look at Trebek. He's acting like Clement Attlee is a personal friend of his. What a self-righteous SOB. Yeah, you know Clement Attlee, Trebek. He probably buggered you."

Clement Attlee, I deduced, had been the prime minister of England from 1945 to 1951. I decided that I'd heard enough about buggery, Alex Trebek, and Clement Attlee, and ended the call.

And then I was forced to think about the real Final Jeopardy question and Langston Walker, and wished that it wasn't so.

* * *

Seth opened his door and said, "I'm sorry about what happened to your friend, Michael."

"I won't pretend he was a friend," I said, "but in the short time we spent together, I grew to respect him, and I couldn't help but think he was a real stand-up guy."

I found a seat in my usual chair, while Sirius took to his hemp doggie bed. My partner sensed the seriousness of the situation and wasn't as buoyant as usual, even when Seth brought him his dinner.

Seth went to the bar to get us our drinks. Before he began his pour, I asked, "Do you happen to have Hennessys?"

"I do," he said.

"If you don't mind, barkeep, I think I'll have that."

Seth replaced my usual bourbon rocks glass with a snifter and poured two fingers of cognac. Then he chose his drink, filling a wineglass with cabernet sauvignon.

He handed me my cognac, then tilted his glass my way. "Auld lang syne," he said. I echoed his words, and we clinked glasses and sipped.

"His choice of drink?" asked Seth.

"It was on the night we had dinner."

I took another sip. Even though I'm not much of a cognac drinker, the drink was certainly smooth.

"I printed out a few articles on Walker and his death," said Seth. "They're on the table."

"I appreciate that. I meant to catch up on that today, but my lost-dog, lost-human case kept me running. I did call a detective in Robbery-Homicide hoping to get an up-to-date account of how Walker died, but he didn't know much."

"From what I read, Walker was by no means the first to die on that trail. Apparently half a dozen other hikers have died from a variety of causes."

I nodded. "The night we dined, Langston told me how difficult the hike was, but he did it as his way of spending time with his dead son."

"What's going to happen to his club?"

I shook my head. "His nickname was 'The Speaker for the Dead.' I don't know who's going to speak, or advocate, for them now."

"He must have had an assistant."

"I'm not sure about that," I said. "During my visit it looked as if he was the club's glue, organizer, and motivator. It will be a real loss if the club falls apart."

I looked into my drink. Maybe I was looking for Langston Walker.

"Did I tell you that Detective Walker was black?" I asked.

"You didn't," Seth said, "but there were pictures of him in the articles."

"One of the reasons he started the club was that he was sick and tired of how many young black men were dying violent deaths. That's what happened to his youngest son. He wanted to create a place of healing, and I think he wanted to put a spotlight on the violence and how those deaths were devastating in so many ways."

Seth nodded, happy to serve as my sounding board.

"Before giving my talk to the club, I wasn't looking forward to it, and I sure wasn't looking forward to having dinner with Detective Walker afterward. But the talk went well, and our dinner went even better. I thought our conversation would be forced and we wouldn't have anything to say to each other. But it turned out to be just the opposite."

I found a smile in a good memory. "We covered a lot of ground, but we also talked shop. You have to expect that when two cops get together. He was still thinking about some of his old cases. It sounded to me as if there was one case in particular that was gnawing at him. I got the impression he was actively working it. 'There's this ghost that's been haunting me,' he said."

"What kind of case was it?"

I shook my head. "I don't know. He didn't tell me the particulars. I wish he had."

Both of us drank in silence for a few minutes. Finally I said, "He was big on special remembrances and making occasions out of dark days. That was why he did the Skyline Trail walk on the anniversary of his son's death. He said it was a way of taking some of the sting out."

"I wish I had met him," said Seth. "He was practicing what I like to preach."

"Why is it the good die too young," I said, "and scumbags live as long as Methuselah?"

"It does seem that way, doesn't it?"

"I wonder how Walker's wife is going to cope with this. Every year she's going to think about how she lost her son and her husband on April 15. That's a bad enough day in most people's minds to begin with."

"Are you going to go to his service?"

"I haven't even thought about it. You said it was this Saturday?"

Seth nodded. "Some people, and some faiths, don't like to delay."

I remembered how Seth, Father Pat, and a few other good friends had done most of the organizing for Jennifer's funeral service. I hoped Walker's wife had people like that in her life.

We went back to our individual wells, each of us drawing from our glasses. Seth eventually broke our comradely silence.

"I couldn't help but notice you only came home with one dog. I assume you found Annie's owner."

"Her name is *Angie*," I said, "and I'm afraid that I'm still looking for her lost human."

I told him the story of Angie and her missing human, concluding with the tracker being found on Pico Boulevard. Then I took another drink and ground some ice between my teeth.

"Heather's out there," I said.

"You believe she's still alive?"

"That's what I *want* to believe. In her lifetime she's already been through hell and back."

"If she's the survivor you say she is, then you know she won't quit."

"That's what keeps me going. She is a survivor. Because of that I'm going to keep believing she's out there, and I'm going to keep beating the bushes in the hopes something will surface."

"Isn't that what you always do?"

"This is one case I don't want to go unsolved. It's got its claws and its paws in me. I got a dog counting on me."

Sirius's ears perked up.

"Excuse me," I said, "I have two dogs counting on me."

"I'm not sure if you found Angie or if she found you. Maybe it was meant to be that your paths crossed during her walkabout."

I'd leave that mysticism to Seth. "Angie sacrificed the pads of her feet," I said. "I better be able to do the same with my shoe leather."

Seth stood up and went over to his prized stereo system. He owns thousands of vinyl albums, and probably as many compact discs. His library is alphabetized and color coded, and it didn't take him long to find what he was looking for.

"This is for you and Angie," he said.

Sometimes nothing revives you like the right music. I started smiling from the opening beat. There's no better pick-me-up than listening to the Scottish duo the Proclaimers emoting their song "I'm Gonna Be (500 Miles)."

Ten seconds of listening was enough to push aside the disappointments of the day, at least for the duration of the song. My head was bobbing and my feet were bouncing.

Angie had started the walk, and I would keep it going, even if it meant walking five hundred miles, and then five hundred more, to find Heather Moreland.

CHAPTER 21

STUMBLING OVER HEATHCLIFF

Flames lashed out like spiked whips, their venom making our flesh boil. Sirius was still breathing. That's what kept me going. But he'd lost so much blood.

The Santa Ana Strangler was watching me. His eyes could have passed for the eyes of a demon. The fire had burned away what little humanity he possessed and revealed him. He had set the fire that burned us. He had shot my partner. He had shot me. But now I was the one holding the gun, and he was answering its commands.

He screamed when a wall of flames went up right behind him, the fire scorching his back. He would have dropped my partner, but was stopped by my command: "Don't!"

The only reason the Strangler was still alive was to help me carry Sirius.

Using my gun to signal him, I directed him away from the worst of the flames. But the Santa Ana winds made it impossible to know where to go. They pushed the fire one way, and then another. Our hope for survival meant choosing the way where we might burn less.

The wind gave the fire a rumbling voice that threatened and roared. And burned. Yes, it burned.

And then I was the one who was screaming. The flames had me in their fiery grip. But I wasn't going to give up on my partner. I kept the gun leveled on the Strangler. And what I read in his face was that he was more scared of me than he was of the weapon I was holding.

He saw me as I saw him. The Strangler thought he was looking at a demon. And in the midst of my pain, and in that raging inferno, I smiled at him. By then much of my hair had burned away, and what he saw was a maniacal, skeletal face. He looked at me and trembled, and I was glad to be revealed.

* * *

Sirius awakened me from my fire walk. "Oh, God," I said, words spoken more for the pain I was still feeling than for the relief that was too slow in materializing.

The flames began receding from my mind and body. It didn't matter that there was a part of me that knew my bout with fire was a thing of the past; even years later I continued to burn.

I hugged Sirius. His being there made all the difference, easing me into what I describe as "the moment after." I don't know where these visions come from; they might be a natural reaction of relief from escaping the fire and the frying pan, or maybe they come from another realm that I don't want to believe in. The moment after opens a window; it is my oracle. Sometimes the meaning seems clear; some-times the vision just frustrates me for my inability to understand what is being revealed.

Langston Walker stared at me with concern. Maybe he saw the demon in me, as Ellis Haines had. Walker was dead, but he appeared to be more troubled by my condition than his own.

"You're still carrying a lot of pain, aren't you?" he asked.

"What about you?"

"I'm afraid this is a double haunting, Gideon," he said. "Now you've got me and my ghost."

I shook my head, not understanding what he was saying.

"Maybe ghosts are like birds," said Walker. "Maybe you can kill two with one stone. Or is that two with one moan?"

"That sounds like something I'd say."

"Maybe you're a ghost too."

The vision passed, and I fell asleep. I've never burned twice in one night, and luckily for me, I don't burn as frequently as I used to.

Normally I sleep like the dead after undergoing a fire walk, and I usually don't remember having any more dreams. My subconscious mind must have been working on multiple levels, though, for in my second dream I found myself walking through a valley awash in fog.

I wasn't alone. Someone padded next to me, and at first I thought it was my partner. But when I looked down, I saw that it was Angie and not Sirius. Angie was sniffing intently. She was on the trail of something. But the scent was elusive.

"I am here!" cried a voice, but I wasn't sure if I was hearing words or hearing the wind.

The fog made it impossible for me to see who was calling, but I suspected it was Heather Moreland.

And then I realized we were walking in a valley in the moors. I couldn't see Heather, and Angie couldn't sniff her out. We kept walking and kept looking, but she remained hidden from view.

* * *

When I awakened in the morning, I felt the usual hangover that comes from a fire dream. I was stiff and creaky, and my skin didn't quite feel as if it was my own. My skin grafts itched, and I felt like a harlequin again, a human patchwork quilt.

I drank coffee and tried to feel the new normal, which meant accepting the limitations that came with the aftermath of the fire. Sirius was there to cheer me up. He'd been through the fire as well and had come a lot closer to death than I had, but you wouldn't know it by his attitude.

My partner joined me in some stretching. After the fire I underwent intense physical therapy to try and obtain the best possible range of motion. When you're severely burned, you have to worry about all sorts of things, including muscles and tendons shortening and scar tissue causing contraction of the skin. Sirius did the exercises to keep me company. Whenever I get down on the ground, he considers it an invitation to play. That's probably what keeps me doing the exercises.

The stretching and playing allowed me time to think about the dream that had come in the aftermath of my fire walk. I was still feeling the frustration of walking with Angie and not being able to find Heather Moreland. She was close enough that I could hear her, but not see her. There was some answer there, something in that dream, but I couldn't put my finger on it. Heather remained elusive, lost in the moors. At least I hadn't encountered Heathcliff walking the foggy moors.

I decided that for the time being, it would be better to switch one Rubik's Cube for another. At the moment there was little I could do about Heather Moreland. Reyes had promised he would try and flag any cases that involved break-ins in the residences of young women, or other abductions. I had calls in and balls in the air; sometimes, as much as you want to press forward, you have to wait for the case to come to you.

A few hours earlier I hadn't even considered looking into the death of Langston Walker. I'd been told that Walker had died of natural causes, but that was before my vision, or dream, or visit from Jacob Marley. I had been touched and told, "Tag, you're it." My subconscious mind, in the form of Walker, had passed on a "double haunting." There was that case of his, of course, his ghost case. And now I was curious about his death.

It was time to bust some ghosts, so I said to Sirius, "Who you gonna call?"

He barked, and I said, "Damn right."

CHAPTER 22

THE CRUELEST MONTH

Langston Walker had died somewhere near the ten-thousand-foot mark of Mount San Jacinto on April 15. If Benjamin Franklin was right about death and taxes being the only two certainties in this world, it seemed unfair that the two had ganged up on Walker and his son on the same fateful date.

The night before, when Seth and I had been discussing Walker's death, my shaman friend had solemnly quoted from T. S. Eliot and said, "April is the cruelest month." At the time I didn't ask him about Eliot's rationale for making such a proclamation. In L.A., April is usually the sweet spot of spring, with the daytime temperature in the high sixties and the nighttime in the midfifties. But Walker hadn't died in L.A. He'd died on a hiking trail with Palm Springs below him and the mountain town of Idyllwild above him.

I packed a day bag, thinking about what I might need. Sirius carefully watched my preparations. He knew the day bag meant an outing, but wasn't sure if he was invited.

"Are you ready for a desert getaway?" I asked.

My partner raced to the door, his tail moving like a metronome signaling a tempo of presto. When he saw I was coming, the metronome increased to *presto agitato*. Tails often say a lot more than mere words.

Early in our drive I started making phone calls. While I shot the breeze, Sirius merely enjoyed it. His eyes were half-closed while the wind traveled through his fur. Every so often he shifted his head as if saying, "It's all good." My partner is the epitome of cool without even trying. He is so cool he almost makes me look cool.

I had highlighted some names as well as information in the articles Seth had printed out on Walker's death. The first official on the scene had been a park ranger named Riley Ramsey, who worked out of the Long Valley Ranger Station, which was part of the Mount San Jacinto State Park. After I gave my phone a few voice commands, it connected me with the station. A male voice answered, but there was static on the line, and I didn't catch his name.

"Is this Ranger Ramsey?" I asked.

"Not by a long shot," he said. "You got Ranger Greer."

"This is Detective Gideon of the Los Angeles Police Department," I said. "I'm looking for Ranger Riley Ramsey." The alliterative tongue twister didn't beat me; the pronoun did. "Is he available to talk?"

"No, *he* is not," said the man. "But *she* is. I'll connect you."

A few seconds later a voice said, "This is Ranger Ramsey."

I identified myself and asked if she had a few minutes to talk about Langston Walker.

"Now isn't the best time," she said. "Could I call you back in an hour or two?"

"I'm actually in my car driving to Palm Springs," I said. "In a few hours from now, I hope to be looking over the area where Detective Walker was found."

"If I can clear my schedule," she said, "I might be able to take you there."

"That would be great."

"I assume you're going to take the tram up to the Mountain Station?"

"I'm sure not going to walk."

"Do you have crampons?"

"I don't even know what crampons are."

"They're spikes that attach to your hiking boots."

She correctly interpreted my silence. "I'm guessing you don't have hiking boots either."

"I'm wearing some Air Jordan knockoffs."

"You are aware Detective Walker died when he slipped on ice and hit his head, aren't you?"

"Was he wearing crampons?"

"As a matter of fact, he was."

"I think I'll take my chances with sneakers, then."

"I'll see if I can at least get you a hiking pole."

"Did Detective Walker have one of those?"

"He had two. From what he was carrying and how he was dressed, I would say he came well prepared for his hike, but even experienced hikers have died on the Skyline Trail."

"He called it the Cactus to Clouds," I said.

"Lots of hikers call it that, or C2C, but I think it should be called Fire and Ice. You go from burning to freezing. Honestly, I wish the trail didn't even exist. Most of the rangers think the same. There's always someone getting lost or hurt, and it seems like we're constantly being called out to assist in a rescue or an evacuation."

She avoided saying, "or a death," but it was clear that's what she was thinking.

There was the sound of a hand cupping the phone's mouthpiece, and I could faintly hear Ranger Ramsey tell someone, "All right; I'll be just a second."

Then she relinquished her hand mute. "I've got to run."

"Better put on your crampons, then."

She laughed and said, "See you in a few."

* * *

I knew I was approaching Palm Springs when I saw the spinning wind turbines. Thousands of them line the San Gorgonio Pass, a valley that runs between the San Bernardino and San Jacinto Mountains. Heavy winds flow through the gap, the lifeblood of all those turbines.

"Thar's gold in them thar hills," I told Sirius, "but just not the ore variety."

My partner opened one eye. I was intruding on his sunning.

It wasn't even noon, but the temperature gauge in my car said it was already eighty-nine degrees. Detective Walker had planned for the heat. From what I'd learned, he'd parked in the lot across from the Palm Springs Art Museum, and had then proceeded to the trailhead. His plan had been to arrive around half past five in the morning and then to be on the trail at first light. Because he'd intended to take the tram down, his wife had agreed to move his car to the Palm Springs Aerial Tramway lot so it could be there waiting for him. I didn't know if it was still there.

My GPS directed me to the art museum, and I parked across the street, where Walker had. As I stepped out of the car, I felt the heat of the day and knew it would only get worse. The nickname for Skyline Trail was evidenced by the landscape around us and the peaks above. We were in the midst of cacti, while above us, Mount San Jacinto was somewhat obscured by clouds. I shaded my eyes to get a better look at the mountains. Up high I could see pockets of ice and snow. The day before Walker's hike, a storm had dropped more than an inch of snow on the upper section of the trail. That had made hiking in the high elevations treacherous. There was no good reason to believe that Walker hadn't died in an accident, or at least no good reason other than his enigmatic visit to me after his death.

As scientific explanations go, Langston Walker's appearance could be explained as my subconscious mind's processing information and events. That was the logical explanation for my "moment after." But too many times my oracle offered me insights that didn't seem to fall within the realm of science. And while I would never go around telling anyone that Walker came to me for a post-death talk, neither would I definitively say this was simply a case of my synapses firing and my subconscious sorting.

I took a last look at Mount San Jacinto. In the heat of Palm Springs, it was difficult to imagine that snow country was within reach, but there it was.

* * *

After driving over to the tram's lot, I flagged down a shuttle. The driver pulled up alongside me and apologetically said, "I'm not allowed to transport dogs."

"He's not a dog," I said. "He's a sworn police officer."

The driver still looked dubious.

I showed him my wallet badge.

"I don't know," he said.

Then I showed him Sirius's badge. Some police departments actually give their K-9 officers badges, but not LAPD. Recently the Los Angeles Police K-9 Fund started offering badges for sale that feature a German shepherd holding handcuffs in his mouth. Beneath the picture it says, "L.A. Police," and underneath that is the motto "You can run but you can't hide." It was that fake badge that sealed the deal: Sirius and I were chauffeured to the visitor center.

We walked into the air-conditioned lobby and made our way to the tramway's ticket counter. The young woman working there stared at Sirius as if he was the big bad wolf.

"I'd like a round-trip ticket, please," I said.

She shook her head. "I'm afraid dogs aren't allowed on the tram."

I flipped open my wallet badge, then waited while she sought out the opinion of her supervisor. They had a whispered conversation, during which I heard Adriana ask her boss, "Should I also charge for the dog?"

"Kids three and under ride free," I said, pointing to the sign.

Like just about every parent I know, I lied about the age of my kid. Sirius is almost seven, even though he doesn't act his age. In that he's just like his partner.

I paid for my ticket and was directed to what the young woman called "the lobby area." Around fifteen people waited for the tram's arrival. It was a good thing I'd chosen a weekday and a nonpeak time for our ride. None of those waiting appeared too bothered by Sirius's presence, although one mother took a protective hold of her boy and drew him close.

"I want to see the doggie," the boy said.

"Not now, Cody," the mother said.

As we waited, the flutter in my stomach grew. I'm not sure what scares me more, fire or heights. The prospect of traveling two and a half miles upward on one of the self-proclaimed "World's Largest Rotating Tram Cars" was giving me butterflies. I'd tried to hide my uneasiness from Jenny on the only other occasion I'd taken the tram, but I'm pretty sure she knew, just as Sirius did now. My partner leaned into me, making as much contact with me as Cody's mom was making with her son. And here I was supposed to be the adult in the relationship.

Four other people joined us in the lobby area before the tram arrived, but that still left window viewing space for everyone. As we started the ascent, our gondola was only half-full. *It's only a ten-minute ride,* I told myself. I also told myself I didn't need an airsickness bag, even though it felt like I did. The gondola slowly rotated; there was no need to go from side to side to try and get the best view, as eventually the view came to you. I tried to ignore the loud noises and the vibrations from the tram's operation, and tried not to fixate on the fact that the gondola was suspended from a wire. It wasn't like I was a member of the Wallenda family attempting a wire walk.

Aside from the occasional feeling of weightlessness and the uneasiness that came when the gondola approached the different towers and swung a little too vigorously, after a few minutes my vertigo eased, and I actually began enjoying the sights and the changing landscape. We went from cacti to brush to trees. Looking down and seeing the steep incline showed me the difficulty of the hike that Walker had undertaken.

We landed at the terra firma of Mountain Station. The difference between where we started and where we ended up was kind of like going through a *Stargate* portal into another world. It was at least thirty degrees cooler than in the valley, and I breathed in the aroma of pine trees.

Passing by Peaks Restaurant, we continued along the path to the ranger station. Signs pointed out hiking trails and lookouts. We took a slight detour to a nearby lookout and found ourselves looking more than eight thousand feet down to the expanse of the Coachella Valley.

The ranger station was about a quarter mile away from where the tram had let us out. It was a rustic-looking outbuilding with white siding and a red metal roof. I climbed a few wooden steps and went inside. There was no ranger at the information desk—only a sign that said all hikers continuing up Skyline Trail needed to sign in and get a wilderness permit. A pile of those permits had been left on the desk.

I studied the sign-in book, flipping back a few pages to the entries and signatures that had been made on April 15. Finding Langston's name brought a pang to my stomach. I used my cell-phone camera to take pictures, making sure to get the names of all those who'd signed.

While waiting for a ranger to appear, I snooped around the office, looking at maps and studying posters showing flora and fauna. Half a dozen visitors came and left; two of them signed in and collected wilderness permits.

I was trying to get a cell-phone signal and see if I could reach my ranger when a voice said, "Detective Gideon, I presume?"

Ranger Riley Ramsey looked like a triathlete. She had short blonde hair, was about forty, and was impossibly fit. She probably looked forward to her annual physical and hearing the results of her body mass index.

We shook hands. Her firm handshake didn't surprise me. "Do you want me to call you Ranger, Riley, or Ramsey?" I asked.

"Anything works for me," she said, and then gave a head jerk toward Sirius. "What's the story with the dog?"

"Meet my partner, Sirius," I said.

The ranger looked skeptical, but that was before Sirius decided to charm her with an extended paw, an "Aw shucks" roll of his head, and his earnest eyes. We were in like Flynn.

"I noticed Langston Walker's signature in your register," I said. "Was a ranger here when he signed in?"

Ranger Riley answered my question while running her fingers through Sirius's fur. "I'm afraid he came through when no one was here," she said. "We've been dealing with budget cuts for the last few years, and having someone working this desk full-time was one of the casualties."

"So signing in is voluntary?"

"The wilderness permits are free, so there's no reason not to get one."

"But anyone could bypass this office and continue on the Skyline Trail without signing in, right? Or with no one here, they could sign in with a false name, couldn't they?"

My questions seemed to surprise her, and she stopped scratching Sirius. "Why would anyone do that?"

"I'm just offering up some hypothetical situations."

"If we caught someone without a wilderness permit hiking on trails where it was required, then they'd face a potential fine. But you're right that unless a ranger was here, they could sign in with a fake name."

"Or they could just take a wilderness permit without signing in?"

She shrugged. "I suppose so."

"Since the permits are left out for anyone to take, isn't it also possible that during a previous visit someone could have picked up a spare permit and used it on a later occasion?"

"There would be nothing to prevent that, assuming a date hadn't already been filled in," she said. Then she added with a defensive tone, "But I still don't get why anyone would want to do that."

"Are there security cameras on the trails?"

"There's the Tram Cam that shows the Long Valley Ranger Station."

"Would that be easy to avoid?"

"It wouldn't be hard," she admitted.

"Can you get to the Skyline Trail from above? Is there a road from Idyllwild?"

"There's supposed to be a dirt road of sorts, but from there it would require a long hike to the trail."

But someone who was motivated, I thought, *could have bypassed the ranger station.*

"Did you take photos of Detective Walker when you came upon him?"

"I took a dozen pictures or so, but Officer Daniels took more."

I consulted my notes and saw that Daniels was with the Palm Springs Police Department.

"And Daniels made the call that it was an accidental death?"

She nodded.

"So a crime-scene technician didn't come and look at Walker's body?"

"Officer Daniels took pictures and videos. I heard him consulting with others. It was his conclusion, and one I agreed with, that Detective Walker fell and hit his head. You could see where he'd slipped in the snow, and there was blood on the rock just to the right of the trail."

"I'd like you to email me what pictures you have," I said, handing her my business card. "I'll be making the same request of Officer Daniels."

"It sounds like you think there's something suspicious about Detective Walker's death."

"I wouldn't say that. But detectives are big believers in the Missouri motto: 'Show me.' I need to be sure his death was accidental."

"Were you born in Missouri?"

I shook my head. "I'm an L.A. native. You'd think we would have a city motto, but we don't, unless you count, 'Shop until you drop,' or 'No one walks in L.A.'"

"Well, we're going to need to walk," she said, "and climb. We'll be traversing about fifteen hundred feet up. That's where Detective Walker was found."

"Was he still climbing up to the summit when he died, or was he coming back down?"

"As far as we can determine, he never made it to the summit and was still on his way up."

It seemed silly on my part, but I was sorry to hear that Langston hadn't reached his goal.

"Ready to rock and roll?" asked Ramsey.

"I can do without the rock part," I said.

* * *

Ranger Ramsey was a great tour guide, and I was lucky that she did most of the talking. That saved her from having to hear my gasping.

We were over an hour into our hike, and I was feeling spent. The two of us had climbed past huge boulders and made our way through rock formations. Pine trees provided handholds along the route. The higher we climbed, the more elusive oxygen seemed, and the colder it got. We crossed over a stream that came from melting snow, and had to deal with dripping water and muddy areas.

"It's been relatively warm the last two days," the ranger said. "On the day the detective was hiking, there was snow and ice on this trail from the previous night."

My admiration for Walker's fortitude had grown with each step. Hiking more than ten thousand feet up isn't for the faint of heart or weak of limb. I was getting a small taste of what he'd experienced, and I felt like waving a white flag. My too-fit ranger must have noticed that.

"It's not very far," she promised.

"That's good," I said. "Sirius is clearly exhausted."

My partner was clearly *not* exhausted, and Ranger Riley laughed. "I've heard climbing C2C means going up the equivalent of more than a thousand flights of stairs."

"Do you have any idea how many climbers were on this trail on April fifteenth?" I asked.

"I haven't done a tally," she said, "but I do know on this upper ascent, there were a lot fewer hikers than usual. It was a weekday, and the weather from the day before kept a lot of people from attempting the summit."

"Especially unprepared hikers without crampons," I said.

"Or microspikes or even ice axes," she said.

"Was Langston carrying an ice ax?" I asked.

She shook her head. "He had hiking poles similar to what you have."

Ranger Ramsey had provided me with two adjustable poles. I hated to admit it, but the poles had saved me from slipping in several spots. She was also right about my footwear. My basketball shoes were wet through and through, and I'd be surprised if a few blisters weren't developing.

"Smell the butterscotch?" she asked.

"I thought I was going crazy," I said. "I've been smelling butterscotch on and off since we started hiking."

"It's the Jeffrey pine trees," she said, pointing one out.

"Does the Peaks Restaurant serve butterscotch sundaes?" I asked. "I have a sudden hankering for one."

"I don't think it's on their menu."

"All this subliminal seduction going on, and they don't even take advantage of it."

A gust of cool wind blew, almost enough for me to say, "Brrr." The ranger also took note of the wind. "On the day your friend was climbing, there was some strong gusting. That might have contributed to his fall."

Walker had been climbing a slippery trail on a day when it was windy and icy. I was almost convinced I was wasting my time.

"Do you know if your friend ever hiked the other saints?" she asked.

"What saints are those?"

"In Southern California, climbers always talk about the Three Saints," she said. "This is Mount San Jacinto. The other two are San Antonio and San Gorgonio."

I found myself smiling. "One saint was enough for Langston," I said. "He always did his climb on the anniversary of his son's death. That's why he was here that day."

"I see," she said, and then added, "He was older than most of the climbers who come up here. This trail isn't forgiving, as you can see. Hikers have succumbed to high temperatures and dehydration. And on the opposite end, there have been cases of hypothermia. Slipping and going down an ice chute killed one man. Since 2009 there have been at least five deaths, and I can't tell you how many climbers we've had to helicopter out."

"As long as I'm not one of them," I said.

"We found Detective Walker right around this turn," she said.

There was no yellow police tape setting off the area. Despite that, I approached the spot as I would have any active crime scene.

The turn to the right led to another switchback turn going upward to the left. A series of rocks, both big and small, lined both sides of the trail. Just steps off the trail were boulders and pine trees. If this had been a John Ford western, foreboding music would have swelled. This spot was perfect for an ambush. The bad guy could have emerged from behind a boulder or a tree.

Ranger Ramsey showed me where Walker had been found, and pointed out the rock where he had supposedly hit his head. I listened to what she said and studied the rock, but I was more interested in the boulder just to the right of the trail.

If I was looking at a crime scene, it was contaminated beyond redemption. Detective Walker's body had brought a number of individuals to the scene who, combined with all the hikers who'd come afterward, had left various footprints everywhere. The melting snow and ice had left the area a muddy mess.

I used my hiking poles to help me get up and around the boulder. Anyone could have hidden behind it. I found the best spot to see from while staying out of sight. In my mind I choreographed how I would go about ambushing someone. There were several possibilities. I could emerge from the boulder as Langston was passing and attack from behind. Or I could wait for him to come abreast with the boulder and jump out, striking at his blind side. As I considered potential angles of attack, I also thought about the best way of taking my victim out. By pushing off from the boulder, I could increase the force of my bludgeoning.

Returning to the trail, I walked the likeliest path that Langston would have taken. It didn't take any stretch of the imagination to come up with several scenarios in which he could have easily been murdered. A blow from a blackjack or a rock to the temple might have been enough to kill him. Then his body could have been positioned with his head on, or near, the jutting rock his head appeared to have struck during the fall.

The ranger watched my movements. She could see my murderous choreographing and how I was imagining death scenarios quite different from the fall she had assumed. She looked uneasy. I didn't much like these thoughts myself. I had hoped my visit to the mountain would dispel any qualms I had about Walker's death. Unfortunately, it hadn't.

I took some pictures and asked some questions. And then we walked back down the mountain toward the tram that would take me home. Our descent was much quieter than our ascent, my dark thoughts proving contagious.

CHAPTER 23

THE MANY VOICES IN THE DARKNESS

After being held for days, after being subjected to physical and mental torture, Heather finally heard her abductor. But he was playing games with his voice by using some kind of amplifier, or shifter, to broadcast his words. It was like a bludgeon on her eardrums.

"Beg me to spare your life!"

A single light speared Heather's vision. The burka's mesh wasn't enough to spare her eyes after long hours in the darkness. But the light wasn't as invasive as the voice. The voice was loud and alien, the kind you'd expect to hear in old science fiction films. Would Emilio go to such lengths? He had always liked his toys.

"Who are you?" she asked.

The voice changed, becoming deeper and more powerful.

"I am he who you will worship."

"I only worship God," she said.

"I am your God!" The room shook as he roared. "Do you ever want to see the sun again? I hold your life in the balance. If you have any hope of staying alive, you will do as I say."

Heather didn't answer. As much as she wanted to challenge the voice, she knew that wouldn't help her current situation. She had to play for time and find a way out.

"You are a piece of shit," said the voice. "You pretend that you're special, but all you are is a waste. A trailer-park slut. I want to hear you say that. I want you to confess that to me with your legs spread. I want you to feel your body the way I felt it. Now strip out of that body bag you're wearing!"

Heather made no move to take off her clothing.

"Don't fuck with me!" The bass must have been turned to maximum. His curse was thunderous, and brutal enough to make Heather flinch.

"You try and act all prim and proper, but that's not what you are. You groaned when I did you. You wanted it."

"I was unconscious when you raped me."

"That's not what your body said. It welcomed me inside of you. It showed what a whore you are."

"You drugged me and raped me."

Heather didn't want to be afraid, but she was. The burka kept him from seeing that she was trembling.

"Worship me now and I might spare you. Beg for your life. And you'd better be creative."

She wasn't sure what to say. She was afraid of her voice failing her. "It's h-hard for me to think right now after being d-doped up." Her breaths were hurried, but the oxygen didn't seem to be reaching her.

The voice changed, taking on a sibilant, oily quality. "Maybe you need an incentive. Is that what you want? You'd make good target practice. You want an apple, Eve? I could put one on your head and try and shoot it off."

And then the voice changed again, into an accent that sounded as if it came from the Middle East: "Or is it death by stoning that you want? It happens more often and in more places than you would think. Whole villages like to join in. Everyone from elders to boys take part. That's the price paid for disobedience. That's what happens to whores. Maybe we should play sticks and stones? Is it time to break your bones? Bitch!"

He spat out the last word.

"And don't think if I choose sticks instead of stones you'll get off lightly. I will light the sticks on fire before tossing them." His accent changed again; now he sounded Indian. "You ever hear of bride burning? It's been going on in India for some time. When a husband isn't happy with the dowry that's paid, he decides to get rid of his wife. His family helps with the fun. They douse the wife with kerosene and then set her on fire. And then she's an ex-wife."

Emilio had come from an Old World family, Heather knew. His mother had always waited upon his father. But as Heather had explained to him on numerous occasions, she worked a demanding job. Emilio's mother hadn't worked outside the home.

"And it's only a matter of time before the world rediscovers suttee. What an enlightened insurance policy that was. The husband didn't have to worry about his wife plotting against him, because when he died, his wife burned with him. 'Until death do us part.' Didn't you say those words, bitch?"

"Why are you doing this to me?" she cried.

The voice changed again. Now it sounded like an atonal robot. "Are you ready to play sticks and stones? I think I'll warm up with a few fast ones. Maybe you'll catch one in the eye. That mutt of yours got one there, didn't she? You can be just like her. That's what the two of you are good for: target practice."

The voice shifter couldn't hide his anger. Heather could hear it even through the electronic distortion. Who other than Emilio would know about Angie's having been maimed by a rock? A lump rose in her throat. Angie had learned to love and trust her, but if she didn't come back, Angie would think she'd abandoned her.

"It's up to you. Do we play sticks and stones? Or do you perform a striptease for me? And in the end, emphasis on the end, I want you to present to me like one of those apes in heat. I want you to show me what you really are."

Life or death, Heather decided. That was her choice. She felt sick. She could either buy time or give up. How much more could she take?

Emilio had always said he wasn't a brute. But maybe she'd misjudged him. What if that was just the tip of the iceberg? What if he was a monster?

With trembling fingers, Heather began removing her burka.

CHAPTER 24

SOMETHING IS ROTTEN IN THE STATE OF DENMARK

My sneakers made squishing noises as I walked to my car. Over their sounds I listened to a message Katie Rivera had left on my cell. She spoke in a hushed voice, making it difficult to hear.

"I'm not sure if I should be bothering you with this," she said, "and you can't attribute it to me, but I just heard that Heather had been inquiring into a situation where potential embezzling occurred. She was questioning charges submitted by a producer who worked for us. I can't say any more because I'm here at work, but if you call me on my cell, I'll fill you in on what details I have."

I reached for the car's door handle and opened it. Before taking a seat, I waited for some of the pent-up hot air to escape. I poured some water for Sirius and drank some myself before getting in the car.

My call to Katie Rivera went directly to her voice mail. I told her I was available to talk, and asked her to call whenever it was convenient for her.

On went the AC. It brought relief from the heat but not from what ailed me. The weight I'd tried to ignore all day was back. The Heather Moreland clock was ticking. I wanted to believe she was still alive, and had to operate on that premise. Langston Walker was now an additional weight, but without the time crunch. He had already met his fate. His answers could come in their own time.

I heard back from Katie right before reaching the turnoff for the Garden of Angels, a unique cemetery for abandoned babies. The timing of Katie's call saved me from having to dwell on baby Rose and her burial plot. If not for Rose, I probably would never have gotten together with Lisbet. I owed that poor little one a debt I could never pay. I could only try and pay it forward with the quick and the dead.

"Is it safe for you to talk?" I asked Katie.

"I hope so. Look, this may be nothing, but I heard this morning that Heather might have caught someone with his hand in the cookie jar."

"I'm surprised she never mentioned that to you."

"It was business, not personal. And she was supposedly sworn to secrecy under penalty of death."

Katie gave a little gasp. "That was a bad choice of words. What I meant to say was that there might have been severe repercussions for her had word of the embezzlement gotten out. Movie studios are famous for hushing up anything that might make them look bad."

"And how did you hear about Heather's involvement in this?"

"I'd rather not say. But I do know for a fact that only a few people are even aware of this situation. I can't even tell you how it's being dealt with. Maybe there's already been a resolution. Or maybe everything was swept under the rug."

"Do you know when Heather became aware of this questionable activity?"

"I'm pretty sure it was recently, like in the last week. In our office Heather is referred to as 'the IRS.' Part of her job is going over invoices and receipts associated with our corporate accounts."

Over the years I knew of several prominent examples of embezzlement in Hollywood. Columbia Pictures president David Begelman had been caught forging checks. And recently, a case of purported embezzling at Paramount Pictures had made headlines.

"So you think this unnamed producer might have been involved in Heather's disappearance?"

"I'm told he was upset by her inquiries and that he threatened to have her fired. But I suppose it does sound ridiculous that he'd be involved with her vanishing."

"I wish it did sound ridiculous. What other specifics can you give me?"

"If you come at him, he'll probably demand that a witch hunt take place here to try to find whoever leaked his name. And everyone knows how close Heather and I are."

"I'll cite an anonymous source, and then throw out lots of misdirection. But in order to do that, I'll need to know everything you know."

Katie sighed. "If this was anyone but Heather, I never would have called you."

"I know that."

She sighed again, and then told me what she'd heard, who might be involved, and what she suspected.

* * *

Paul Grauer's assistant carried on a conversation between the two of us. Grauer was the producer whose invoices Heather Moreland had red-flagged, and he was proving an apparent master in self-preservation. When I got tired of the proxy stonewalling, I told the middleman that without Grauer's cooperation, I would be forced to contact the Department of Justice and pass on what information I had. Immediately after that, Grauer agreed to a six o'clock meeting.

His offices were in Studio City, about five miles from my house. My hope was that I'd have time to go home and change into my standard uniform of a blue blazer and gray pants, but heavy traffic nixed those plans. As it was, I arrived ten minutes late, wearing my hiking outfit of basketball shoes, jeans, and a T-shirt. I tried unsuccessfully to make myself presentable, but half the trail seemed to have attached itself to my clothing. I'd gotten too much sun during my hike, a no-no for burn victims who've had skin grafts. I looked in the rearview mirror and did my best to wipe away the dirt. My face was red, my skin was already chafing, and the keloid scarring on my face looked that much more pronounced.

"Dress for success," I muttered.

Sirius was snoring in the backseat, which was reason enough for me to let sleeping dogs lie. He doesn't like Hollywood meetings anyway. I suspect that's because only three dogs—Lassie, Rin Tin Tin, and Strongheart—have been awarded stars on the Hollywood Walk of Fame. That's right, no Toto or Beethoven or Marley. And no Pluto either, I thought, thinking of Angie and Heather Moreland.

It was a secure office building, and I had to check in with a guard before being allowed access to the elevators. Grauer's production company took up much of the tenth floor. As I walked the halls, I could see that most employees had gone home for the day.

A familiar voice greeted me: "Detective Gideon?"

Grauer's assistant was a midtwenties male fashion plate. Suddenly I felt even more underdressed than I was. He didn't extend a hand, perhaps afraid that I might take the gleam out of his manicure. "Please follow me," he said.

He led me through an office into a meeting room, gestured for me to go inside, and said, "Mr. Grauer will be joining you shortly."

Fifteen minutes passed before Grauer joined me, and he didn't come alone. Two men entered the meeting room. Only one of them shook my hand, and only one of them spoke.

"Detective Gideon?" asked the older man. "I'm Saul Levine, Mr. Grauer's attorney."

Levine was around sixty. He sported a skunk-stripe hairdo that reminded me of Paulie Walnuts in *The Sopranos*. His shark eyes also reminded me of Paulie.

Grauer took a seat across and away from where I had been seated. He made sure Levine was situated between the two of us. His disapproval of me was apparent by his folded arms and frown. He was forty, but trying to look thirty with his stylish clothes and hipster haircut. James Dean had been dead for more than sixty years, but he still had his imitators.

"As I understand it, Detective Gideon," said Levine, "you are looking into the disappearance of a Disney employee named Heather Moreland."

"Correct," I said. I felt as if I was in the presence of a ventriloquist, but I refrained from asking if I should direct my comments to Jeff Dunham or to his dummy, Walter.

"And for some reason you want to question Mr. Grauer about this disappearance?"

"It's my understanding that Ms. Moreland identified suspicious invoices and billing statements submitted by Mr. Grauer."

"And how did you come by this information?"

"It turned up in the course of my investigation."

"So what you have is hearsay?"

"I prefer to categorize it as a potential lead."

"It sounds like you're grasping for straws. And your claims come close to constituting defamation of character."

"Are you denying that Heather Moreland found irregularities in Mr. Grauer's billing? And are you contesting that she brought these questionable invoices to her superior?"

"There was a misunderstanding. In case you were wondering, Disney has not filed charges against Mr. Grauer, nor do they intend to."

"I happen to know your client threatened Heather Moreland. He said he would make her 'pay' if word of her findings circulated beyond those she had already made aware."

Grauer whispered in Levine's ear, who nodded. "My client was just trying to impress upon Ms. Moreland the gravity of the situation and the need to keep matters private."

I decided to give Grauer my full attention, staring him down while I talked. "He scared an employee who was just trying to do her job. He dropped the F-bomb repeatedly during his tirade, and did his best to intimidate her. He threatened retaliation, and left it to her imagination as to what that might entail. Bullying isn't a crime, but criminal intent might be. Did you follow through on the threats you made to Ms. Moreland?"

My eyes said what my words couldn't: you're an asshole. I tempered my speech, not wanting another complaint in my jacket. But Grauer knew exactly what I was thinking, and because of that he looked away.

"I am sure my client regrets upsetting Ms. Moreland," said Levine. "But as I said, she didn't know the full picture. When her superiors were apprised of the situation, the matter was dropped. And while Ms. Moreland should be commended for a job well done, the matter in question was above her pay grade."

"Heather Moreland is missing," I said. "That's what I care about. I couldn't care less about her supposed pay grade or mine. I need to be satisfied that Mr. Grauer isn't involved in some way in her disappearance, and the only way that's going to happen is if you tell me what occurred to provoke his malice."

The two men looked at each other and seemed to come to an understanding.

"I am going to offer a hypothetical situation," said Levine. "As you know, public relations are very important in this business. But there is a thin line between what is acceptable and what might be construed as a bribe.

"The film awards season runs from October to the end of February, but the jockeying begins early in the year. In order to have your picture considered for nominations, it's often necessary to plant the seeds early. And how do you do that? Maybe a star agrees to make appearances, or say something, or write something. Handwritten notes from the right person can be a very effective tool. And while this star is sincere about what he or she thinks, their approbation is an investment in time. Sometimes priming the pump is necessary. Rewarding these efforts is a way of making sure they get done. For the sake of appearances, though, these business expenses can't be directly linked to the promotion of one particular picture."

"Caesar's wife," I said.

The mouthpiece didn't get my reference. I tried another. "The Golden Bribes," I said.

"These were not bribes," said Levine. "I strongly object to that categorization."

"Isn't that what they used to call the Golden Globes?" I asked.

"I hope you're not implying my client in any way targeted the Hollywood Foreign Press Association, because he most certainly did not."

Just about everyone in Hollywood believed the fix was in when Pia Zadora was awarded a "best new actress" Golden Globe in 1982 for her role in *Butterfly*, beating out such actresses as Kathleen Turner in *Body Heat* and Elizabeth McGovern in *Ragtime*. It was commonly thought that Zadora's moviemaker husband, Meshulam Riklis, essentially bought the award. As for her acting, Zadora was also awarded two

Golden Raspberries, also known as Razzies, for "worst new star" and "worst actress."

That was the nadir for the Golden Globes. In the years since, they'd changed their ways and mended their reputation.

If I could believe Levine's double-talk, Grauer had been trying to create early buzz for his picture. What he'd done was probably not illegal, but neither he nor his clients wanted details of his payola reported in *Variety, TMZ,* or the *Hollywood Reporter.*

I had a smoking gun, but not the gun I wanted. I stood up and said to Grauer, "It's been a real pleasure talking to you."

CHAPTER 25

LOOKING FOR SMOKE SIGNALS

Lisbet had left on my front-porch light. It was nice not coming home to a dark, empty house. I sat in my car for a few moments, pretending I was decompressing in a hyperbaric chamber. I breathed in and out, trying to put the disappointments of the day behind me. It wouldn't do to inflict my mood upon Lisbet.

The aroma of chicken greeted me as I stepped into the house. A second greeting was the sound of Ed Sheeran's "Thinking Out Loud." Lisbet and I haven't decided upon "our song," but that's definitely a contender. The third greeting was Lisbet. She emerged from the kitchen and offered a hug.

"Glass of wine?" she asked.

"That would be great," I said. "Just let me change out of these clothes."

I went to my bedroom, stripped out of everything, and then put on my most comfortable sweatpants and one of my haiku shirts. Lisbet could only blame herself. She's the one who's been supplying me with the haiku T-shirts. This one read:

This is my haiku

You can call me Ishmael
Radioactive

"I like your shirt," said Lisbet, handing me a glass of white wine.

In the background Ed Sheeran sang of falling in love and staying in love. We both took seats on the couch. Sirius joined us, curling up at our feet.

"I'm not sure about the shirt's last line," I said. "I mean, if you're going for a five-syllable word and a non sequitur, couldn't you come up with something better than 'radioactive'?"

"How could you improve upon 'radioactive'?"

I took a sip of wine and thought about it. "That's *el-e-men-tar-y*, my dear Watson."

Lisbet shook her head. "I would have expected a better five-syllable word from you."

"Give me an *op-por-tun-i-ty*," I said.

"I think I've created a monster."

"You mean like the *a-bom-in-a-ble* snowman?"

"You have a talent for this game," she admitted, "but I wish you'd use your *i-mag-in-a-tion* for something else."

I raised my wineglass to her, but then the five-headed monster showed itself again: "*Con-gra-tu-la-tions!*"

Lisbet rolled her eyes, which was certainly the appropriate response. Try as I might to come up with some other five-syllable words, the well seemed to have run dry.

"Hungry?" Lisbet asked.

I had to think about it. When I'm on the hunt, I usually don't think about food. Up until now I'd attributed the ache in my stomach to disappointment, but realized that in part it was from not having eaten.

"I am."

"I'll serve up the meal."

"And I'll feed Sirius."

Her hand reached out and stopped me from getting up. "I already have his dinner set aside. You stay put."

Sirius must have known what we were talking about, because he followed Lisbet into the kitchen. I put my feet up on an ottoman, stretched back into the sofa, and did my sipping.

Comfort food was on the night's menu. Lisbet filled the table with fried chicken, baked potatoes, and broccoli. I joined her there, and we both started eating. The food helped to fill some of the void I was feeling.

Lisbet refilled my wineglass. It's rare for her to have more than one glass. She knows her limits and knows what is good for her. I believe in a sliding scale, which I hope won't lead to a slippery slope. The wine loosened my tongue, even if I wasn't sure if that was a good thing. I had planned to spare Lisbet the details of my day, but found myself talking about it anyway.

I told her about climbing Skyline Trail and wondering if I was crazy for thinking that someone might have ambushed Langston Walker and then tried to make it look as if he had slipped and hit his head.

"Everyone believes it was an accident," I said. "I seem to be the only one with doubts."

"Why would anyone want to kill a retired cop?"

"There's only one reason I can think of." I told her about Walker's ghost remark and his looking into a closed case.

"And you think this individual was so threatened by the possibility of Detective Walker's reopening the case that he murdered him?"

"If you've already murdered someone, is it such a stretch to think you might be capable of committing a second murder?"

Lisbet shook her head. "It's hard for me to envision that."

For her sake, I was glad that was so. I wished that it wasn't so easy for me.

"Everyone knew Langston would be hiking the trail on that day. If I was to choose a spot to ambush him, I would have picked the area where he died."

"That might just be a coincidence."

"I know."

"So what are you going to do?"

"I'm going to attend his funeral service tomorrow. And I'm going to try to arrange a time to talk to his wife. Maybe she'll have some insights, or maybe she'll let me look through his paperwork to see if I can find her husband's ghost."

"Now you're the one who's haunted."

"I am frustrated," I admitted, "but not so much about Walker. I can't be sure if I'm making something out of nothing. What I am sure about is that I want to study his death further. It's not his case that has me in a funk, though. It's Heather Moreland."

"How can you even be sure that she's been abducted? Isn't that still in question?"

I shook my head. "Angie made me sure. Heather Moreland is a stand-up woman. She never would have abandoned her beloved dog."

I let out some air and made a small confession. "I dreamed about Heather Moreland and Langston Walker last night."

"You had a fire dream?"

I nodded. Lisbet knows I don't like to talk about my dreams and the visions that come with them, but on a handful of occasions, she's been sleeping next to me when they occurred. She's never pried. The only thing she's tried to do is catch me during one of my difficult landings. Once or twice I have talked about the moment after. Confession might be good for the soul, but I find it distinctly uncomfortable. Talking about my dreams is tantamount to admitting to PTSD, and that's something I don't like doing. I don't even like to admit it to myself.

"I suspect the dream had something to do with the fake building in West L.A. where I found Angie's tracking device. I was disappointed it didn't lead us to Heather, but it also provided me with a ray of hope that she's alive."

Lisbet nodded, but I sensed she thought mine was wishful thinking. I explained why I hoped it was not.

"The tracking device was planted at a specific spot. It wasn't crushed and tossed out in the trash, but instead was purposely situated in West L.A. To my thinking, that's a good thing. If she was already dead, I don't think the abductor would have gone to such lengths."

"Was she—alive—in your dream?"

I didn't like Lisbet having to tread so carefully and feel the need to be so selective in her choice of words.

"Yes," I said, "although I never saw her. I could faintly hear her calling for me. But I couldn't see her. She was obscured by fog."

"There were no—insights—then?"

I wanted to tell Lisbet to stop walking on goddamn eggshells, but instead took a breath and shook my head.

"At least she was alive in your dream," said Lisbet.

"There is that."

I didn't need to tell Lisbet about the additional pressure I felt with each passing day. She knew. I could feel it in her touch as she stroked my arm.

"This chicken is great," I said, taking another bite.

She seemed to find that funny. "Save some room for dessert."

"What did you make?"

"Key lime pie," she said. "You'll have to tell me if you want it with whipped cream."

I remembered how Walker and I had both eschewed whipped cream on the sweet potato pie we'd split.

"There's a restaurant I want to take you to in the next week or two," I said. "It's sort of a fusion soul place."

"That sounds great."

Our talk took some of the weight off me. The pressure in my neck eased, making swallowing easier. The food began tasting better, and I didn't have to fake my enthusiasm. After both of us finished eating, we sat around the dinner table, passing the time in each other's company. For a few minutes at least, I wasn't ruminating about the disappearance of Heather Moreland.

I insisted upon doing the dishes, and Lisbet sat in the bar area to keep me company. As hard as she tried to fight off her yawns, several of them surfaced. It was late and she was tired.

When I finished with the dishes, she said, "Coming to bed?"

"In a little while," I promised.

We hugged, did a little dance, and then she went off to the bedroom. As is our nightly habit, Sirius and I went for a short walk, even though both of us were stiff-legged from our exertions earlier in the day.

When we returned from our outing, I decided it was time for a nightcap and some music. There was still some wine left in the bottle, so I settled into the sofa and donned earphones so as to not disturb Lisbet. I went with a recent release I'd heard: Adam Lambert's "Ghost Town." The lyrics struck close to home. The song's opening, where Lambert talked about dying last night in his dreams, could have been biographical. Every time I had a fire dream, it felt like a little death. There was also the song's lyric about walking into the flames. Everything that was being sung seemed a little too close for comfort.

Normally there's a part of me that's afraid to sleep. It is the "perchance to dream" part. Almost burning to death once was enough. Continuing to do it is sometimes such a scary prospect that I struggle against sleep.

But not tonight.

I joined Lisbet in bed, feeling defiant. *Bring on the flames,* I thought, *and let me burn.* I was willing to have my dream if it would reveal some hidden insight that could assist me in finding Heather Moreland.

An-ti-ci-pa-tion, I thought, coming up with one last five-syllable word. It didn't help, though. I slept through the night.

There was not even a hint of smoke. Nor were there any smoke signals to be divined.

CHAPTER 26

GIVING UP THE GHOST

Langston Walker's memorial service was being held at the First African Methodist Episcopal Church, called FAME by some and First AME by others. By the time I arrived, both the regular parking lot and the overflow lot were full. I had to settle for street parking in the Jefferson Park neighborhood, an impoverished area in southwest L.A. My car "alarm" was at home; I'd given Sirius the morning off. There were enough elements about my vehicle to suggest it was an off-duty police car, but I wasn't sure if that would deter would-be thieves or make it a magnet for vandals. As I passed by my car, I fondly tapped it twice and hoped it would be there when I returned.

FAME is one of the larger megachurches in Los Angeles and an important hub in L.A.'s African American community. When I worked Metropolitan K-9, I was called to the Jefferson Park area on several occasions, but I'd never had reason to go inside the church. As large as the building was, it appeared that those mourning Langston Walker were going to fill its interior real estate.

I thought of my wife's memorial service but remembered few specifics. I'm sure I was in shock, and it was all I could do to be there in person. In the days following Jennifer's death, it was an accomplishment just getting out of bed. My good friends drove me to the service, guided me as to what to do and how to act, and then took me home. Sirius was there waiting for me, and the two of us mourned together.

The number of people in the church said a lot about Langston, and I couldn't help but wonder if I would have even a tenth as many mourners when I died.

I walked down the aisle, and as I looked for a spare seat, I saw plenty of familiar faces. The 187 Club was well represented, as was LAPD. Art Epstein was there and had his arm around a young man who had to be his son Joel. We nodded to each other, but there was no space in his pew, which was just as well. This wasn't a day to talk about Ellis Haines.

An African American family of five waved me down to join them. The family closed ranks, allowing room enough for all of us. I nodded my thanks to them. They happened to be standing from tallest to smallest. Right next to me was the mother, a tall, heavy woman who looked to be in her late thirties. Her husband, a few inches shorter and a few years older, stood next to her. The two daughters were next in line. They looked to be fraternal twins, each on the cusp of being a teen. At the end was a boy, who was perhaps ten.

"We're the Williamses," said the mother. "I'm Grace, and this is my husband, Dion."

"Sometimes Grace forgets I can speak for myself," said Dion. He extended his hand, and we shook.

"I'm Michael Gideon," I said.

"This is Mr. Gideon," Grace told her children. "And this is Destiny, Amity, and Justice."

"Those are great virtue names," I said, "just like yours."

"I thought I would continue the tradition of my mother and her mother before her," said Grace.

"I suggested we name one of the children Silence," said Dion, "a greatly underrated virtue."

Even in the somber setting of a memorial service, I couldn't help but laugh. The twins rolled their eyes, while Justice dismissively said, "Dad." It was clear they'd heard their father's observation before.

"How do you know Langston?" Grace asked.

"I work LAPD," I said, deciding on the shortest explanation.

"You hear that?" said Dion. "You kids act up and I'll have Mr. Gideon arrest you."

There was more eye-rolling, and another aggrieved, "Dad."

"And how do you know him?" I asked.

"Langston and Savannah live just down the street from us. And we go to the same church."

We were all still speaking in the present tense, I noticed. We were all reluctant to let Langston go.

"Not this church?"

She shook her head. "Our church is too small to accommodate this many people. That's why the service is being held here. And that's also why the service won't be adhering to the usual AME program. Savannah wanted to do it Langston's way."

"That's as it should be," I said.

"Amen," said Grace.

Despite our being toward the back of the church, the space still felt intimate, something rare in big buildings. A woman who I assumed was Savannah Walker was sitting in the front row, flanked by her family. Every so often she dabbed her eyes with a tissue, but it was clear she was resolved not to break down during the service. Her children and grandchildren were not as inclined to rein in their grief; there was a lot of quiet sobbing going on.

Before the service began, I tried picking out which mourners were members of the 187 Club. I was pretty sure on most of my selections, identifying them by their thousand-yard stare. They were thinking about another memorial service, just as I had been. I suspected many were reliving that awful time surrounding the murder of their loved ones. There was no getting over that; there was just learning how to cope in its aftermath.

The sound of a musical introduction signaled that the service was about to begin. "They have three or four choirs at First AME," whispered Grace, "and I think Savannah was able to talk all of them into singing."

I was used to memorial services being somber events, but from the first this seemed more like a celebration than a solemn remembrance. The service started with the song "Stand." It was new to me, but not to most who were there. The song's lyrics commanded that everyone get to their feet. Stand we did. Clap we did, fast and loud. Hope we did.

There were prayers, of course, and a moving eulogy, but mostly there was up-tempo music. The different choruses would not let us be passive, exhorting us in their refrains to get out of our seats and move our feet and clap our hands. As different as all this was from the services I'd grown up with in the Catholic Church, I didn't feel out of place. There was no "Ave Maria," but there were gospel standards with choruses perfect for the mourners, including "I'll Fly Away," "I'm Free," and "Swing Low, Sweet Chariot."

The recessional of "Amazing Grace" was familiar to all. John Newton had written the hymn, and I wondered how many people in the church knew that he'd been a slave-ship captain before realizing the error of his ways and becoming an abolitionist. Everyone held hands and sang. I thought about Newton's journey as we sang the refrain, "I once was lost but now I'm found, was blind, but now I see."

I felt that blindness. For the sake of my cases, I hoped it would pass. I hoped I'd be able to see.

After I reclaimed my hand from Grace, she asked, "You'll be going to the repast, won't you?"

I opened up my mouth to offer up some excuse, but Grace could read my intentions and intervened. "You know Langston wouldn't want his LAPD friends to leave hungry."

"He did like good food," I said, remembering our dinner. "But I really . . ."

Grace was already shaking her head. "And you wouldn't want to offend Savannah."

"I'm afraid I don't know her," I said.

"That's all the more reason for you to stay and meet her. I'll be sure to introduce the two of you."

Talking with Savannah Walker was on my follow-up list, but I hadn't planned on talking to her on the day of her husband's memorial service.

"Welcome to your new family," Dion said.

* * *

The repast was being held in the biggest of the church meeting halls. There were several catered carving stations, but there was also an abundance of home-cooked casseroles, greens, salads, and desserts.

I regretted having come empty-handed, and wouldn't have eaten but for Grace. She brought me a heaping plate and ignored my protests. By this time she'd learned I was a widower (it's a word she used, but one I've never been comfortable with), and had decided I wasn't really capable of looking after myself. It didn't surprise me to learn that Grace was a first-grade teacher. At least she didn't cut the meat on my plate.

Dion and I made small talk. I learned he worked in human resources for UPS, having transitioned from being a driver.

"I used to get a lot more exercise," he said, patting his stomach, "but after almost twenty years of all that running, I'd had enough."

"Was that your decision or Grace's?" I asked.

He laughed and started nodding. "I remember coming home one day and seeing some textbooks on the table. 'What are these doing here?' I asked. And that's when I learned I was going to night school."

Both of us looked over to Grace. She was in the process of separating Justice from his first course of dessert and insisting he eat "real food." Dion looked at me and raised his eyebrows. We both hid our grins.

Around us all the tables were rapidly filling up. At the table directly across from us, I recognized a familiar face. It took me a moment to place Ronaldo from the 187 Club without his soccer jersey. He was wearing a black suit. The two of us nodded at each other.

Dion noticed the exchange and asked, "Cop?"

I shook my head. Everyone at Ronaldo's table, I realized, was a member of the 187 Club. I wasn't sure if I should explain how I was acquainted with him and the others at the table. As far as I was aware, the 187 Club wasn't like AA, where you were supposed to respect the privacy of its members, but I couldn't be sure.

"He's one of Langston's friends," I said.

Seated next to Ronaldo was Catalina Ceballos. And not surprisingly, next to her was James, the man who had comforted her when Catalina became upset while talking about her husband's status as a "cleared other." It seemed to me that in the wake of Walker's death, most of the 187 Club members looked shell-shocked. There didn't seem to be much talking going on at their table, or at several of the other tables filled by club members. The introspection I'd noticed during the service seemed to have carried over to the repast. Maybe the membership was realizing the additional void in their worlds created by Langston's death.

My ulterior motive for staying at the repast was to have the chance to talk with Savannah Walker. As I sat there second-guessing my strategy, the decision was taken out of my hands. In her time of grief, Mrs. Walker had taken it upon herself to go from table to table thanking people for being there. She began her rounds at the table two down from where we were, and then she continued to the table right next to us. Even before she reached us, everyone at our table got to their feet. Grace remembered her promise to me and came to my side.

Most at our table seemed well acquainted with Mrs. Walker, and before she reached me, everyone offered her words of sympathy and hugs. Grace embraced her, then introduced me as if I were an old friend.

"This is Michael Gideon," she said. "He knows Langston from the force."

I had assumed Savannah Walker wouldn't know my name and was surprised at her recognition of it.

"You're the detective who just spoke at the club," she said. "Langston said you brought your dog to the meeting, and then to the dinner. My husband told me your dog kept looking at him with these beseeching eyes, and he found himself throwing him more and more of his dinner."

"He's quite the expert at getting handouts," I said. "And your husband had a great big heart that he showed to both the two-legged and the four-legged. I'm sure I don't have to tell you how much I respected him, and how I'm sorry I never got the chance to know him better."

"He came home in a wonderful mood after the two of you had dinner," she said, "so I know he enjoyed getting to know you as well."

As we nodded and smiled, I knew the moment had come when Savannah Walker was ready to move on. There was a room full of people waiting to offer her their condolences and their love. I almost let her pass by, but I reached out with my hand, gesturing for her to bear with me a little while longer.

"In only two short hours, it seemed as if Langston and I discussed just about everything," I said. "But since hearing about his death, there's one thing I keep thinking about: his ghost."

I thought I'd have to explain further, but Savannah was nodding. "I'm surprised he opened up to you about the ghost. I could tell something was bothering him this last week or so, and I kept pressing him to tell me what it was. He told me about a closed case that was haunting him."

"So he was actively working the case?"

"For most of this week, he was holed up in his office. Langston would only say he was 'doing some chewing.'"

"I hope you don't think it's presumptuous of me, but I'm wondering if I can pick up on this case where Langston left off."

She squeezed my hand. "I'm sure Langston would have liked that, but I don't know much more than what I've already told you. Tell you what, though—why don't you stop by the house? Maybe you can make sense of what he was working on from what's on his desk. I learned not to touch his desk and upset his system." She smiled. "Of course, I always thought his *system* looked more like clutter than anything else, but maybe you can decipher what's there."

"I'll do my best," I promised.

I knew better than to tell her my suspicions that her husband's death might be anything but accidental. In the days to come, there would be a better time to discuss that with her. For now she had to deal with more pressing obligations.

It was only as Savannah moved on to the next table that I noticed a lot of curious eyes watching us. Those at the nearby 187 Club table looked particularly interested. They were certainly close enough to have heard our conversation.

I wondered what they thought of Langston's ghost. And I wondered if Langston's spirit still cared now that he himself had given up the ghost.

CHAPTER 27

VENI, VIDI, VICI, AND VENTI

I drove home in silence. Sometimes even the best music can't improve upon that. I could still hear the church music in my mind, and I wanted it to keep playing in my mental background while I thought about the odd couple I was obsessing over: Langston Walker and Heather Moreland.

It was time to work Heather's case. I put in a call to Sergeant Reyes, hoping he'd had time to red-flag cases that might have some similarities with ours.

"I was just going to call you," he said.

"I'm hoping that means you have something."

"Negative," he said. "Over the last year there have been a few abduction attempts, but they were vehicular related and not home invasions. The suspects tried to snatch the women off the street."

He heard my sigh, interpreted it correctly, and said, *"La compañía en la miseria hace a ésta más llevadera."*

"What's that mean?"

"Basically I'm saying we're companions in misery."

"Misery loves company?"

"Yeah," he said. "We share in the failure."

"I'm not a fan of that expression in either language."

"What are you going to do about it?"

"Lots of body shops are open on Saturday. I'm going to find out if Emilio is working, and try to get him to talk to me."

"You want company?"

"I think we'd be better served by your looking at suspicious break-in cases. Besides, I'd stay off that foot of yours. But I will bring my partner along."

"You think Emilio likes dogs?"

"I'm hoping he's scared of them."

* * *

I called Emilio Cruz from the driveway of my house. He answered on the fourth ring. The background sounds told me he was at work.

"Emilio, this is your favorite cop, Detective Gideon."

"I don't have a favorite cop. In fact, I'm still waiting to meet the first one who isn't an asshole. And I thought I told you not to bother me anymore, especially at work."

"I just need a few minutes of your time, Emilio. There are some loose ends that need tying up. How about I buy you a cup of coffee so that we can have a chance to chat?"

He didn't answer for a few seconds. If not for the noise of grinding metal, I would have suspected he'd hung up on me.

Finally he said, "I'll call you back in a little while after I decide if we should meet."

I assumed he was blowing me off, and tried to stop that door from shutting on me. Unfortunately, I only had words and not my foot.

"I am available to meet anywhere, anytime . . ."

The noise from the body shop was no longer on the line, and neither was Emilio Cruz.

* * *

I was making Sirius a meal when my cell started ringing. I looked at the display, surprised to see that Cruz was actually calling me back.

"I'll meet you at three thirty at the Starbucks on Sherman Way and Sepulveda," he said. "There's a strip mall there with a bunch of Asian restaurants, but usually it's not a problem getting parking during the day."

"Three thirty," I said, repeating his words so that I would remember them. "Starbucks on Sherman Way."

"I'll take you up on the coffee," he said. "I'll have a soy caramel macchiato with four shots."

There was no way I was going to remember his order. "Let me get a pen and write that down."

I grabbed a piece of paper and had him repeat it. "And I want a venti," he said.

I didn't know what that was, but I wrote it down as well. The problem with taking down his order was that I had forgotten the street address, so I asked, "So is this the Starbucks with the charter school across the street?"

"No. That's the reform-school Starbucks on Van Nuys Boulevard."

"Reform school?"

"Try waiting behind those kids and tell me differently," he said. "They're the reason I go to the Starbucks on Sherman."

Sherman Way, I remembered, writing it down.

"Four shots," he said once again, and then hung up on me.

* * *

Construction and detours forced me into taking a roundabout route to coffee. I turned on Cedros Avenue and drove by Van Nuys High School, one of the schools used as a setting for the movie *Rock 'n' Roll High School*. I probably should have found a Ramones song and cranked it up, but I resisted. During the movie's filming, the band had visited the high school. Of course, lots of other famous people had actually gone to the school. Norma Jeane Baker—also known as Marilyn Monroe—had spent most of her sophomore year there.

After turning left on Sherman Way, I drove a few blocks west and found the strip mall. There was plenty of parking available, but nothing near the Starbucks. Sirius and I set out across the parking lot. One of the outdoor tables was unoccupied, so I had Sirius snag it. I made it official by offering up my commands in German and telling him, *"Sitz! Bleib!"* Like almost half the residents of L.A., Sirius had been born in a foreign country. You wouldn't know it by his accent, though.

A friendly barista took my order: one small black coffee and one venti soy caramel macchiato with four shots. Over the years I've had enough coffee in Starbucks to know that "tall" means "small." No barista has ever had a problem with understanding my order of a small coffee, however. From the signage I learned that "venti" meant twenty-four ounces. I wondered if it also translated to insomnia.

The barista pointed outside to the waiting Sirius. "Does your dog want a puppuccino?" she asked.

I'm sure her intentions were good, but I was afraid to find out what a puppuccino was.

"He'd like an ice water, please," I said.

I waited for our orders and then carried them out to the table. "Thanks for keeping democracy safe from the squirrel invaders," I told my partner.

Sirius modestly accepted my thanks. I probably should have gotten him a puppuccino.

I sipped my coffee; Sirius sipped his water. After fifteen minutes I began wondering if Cruz was a no-show, or whether he liked the idea of keeping me waiting.

Five more minutes passed before Cruz appeared. He had changed out of his work uniform into a cotton oxford shirt and designer jeans, the kind of look you'd expect from an off-duty lawyer. He took his time approaching our table, his leisurely stroll demonstrating that he was the one in charge. When he noticed Sirius, he came to an abrupt stop, and then cautiously took a seat at the table as far away from my partner as possible.

"I wish you hadn't brought your mutt," he said. "I'm allergic to pet dander."

The nickname for German shepherds is German shedders. I had never appreciated all their shedding until now.

Cruz picked his coffee up and acted like an oenophile, swirling the brew, then sniffing it, and then taking an exploratory sip. One of my father's favorite expressions was, "He acts as fussy as *El Exigente*." My dad had explained the meaning of his words to me, saying his phrase came from years of watching coffee commercials that featured a white-clad, linen-suited character known as "*El Exigente*—the demanding one." As Cruz took another sip of his coffee, I could hear my father's phrase in my head.

El Exigente nodded. The coffee passed muster. Strangely enough, his approbation wasn't enough to make me feel as if I could die happy.

"Before I came here," said Cruz, "I decided to write up a statement. I expect it will answer all of your questions."

He reached into his shirt pocket, unfolded a piece of paper, and handed it to me. I read what he'd written:

1.   *I had nothing to do with my wife's disappearance.*
2.   *I don't know anything about my wife's disappear-ance.*

3. *I can't direct you to my wife's whereabouts.*
4. *Up until now I have cooperated with the police and answered all their questions. Any future inquiries will be considered police harassment. As I've already requested, I want all future communication to go through my lawyer.*

He had signed his statement and noted today's date. I nodded to show that I'd read it, and then I did my best to ignore what I'd read.

"Did Heather ever mention someone threatening her, Emilio?"

"Not that I recall. And I'll refer you to what I wrote on point number four."

"Did you write this up yourself, Emilio?"

My question seemed to catch him off guard. "That's my handwriting you're looking at."

"I'm sure it is. But you didn't answer my question."

"Look at point four."

"I don't know you that well, Emilio, but it's pretty clear you're not the sharpest knife in the drawer. You understand what I'm saying? And your being slow couldn't have been much of a turn-on for Heather. Looks only go so far. You know what they say about the brain being the most important sex organ. That sort of suggests you're impotent."

Emilio was no longer enjoying his coffee. "Fuck you," he said.

I shook my head and sighed. "You're making my point for me. You see, profanity shows a limited vocabulary. That's why I suspect you didn't write your letter by yourself. So who helped you?"

"You're full of . . . it."

At least I'd managed to curb his swearing.

"It seems like I hit a sensitive spot, Emilio. You overreacted when we talked about Heather growing weary of your tiny brain. I guess over time that became a turnoff for her, especially when her career started taking off."

"That shows you how much you know."

"What don't I know?"

"Heather couldn't get enough of me in the sack. I was large and in charge, and she loved it."

"So explain to me again why it is that she wants a divorce?"

"Number four," he said.

"Funny, that answer sounds more like number two."

He sat at the table doing a slow burn.

"You see, Emilio, that's how you use profanity without being profane."

"If you're so smart, then why haven't you figured out what happened to my wife?"

It was hard to tell if his taunt implied that he knew things about that disappearance. Maybe my goading could get him to say more.

"I'm working on that. And since I'm pretty sure you're not smart enough to have abducted her by yourself, I'm wondering who you might have gotten to help you. Working in an auto shop like you do, I'm guessing it wouldn't be that hard finding some muscle for hire. If that's the case, you could have kept your hands clean and distanced yourself from Heather's abduction."

"Number four," he said.

"Did a lawyer help you draft your statement, Emilio? Is that who you talked with before agreeing to meet with me?"

"I didn't talk with no one. I didn't need to."

"So after Heather drops the bombshell on you, after she tells you tough luck, after she says your year of counseling and anger-management classes still wasn't enough to cut it for her, you lost it, didn't you, Emilio?"

"I'm beginning to think you're the one who can't read," he said. "Do you want me to read points one and two?"

"No need," I said. "But I'm wondering why you settled on only four points. Is it because that's as high as you can count?"

Cruz's voice constricted, and his clenched fingers turned into fists. "You're such a tough guy hiding behind your badge and gun."

"I'm not hiding behind my badge and gun," I said. "I'm hiding behind *him*."

Sirius had picked up on the threat in Cruz's voice and was raising him one. His growl was deep and his teeth were bared. Hell, even I found it scary, and he was *defending* me.

"Call him off," begged Cruz in a frightened whisper.

"*In Ordnung,*" I told my partner, telling him "okay" or "enough" in German.

Sirius stopped growling.

Cruz got to his feet, albeit a little unsteadily. He backed away from us until he'd retreated to what he must have thought was a safe distance, and then quickly began walking to his car.

"Let's do coffee again soon!" I shouted.

He flipped me off.

"I guess that must be point number five," I told Sirius.

I watched Emilio get in his car and then drive off. For once, I wasn't in a rush to be somewhere. My coffee was cold, but I sat there sipping it anyway. I pulled out Cruz's note and looked at it. Why he'd even bothered to meet with me didn't make sense. He'd pretty much refused to discuss his wife's disappearance.

Maybe he'd just wanted me to pick up the tab for his venti soy caramel macchiato with four shots. I finished my own cup of coffee. There were no dregs at the bottom, even though I imagined I tasted them.

CHAPTER 28

THE SCENT OF A WOMAN

Since there wasn't anything I could do at the moment for Heather Moreland, I decided to do something for her dog. I called Doggy Doreen. Despite her putting a positive spin on it, she couldn't hide the fact that Angie was still unsettled and hadn't yet adjusted to her new situation.

"What do you think about my coming over and taking her somewhere for a walk?" I asked.

"That would be wonderful," she said. "If you get her tired, maybe she won't be pacing back and forth all night."

"Is that what she's been doing?"

"I'm afraid so."

"A walk can't hurt, then. Is there anything I can do for you?"

"It's sweet of you to even ask, but there's nothing I can think of."

"How about I bring some dog food to save you a trip to the store?"

Doreen did her best to talk me out of it, but then owned up to a few favorite brands of dry food.

* * *

For the dogs I bought a few large bags of premium kibble; for the human I brought two bottles of wine. As I began carrying my offerings inside, Doreen effusively thanked me.

"Just make sure you remember that the wine is for you and the kibble is for the dogs."

Laughing, she said, "I'll try not to forget that."

While I went to my car to get another bag of kibble, Doreen got Angie ready for our walk. My rescue dog was happy to see me and wagged her tail nonstop while sniffing me. As Angie took stock of my scent, I was sure she was privy to all my movements since dropping her off.

Sirius was in the car, and Angie was even happier seeing him. My partner matched her, tail wag for tail wag. After getting Angie settled, we took off on our drive.

The Silver Lake Recreation Center is dog-friendly. They even have two dog parks, one for little dogs and one for big dogs. On this occasion I decided to bypass the parks, opting for the two-mile walk around the reservoir.

In Germany they have strict rules concerning breed suitability. Sirius came to LAPD as a *Schutzhund* I, their highest ranking. In German, *Schutzhund* means "protection dog." To earn his designation, Sirius had to pass a number of tests involving tracking, obedience, and protection. The character of the dog is carefully judged. They have to show enthusiasm for the tasks given to them, and need to demonstrate courage in the face of perceived danger. Dogs also have to display appropriate levels of aggression. You don't want a timid dog, and you don't want Cujo. You want the right Goldilocks porridge.

I decided to use the walk to work on Sirius's skills, not to mention my own. At least once a month, we try and train with Metropolitan

K-9 and go through drills that include suspect apprehension, bite work, attack simulations, and tactical deployment. Though we couldn't do any of those things on the walk, we could still do some obedience, agility, article search, and tracking. The problem was doing all those things while also walking Angie.

Over the years I've tried to make our workouts fun for Sirius. Because of his intelligence, I try and mix up the training so he doesn't get bored. In my daypack I keep tennis balls, discs, stuffed animals, treats, and water. All of those items, and more, come into play during our training.

At the onset of our walk, we started with the command "Sit." While Sirius waited, Angie and I continued forward until we were out of sight. My command was for Sirius to stay put until he heard from me. Some dogs struggle when they can't see their handler. Five minutes passed before I finally whistled. It was the sound Sirius was waiting for. When he came bounding up to us, I praised him, and then brought out a tennis ball. While Angie and I kept walking, Sirius and I managed to play fetch. I had thought Angie would want to join Sirius in his games, but she actually paid him very little mind. Once again she seemed to be captive to her nose. It was hard to tell if she was following a scent or looking for one. Either way she pulled me along. "Heel" did not seem to be part of her vocabulary.

Along our route I hid a Frisbee, and then had Sirius find it. His reward was my throwing some discs to him. Then it was back to more obedience and some agility training; I had him running in and out of bushes, much like coaches have their athletes making cuts around cones. Now and again Angie wagged her tail at his displays, but for the most part she remained preoccupied with her nose work. I'd had few dealings with bloodhounds, and didn't know if the breed was obsessive-compulsive, or whether just Angie was. Sirius wanted to please; Angie couldn't care less about Brownie points. She had her own agenda, or seemed to.

The sun was about half an hour from setting when we finished our walk. I wasn't sure if I'd succeeded in wearing out Angie. As we drove her back to Los Feliz Hills with the windows a few inches down, Angie's nose was still on the job, tilting one way and then the other. From the rearview mirror I watched her. On a few occasions it looked as if she was on to something, but then whatever scent she had honed in on disappeared, and once more she returned to her olfactory hunt.

Her sniffing brought to mind one of my all-time favorite movies: *The Scent of a Woman*. It also brought to mind Heather Moreland.

"I bet you're looking for the scent of one particular woman," I said.

Angie answered by continually testing the air.

"I'm looking for that same scent," I confessed. "And if you don't give up, I won't either."

CHAPTER 29

SLEEPING BEAUTY, WEEPING BEAUTY

When he'd last appeared in front of her, Heather had been forced to listen to his lies and insinuations, his horrible toxic comments, for the better part of an hour before he showed himself. But even then her captor had hidden behind a mask, wearing something that resembled the face of a mandrill, with a long red nose, bluish lines, fierce teeth, and feral eyes. The mask was like one a witch doctor might wear.

And his blowgun was a weapon a witch doctor might use.

She'd wondered if the weapon was for show or if he really intended to use it on her. She hadn't had to wait long to find out.

"Do you have any last prayers?" he'd asked, his voice muffled behind the mask.

Then he took in a breath, found a space for the blowgun through the serrated teeth of the mask, and blew. Though the dart missed, she could see its sharp point as it skidded along the concrete floor.

"What the hell is wrong with you?" she screamed.

He answered by sending another dart her way.

Heather looked for something she could use as protection. She had to settle for the mostly empty pitcher of water, trying to use it as a shield. The darts came faster and faster, and his aim improved. Heather tried picking up some of the darts to throw back at him, but she couldn't throw them as far as he could shoot them, and her efforts only exposed her all the more. She didn't know if the tips of the darts were poisoned. She only knew it was terrifying being a target.

"Bastard!" she screamed at him. "Bastard!"

One of his darts finally struck, burying itself deep in her thigh. She pulled the dart out as fast as she could, but she was afraid the damage had already been done.

"You fucking toad!" she cried.

"Do you want those to be your last words? If I was taking my leave of this earth, I'd try and do a little better than that."

"I pray that you burn in hell."

"That's a little better. But perhaps you should be praying that I didn't coat that dart's tip with deadly poison. Did I, or didn't I? I really can't be sure. And neither can I tell you what makes for a lethal dose."

It hurt where the dart had struck her; pain and heat radiated throughout her thigh. Heather was feeling wobbly, but the rational part of her mind, which she was trying to cling to, wondered if his power of suggestion was making her feel that way.

Am I dying? she thought. She didn't know. She began to silently pray, but he must have noticed the movement of her lips.

"Let us prey," he said, laughing.

His words were the last thing she remembered before swooning.

* * *

When Heather finally awakened, being alive didn't feel like a victory. It was just a reprieve before more torture.

There had always been a part of her that resented her mother, that wondered why she hadn't simply called the authorities and had her father locked up. Heather had grieved when her mother had been murdered, but she'd also blamed her mother for not acting and saving herself, not to mention saving Heather and her brother. She was more sympathetic to her mother's plight now. She'd learned what it was like to constantly be afraid, and how when hope is the only thing you can cling to, it becomes all the harder to hold on to.

She didn't know how long she had been out. In her prison, days and nights were difficult to distinguish. She found herself naked and sprawled out on the concrete floor. The burka was gone; in its place he'd left skimpy lingerie.

It was the sound of heavy breathing, Heather realized, that had awakened her. The sounds were magnified, almost as if he was breathing through a respirator. It was like listening to Darth Vader. Maybe that was the effect he was going for. It wouldn't have surprised her to see him wearing a Vader mask.

The breathing dominated the space around her. It was a sound designed to make her anxious. Heather tried to control her own breathing and not succumb to panic. Her captor enjoyed terrifying her and demeaning her and hurting her. He wanted to break her. She couldn't let him, for she suspected resisting him was the only thing keeping her alive.

With nothing else to wear, she put on the sheer Chantilly lace teddy. It didn't do much to lessen the bite of the cold, but then the lingerie clearly hadn't been designed for warmth. It came with a plunging neckline and an exposed backside that made her feel like she was wearing dental floss. She doubted whether a woman could have designed such an outfit.

The breathing grew louder and more intense. It echoed around the room.

As she finished dressing, she examined the puncture on her thigh. It was red and ulcerated. She was afraid it was in danger of festering. There was nothing to treat the lesion; there was barely any water left.

Heather turned her back to where the camera was, and where she suspected her captor was watching her from. She didn't want to give the voyeur any more images of her than necessary. She peed in a small trash basket, then ripped off a piece of the lingerie, dipped it into her urine, and tried to clean the wound as best she could. It stung, but she forced herself to saturate the wound with urine. She'd heard that was how you treated the puncture wound from a stingray if no other antiseptic was available. Her sterile urine might stave off any potential infection. That didn't make what she was doing any less repulsive, but she refused to succumb to an infection, or to him.

His overly loud breathing almost sounded like the beating of drums. She did her best to ignore the auditory invasion. Because she knew his eyes were on her, Heather didn't address her sticky inner thighs. While she'd been drugged, he had once again raped her.

It was hard to think over his amplified breathing. Her captor preyed on comatose women. When stories of Bill Cosby's sexual predation had emerged, Heather had been repulsed. The whole idea of date rape, of trolls abusing unconscious women, was beyond repugnant. Along with the Cosby revelations had been articles detailing his suspected somnophilia. Some had tried to categorize Cosby's sickness as a fetish, as Sleeping Beauty syndrome, but that was ridiculous. No one called pedophilia a fetish. Somnophilia was a dangerous sickness, a psychiatric disorder. Emilio had wanted to try things sexually that she had spurned. She'd refused to entertain his desire for a three-way. On one occasion she remembered passing out and not waking until morning. She blamed it on a reaction to an over-the-counter medicine. But what if Emilio had drugged her? What if he was a somnophiliac?

"Did you sleep well?"

The amplified voice made her jump. There was a nasty tone to it, but more than that, it didn't sound quite human. He was using a voice changer again, and his laughter sounded like that of a troll or ogre.

"Emilio?" she asked.

He didn't respond other than to say, "Are you ready for more games?"

CHAPTER 30

LISTENING TO GOD, LISTENING TO DOG

During my years with Metropolitan K-9, the cops went through as much training as the dogs did. We were coached on becoming more effective handlers, with the instruction designed to improve our vocal techniques and physical cues so as to maximize the understanding between handler and dog and the effectiveness of the team.

There came a time in K-9 when I thought I knew it all. That's when one of my instructors decided to give me a comeuppance. "What the hell is wrong with you, Gideon?" he asked. "Are you going to wake up sometime today and notice the gimp in your dog's giddy-up? What do you need, a waving red flag? Until you learn how to listen to the dog, you're always going to be a second-rate handler."

My first reaction was defensive. I wasn't going to buy into any Zen crap. Listen to the dog—sure. Ohm. Ohmmmm. But as it turned out, during the day's training, the dog had gotten a foxtail in his paw, and I had missed what he was telling me. From that day forward, I've tried to take the time to better read whatever dog I'm working with. You can't rely on a dog's bark to tell you everything. Because of that I began to more closely study the position of a dog's head, ears, eyes, and tail. I gauged attitudes and posture, and interpreted sounds and body language and what the dog's eyes said. I became a better listener.

I thank my lucky stars that I landed a partner like Sirius. He "speaks" in a way that makes it easy for me to understand. I usually know what he's up to and what he wants. I don't need to interpret much, and we always seem to be on the same wavelength. But it wasn't Sirius I was thinking about as I settled into bed; it was Angie. Had I been listening to her?

I had categorized her as OCD. I had thought she was a nose with a dog attached. It was easy to write her off as instinct bound. But had I paid the proper attention to what she was trying to tell me?

Her behavior offered clues, I was sure, but I was slow in picking up on them. There was something there, or I sensed there was, but I couldn't put my finger on it, and the more I tried, the more frustrated I became.

It says something about your day when the highlight is attending a memorial service. Tomorrow, I thought, I would call Savannah Walker. Asking to meet with her so soon after her husband's service felt wrong and discourteous, but Emily Post never ran a potential homicide investigation. Besides, Mrs. Walker had been married to a cop for more than thirty years. If anyone would understand my intrusion, she would.

My unsettled mind wasn't making it easy to sleep. I wanted oblivion. I wanted an escape from that weight, that pressure I was feeling that came from Heather Moreland's disappearance. My Saturday-afternoon coffee with her ex-husband hadn't yielded anything. I was still puzzled as to why he'd met with me. What was his motive other than wasting my time?

For the second night in a row, I all but welcomed a burning dream. I had too many questions and not enough answers, and because of that I was willing to spend time in hell to get them. That spoke to my desperation. In the not-too-distant past, there had been nights when I'd purposely gone without sleep in order to avoid another fire walk. What I experience doesn't just *feel* like I'm burning. I *am* burning.

I almost called Lisbet, but didn't. I told myself that I wasn't bothering her because of how heavy her workload was. The truth was that I didn't want to look weak.

Sleep finally came. I don't know if the night would have brought with it a burning dream, because as it turned out, my sleep was interrupted. At a little after two, my cell phone began ringing. Without reading glasses, I couldn't make out the readout of who was calling.

"Detective Gideon?"

The woman's voice sounded apologetic and unsure. It also sounded familiar, but I couldn't place it at first. I growled some acknowledgment of my identity.

"This is Doreen Phelps," she said.

"Who?"

"Doggy Doreen," she said.

"That Doreen," I said, trying to sound friendlier.

"I wouldn't have bothered you at this hour except for something that happened to Angie."

Now I was awake: "What?"

"The vet is looking at her now. I was afraid she wouldn't make it. But it's looking better now."

I tried to rein in Doreen, and her story. "Take a deep breath, and then tell me what happened from the beginning."

Her breath sounded shaky, but at least she took my advice. "About an hour ago I heard this loud ruckus," she said.

"So that would have been around one in the morning?"

"That's right." Her voice steadied. "At first I thought a raccoon or possum must have gotten into the backyard and was driving the dogs wild. But then I realized all the noise was coming from Angie. She was barking and baying and growling. Naturally that riled up the rest of the dogs, most of which were asleep in the master bedroom.

"It sounded like Angie was having a run-in with something, so the other dogs and I went to investigate. By the time we got to the backyard, though, the sounds had stopped. That seemed strange to me, what with the way Angie had been going crazy. I started calling to her, but she didn't respond. There are motion detectors out back, but it's a good thing I had the dogs with me. Without them I don't think I would have even seen Angie. We found her in a heap hidden under shrubbery near the fence. She was barely breathing. My first thought was that she'd stumbled on a baby rattlesnake. They show up around this time. But then I noticed she was bloody, and that whatever she'd tangled with had taken half of one ear."

I'd heard enough. "Where is she being treated?"

"It can wait until the morning," she said. "I just thought you might want to know—"

"You did the right thing by calling me. And I do need to see her. What's the address?"

Doreen went to find a business card in the reception area, and then read me the address. I entered it into my phone's GPS and said, "I'll be there in twenty minutes."

* * *

The vet's clinic looked closed except for the three cars that were parked in the lot. I lowered the car windows until they were half-down, and then I gave Sirius the command to "Stay."

"I would tell the doc that you and Angie are family," I told him with a scratch, "but I don't think the vet would buy the resemblance."

The doors to the animal hospital were locked, but there was a buzzer, which I pressed. Doreen appeared with a young Hispanic male in blue scrubs who unlocked the door for me.

"Thank you, Hector," she said.

"No problem."

"Hector is a lifesaver," she said to me. "He carried Angie in and got her ready for Dr. Green."

The vet tech smiled and shrugged, and then took his leave of us. Doreen had me follow her into a treatment room, where Angie was being tended. Dr. Green looked up from her work and acknowledged us with a curt nod. She had short, gray hair, with scrunched eyebrows that angled downward to a V and looked almost owl-like. Her glasses were perched precariously on the very end of her nose.

"I've had visits from animal control before," she said, "but never from a detective."

"Just think of me as animal control for the two-legged. How's our patient?"

There were two IV tubes feeding into Angie. She was sprawled on a table, and her eyes were closed. An oxygen mask covered her muzzle, and misted up with every breath she took.

"She'll live," said Dr. Green.

I moved closer to Angie. One of her floppy ears was no longer as floppy. Half her left ear had been cut off.

"What the hell?" I said.

"My words exactly," said the vet.

"What happened?"

"I'd be guessing," she said.

"Guess away."

She pointed to a series of indentations around Angie's neck. "I'd say these are ligature marks."

"From what?"

"They likely came from an animal-control pole."

I caught myself reaching protectively for my own neck. It hadn't been that long ago that I had found myself on the wrong end of one or two of those poles.

"So someone tried to strangle Angie?"

She nodded. "But that's not all. I've identified a possible puncture mark on her body. Based on her condition, I believe Angie was drugged."

"Any guess what kind of drug was used?"

Dr. Green raised her glasses from her nose and nested them in her hair. "Based on Angie's respiratory depression, overall sedation, and muscle relaxation, it was likely some kind of barbiturate. My best guess would be phenobarbital."

Doreen entered the conversation. "I probably should have mentioned this before. There were some cubes of meat on the ground near to where I found Angie."

"I hope the other dogs didn't eat them," I said, "or are in danger of eating them."

Doreen shook her head. "As soon as I noticed them, I rounded up the troops and locked them inside. I can't be sure, but I don't think Angie ate any of the meat."

"Whoever did this was likely counting on Angie bolting down the food," said Dr. Green. "When that didn't happen, her attacker likely shot her up with phenobarbital. If you can bring me the meat, I'll have it tested."

"If I know Angie," I said, "putting the bite on the trespasser interested her a lot more than the food did. So that's when the bad guy went to plan B with his animal-control pole, but Angie fought him so hard he had trouble injecting her with anything. And she raised such a ruckus, he couldn't stay around to make sure she was dead."

"Why would he cut off part of her ear?" asked Doreen.

"It might have happened during their struggle," I said. "Or maybe this guy is just a sick psychopathic scumbag who got pissed off by Angie's will to live."

I reached out and stroked the unconscious dog. Against all odds, Angie kept surviving.

"Do you have home-surveillance cameras?" I asked.

Doreen shook her head. "I'm afraid not."

"What about your neighbors?"

"I don't think they have them either. Until now our neighborhood has always been very safe."

"Why would anyone want to hurt Angie?" asked Dr. Green.

I shook my head. "I don't know why. The only thing I can think of is that there's a tie-in with the case I'm working." Then I offered an abbreviated explanation: "Angie's owner is missing under suspicious circumstances."

"But how could anyone have known where Angie was to target her?" asked Doreen.

It was a good question, and I didn't have a good answer. "Did you tell anyone that you were boarding her?"

"Not a soul," she said.

"I didn't either." The only other person who knew where Angie was being boarded was Lisbet, and I knew she wouldn't have passed on that information.

"So maybe it was the act of some crazy," said the vet.

"Maybe," I said. But I didn't believe it.

CHAPTER 31

WHEN TO HOLD THEM, WHEN TO PHO'LD THEM

On doctor's orders, Angie had to stay over at the clinic. I was reassured that there was someone on staff twenty-four hours a day, and Dr. Green agreed that only Doreen and I would be allowed to visit with Angie.

"I'd like to be the one Angie is released to," I said. "With everything that's gone on, I think it's best that she be under my protection."

"I'm afraid you might be right," Doreen said.

Hector was called to accompany Doreen and me out, and I was glad to hear him lock the door behind us. I walked Doreen to her car, but it was clear she was still spooked.

"How about I give you a police escort?" I said. "I'll meet you at your house and make sure everything is fine there."

"That's silly," said Doreen, but I could hear the relief in her voice.

"You're going to have to humor me," I said. "I'll be waiting for you out front of your house."

She took a little more cajoling before getting into her car and driving off. As planned, I arrived at Doreen's house before she did. That gave me time to scout her neighborhood. From what I observed, there were no security cameras in the four other homes on the street.

Flashlight in hand, Sirius and I walked around Doreen's front yard. Nothing looked out of the ordinary. Our scrutinizing roused the pack of dogs inside, and a lot of excited barking.

At the approach of headlights, Sirius and I moved toward the driveway. I signaled with my flashlight, and then shone it on my face so that Doreen could see it was me. She turned into the driveway and parked in the garage.

"You really should get home," she said. "As you can hear by the ruckus, my Praetorian Guard awaits me."

"I need to look around your backyard," I said. "And since Sirius and I are already here, we might as well make sure your house is secure."

I had to talk loudly over the noise of the waiting dogs. "Behave, everyone!" Doreen yelled through the closed door, but the clamor continued. When she opened the door, the dogs streamed out into the garage. Two sniffed me while the rest took stock of Sirius. He stood there imperiously, letting them get their sniffing in while ignoring their yips and growls.

"Stop that, Wilbur!" shouted Doreen, directing her words at the smallest but most aggressive of the dogs. The pug-mix backed away with a last growl at Sirius.

"Wilbur has a Napoleonic complex," said Doreen.

"*Sois sage!*" I told him. My one year of taking French in school finally bore fruit. Of course I only remembered those words because my poor teacher, Miss Durand, had found it necessary to keep directing them at me.

After Sirius and I passed the inspection of the guard, we followed Doreen into the house, and then went about examining every room and closet. The six dogs followed us everywhere and double-checked everything we did.

When we gave the house the all clear, Doreen turned on the backyard lights and took me for a tour. Much to their disappointment, all the dogs were left inside, including Sirius.

"Here's where I found Angie," said Doreen, pointing to a spot near the wrought iron fence.

The vegetation around the area had been disturbed, with most of the ground cover dug out. I imagined Angie being suspended with an animal-control pole and desperately looking for any kind of purchase with her hind legs. I shone my light on the wrought iron fence. There were visible scratch marks in the posts and pickets, and I felt the anger spreading from my chest into my body. Angie was lucky to be alive.

I took pictures with my cell-phone camera. The ground outside the fence was compacted, probably from the intruder's effort in trying to strangle a sixty-pound dog, but there were no visible footprints.

On our side of the fence were two cubes of meat about a square inch around. Sandwiched inside the cubes, I could see white tablets. I bagged the meat as evidence, and then Doreen and I carefully searched the area looking for any more. Another doctored two cubes turned up that must have scattered during Angie's struggles.

"That poor dear," said Doreen, shaking her head at the signs of the fight that had taken place.

* * *

After securing the evidence, I arrived home with dawn about an hour off. The Sunday paper was already in the driveway. I've joined the digital world, but I still like reading my Sunday newspaper the old-fashioned way. Normally once I'm awakened, I'm up for the rest of the day. I took the paper and a cup of coffee to the sofa and did my reading and sipping. I was halfway through the sports section when I fell asleep.

Four hours later I woke up with Sirius conked out on the floor next to me. I managed to move through his obstacle course without stepping on him, and from the kitchen called Lisbet's home number. After half a dozen rings, I was forced to talk into her message machine.

"I'm just making sure you're coming over for dinner tonight. Seven-course meals take time to prepare, you know. It takes a lot of thought and effort to get a six-pack and takeout. Actually, I was thinking of getting us some pho to go. Does that work for you? There's a place nearby that's un-pho-gettable. I kid you not, it's pho-nomenal."

I smiled at the thought of Lisbet's groaning. My tone became more personal. "I miss you," I said.

But I could be neither romantic nor serious for long, and finished my message by saying, "Pho sure."

My next call was to Savannah Walker, where I got another message machine. I also got a bit of a jolt. It was Langston Walker's voice I heard asking me to leave a message at the beep.

I debated over hanging up or leaving a message, and then found myself trying to say something intelligible: "Mrs. Walker, this is Michael Gideon. I know this is probably a terrible time to be disturbing you, but I'm wondering if you could give me a call back." Then I left her my home and cell numbers.

By that time Sirius had joined me in the kitchen, and I decided to make us some eggs and hash browns. Because that's my go-to breakfast, I had boiled potatoes earlier in the week, and they were waiting for me in the refrigerator. I heated up a little olive oil, grated two potatoes, and threw them in the pan. After browning the hash browns for about a minute, I turned them over, and then cracked three eggs and added them to the hot skillet. Then I applied a little salt and pepper to everything. When I have the time and I'm feeling particularly creative, I whip up a side of homemade salsa, but since I didn't have the ingredients, I opted for ketchup. My healthy cooking wasn't only for me: Sirius got half of what was in the pan, minus the ketchup.

After breakfast I went back to reading the newspaper and hoping for returned calls. Lisbet was the first to ring me back. "Isn't it a pho-ntastic day?" she said.

"You very pho-nny," I told her.

"I wish you'd been able to come with me to the Earth Day sunrise service at Eagle Rock Park. It was beautiful."

"You were up with the birds," I said. "I was up with the dogs." Then I told her how I'd spent half my night.

"Are you sure you'll even be awake when dinner rolls around?" she asked.

"I actually took a nap."

"Well, at the risk of prompting another one of your puns, pho sounds great. What time should I be over?"

"Unless you hear differently from me," I said, "why don't you come over at pho thirty?"

* * *

Savannah Walker called me back a little after one. Like Lisbet, she told me that she'd been attending a church service.

"I'm hoping you can forgive my timing in all of this, Mrs. Walker," I said, "but I want to pursue your husband's ghost as soon as possible."

"Is it only a ghost that you want to pursue, Detective Gideon?" she asked.

"What do you mean?"

"I get this sense you're not telling me the full story. When you've been married to a detective as long as I was, you pick up on undercurrents. When Langston was onto something, I could hear it in his voice, and see it in the way he was acting. He was on the scent, he said. You're no different in that regard. But what scent is it that's driving you?"

"I have no proof. I only have some half-baked suspicions. And I don't see the reason to bother you with those."

"I'm grieving, Detective. But I don't want you working behind my back. I want to be involved."

"Then I'll ask your forgiveness ahead of time if I'm wrong about this matter, which I probably am."

"As long as your heart is in the right place, there will be no need for forgiveness."

"I hope it is," I said. "And I hope you won't think I'm crazy when I tell you that I'm not completely satisfied with the explanation that your husband slipped on the trail and died of natural causes."

"You think someone murdered him?"

"With your permission, I want to look into that possibility. Langston was investigating his old case, his ghost case, and I'm wondering if that investigation could have had anything to do with his death."

Savannah Walker didn't answer right away, and every second of her silence made me feel worse for even having broached the subject. I said, "I'm sorry that I bothered you with such speculation—"

She interrupted me: "Please don't apologize. All this time I felt bad that I was thinking along those lines. Everyone assured me it was an accident. So I said nothing."

"It probably was an accident, but I went up the Skyline Trail with a ranger. We looked at where Langston died, and I came away with questions."

"And you want to look into it more now?"

"I do."

"You have my blessing, Detective Gideon."

"I appreciate that."

"You and Langston," she said. "The two of you are anxious to go where angels fear to tread."

"It's an occupational hazard."

"I'm not sure if it is. There was no stopping Langston when he thought he was onto something. He always worried that he wasn't a very good detective, although he had one of the highest closure rates in RHD."

"He told me about his doubts, but said he outworked everyone."

"He did that."

She laughed softly, then sighed. "Let's talk about what you've patiently tried not to ask. You want to look at my husband's files as soon as possible."

"I do."

"I have a few dozen people coming over to the house to pay their respects. If you don't mind the noise and distractions, you are welcome to come over now."

"Thank you. I'll do my best to not impose on your gathering."

"Do whatever you need to do."

She gave me her home address, and I told her I would be there within the hour.

I've always had trouble grieving, and have never been comfortable at funerals.

"This is my way of paying respects, Langston," I said. "This is my way."

CHAPTER 32

DOGGIE BAGS

On the drive over to the Walker house, I thought about my dinner with Langston and what we'd talked about. It was possible he'd already cued me in to his ghost and provided me with suspects for his murder. He'd referenced the Spook Town Compton Crips killing Catalina Ceballos's husband. A spook is a ghost. The fact that Walker was trying to reopen the investigation couldn't have made him popular with the gang. Catalina had already claimed the gang had made threats on her life. Would they go so far as to kill a cop, albeit one who was retired? And what was it about this ghost case that had haunted Walker?

From what Walker had implied, Catalina hadn't believed her husband was involved in dealing drugs. The two of them had been college students at the time. Was there another reason he'd died? And was it possible the gang had been set up to look like the murderers?

I had lots of questions and couldn't wait to look at the case notes.

My GPS directed me to the Walker residence on South Sherbourne. During our dinner conversation, Langston had asked me if I'd ever been to Ladera Heights, and I told him I hadn't. I wonder what that said about my social circle and the racial divide. This was my first foray into what he said was often referred to as the "Black Beverly Hills."

The houses I drove by were well kept up, and most of the residents I saw were African American. It was nice to see the American dream on display in a form that wasn't lily-white.

Cars lined the Walkers' circular driveway. Savannah's visitors had already arrived. I parked on the street and walked up a driveway bordered by rosebushes. Even though it wasn't yet May, all the roses were in bloom, and the air was awash in their fragrant scent.

I rang the doorbell and waited. When the door opened, I was expecting to see Savannah Walker, but instead was greeted by Catalina Ceballos. She looked as surprised to see me as I was to see her.

"Detective Gideon," she said, extending her hand.

"Ms. Ceballos," I said.

It was clear she hadn't expected me to remember her name.

Her furrowed brows also made it clear she wondered what I was doing there.

"Are you here for our meeting?"

"Actually, I came by to have a word with Mrs. Walker," I said. "But seeing you here, I wonder if I might also talk to you."

Her brows were still furrowed. "About what?"

"I know Detective Walker was trying to help you reopen your husband's homicide. Was he dealing with LAPD, or the Los Angeles Sheriff's Department?"

I asked the question because LASD had jurisdiction over Compton.

"Carlos's murder happened just outside of Compton," she said. "The South Bureau's Criminal Gang and Homicide Division were assigned to it."

I nodded. "Who was the lead detective?" I asked.

"Why do you want to know?"

She didn't try to hide being suspicious of my motives. "I know Detective Walker was advocating for you in reopening the case. Now that he's gone, I thought I might look into the situation."

What I said was true enough, but far from the complete story. Still, it changed Catalina's tone and attitude. "I would be very grateful for that."

She gave me the name of the detective. Without my asking, she also provided me with her cell number, volunteering to answer any questions I might have.

"I'll be sure to follow up with you," I promised, at which time Catalina seemed to realize I was still standing on the stoop.

"Please come in," she said. "I'm answering the door because the club is here today to pay its respects. Savannah was also nice enough to allow us to use her house for an emergency meeting. With Langston's death, everything's crazy."

"I hope you're making plans to keep the club going."

"That's what we all want, but no one seems to know how to make that happen."

"At least you've started planning."

She nodded, but didn't look convinced. "Langston was the club's glue. If we didn't know how indispensable he was before, we sure do now. But let me take you to Savannah."

I followed Catalina, assuming I would be taken to a quiet location where Mrs. Walker was waiting. What I wasn't expecting was to find her sitting in the living room with at least a dozen members of the 187 Club. Everyone stopped talking when they saw me, and I offered a nod to the room.

Mrs. Walker rose from her chair and said, "Please excuse me."

She came up to me and offered me a pleasant as well as circumspect greeting: "Thank you for coming, Detective."

"My pleasure," I said.

We escaped the room's scrutiny by starting down the hallway. Paintings lined both sides of the corridor. There were spiritual scenes, and folk art with mostly black subjects.

"You have a beautiful house," I said.

"Thank you," she said. "We've lived here for almost thirty years. When we first looked at this house, Langston said we couldn't afford to buy it, and I said we couldn't afford not to buy it. The backyard was always my refuge. It looks out over Marina del Rey, and on clear days you can make out Catalina Island. I wanted to have a mortgage-burning party this year, but Langston wasn't convinced. He said no one did that anymore."

"That's only because in California no one ever pays off their mortgage," I said.

"You're probably right about that."

She opened a door, and I was shown into a small room that had been made into an office. The desk had stacks of paperwork. There were composition notebooks, files, and computer printouts. In the center of the desk was a laptop, which was attached to a three-in-one printer. Next to the desk was a filing cabinet.

"Welcome to Langston's inner sanctum."

"Is his computer password-protected?" I asked.

Savannah shook her head. "I've used it on a few rare occasions, so I know it's not, but that's about all I can tell you about anything in this room. Langston didn't like his work space disturbed. That's why you'll have to excuse the mess."

"It's a lot neater than my own work space," I confessed.

She began to take her leave of the room, but paused at the doorway.

"Langston always liked the door closed, even when it was only the two of us in the house. I always said, 'Why do you need the door closed?' And he would say to me, 'I think better that way.' Would you like the door opened or closed?"

"I'm with Langston. If you don't mind, I'd prefer it was closed."

"I should have known," Savannah said. As she closed the door, I noticed the small, sad smile on her face.

* * *

Even though I'm a cop, and even though I had permission to go through Langston Walker's papers, it still felt like a breach of privacy. To sit at someone else's desk is revealing, even before you start digging through the contents. You get a feel for the person by what's on the walls, what pictures they value enough to place close to them, and what items are within reach. Walker's love of family was on display, but his desk was first and foremost a work area. At first glance the area might have looked disorganized, but everything was functional. He had sorters, trays, and organizers filled with paperwork, pens, highlighters, tape, staplers, and such essentials as glue and scissors.

Early in my scrutinizing, I realized Walker was definitely old school. I went into his computer and searched its history. He hadn't cleared its cache for some time, if ever, and I was able to look at all his browsing data. Nothing immediately jumped out at me as relevant to the case. I studied all the computer documents he'd worked on during the last month.

These days police work, like so many other professions, is electronically dependent. Walker had risen through the ranks writing reports rather than inputting data. That would have changed at the end of his tenure, but in his retirement he had reverted to what was most comfortable for him. There were lots of handwritten composition notebooks piled atop one another. Each seemed to serve a different purpose, and I spent some time getting used to his system.

I pulled out my own notebook. In that regard, Walker and I weren't too different. I noted the date and time. One section of my notebook was for taking notes, and another section was for compiling questions or making notations for things I would need to do. My first entry was: *Get Walker's cell phone and make list of incoming and outgoing calls.* Then I wrote down: *Find out why Walker was late to our dinner.* He had apologized for being late, and had told me that he'd had to put out some fires. I needed to know what fires those were.

Walker was also a believer in file folders, in which he stored articles and printouts. The folders weren't color-coded, and some weren't even labeled. Sifting the wheat from the chaff wasn't going to be easy.

I made my own priority pile of those folders and notebooks that interested me most. One folder contained half a dozen maps of L.A. In two of the maps, *X* didn't mark the spot, but instead marked half a dozen spots. Judging from where the *X*s were, I was looking at Santa Monica, Westwood, Hollywood, La Brea, Northeast L.A., and Central L.A. There were no street addresses, and nothing to designate what the *X*s meant except that on one of the sheets, the number "480" had been written, and the Central L.A. *X* had been circled. Walker apparently liked his maps to be enigmatic. There was a map of L.A. and the surrounding area marked with red lines, and a map of Westside and Central City with red, green, blue, yellow, and purple lines. It would have helped if Walker had printed out a key of what I was looking at.

On one piece of paper in his map file folder, Walker had written the words "comfortable street." He'd underlined the word "comfortable" twice. Not only maps were in the folder. I found a piece of paper where he'd written, "It's like the line from Hamlet about protesting too much."

While thinking about Walker's Shakespeare reference, I suddenly started. It was already four o'clock. I called up Lisbet, and when she answered, the first thing she said was, "Why do I get this feeling I'm being stood up?"

"I'm going to be late," I admitted.

"How late?"

"Six o'clock," I said, but Lisbet heard my wishful thinking in those words.

"More like seven?" she asked.

"Maybe," I said.

"I have work I should be doing anyway. How about I come over for pho tomorrow night at six thirty?"

"I am pho-tunate to have an understanding girlfriend like you."

"I am going to pretend I am deaf in one ear."

"I promise to nibble both your ears tomorrow."

"I'm going to hold you to that promise."

We said our good-byes, and each of us offered a last smooch over the phone. Then I went back to Langston's paperwork, picking up the largest of his folders. On its cover he'd written "187"; inside was a hodge-podge of material that pertained to the 187 Club. Near the front of the paperwork, I found my name and telephone number and the notation, "April's speaker." There were inspirational articles about overcoming grief, notes about meetings, and reminders of things that needed to be done. Deeper into the folder was a list of the members' names, addresses, and phone numbers. Still deeper were photocopies of police reports, along with notes pertinent to some of those cases. Altogether there were five reports, each detailing a homicide.

The contents of the folder couldn't be hurried through. There was a lot inside, and I settled down to my reading and note-taking. The common denominator was a lot of death. *It was the 187 Club, after all,* I thought.

The case that interested me most was my potential ghost case, which was held together with a large binder clip. I flipped through the pages and read about Carlos Ceballos's death. The DA had opted not to prosecute the gangbangers from the Spook Town Compton Crips, telling LAPD there was insufficient evidence to get a conviction. LAPD said they had the shooters. Gang graffiti bragged about the killing, and the word on the street also fingered the shooters.

A knock at the door almost made me jump. I'd been so absorbed in the material that I'd lost track of place and time.

"Come in," I said.

Savannah Walker opened the door. On her face was the same sad smile I'd seen earlier.

"How many times do I remember seeing a dazed expression just like that one?" she asked. "I'd always have to awaken Langston from his other world."

Time had gotten away from me. It was now dark outside, and my surprise showed.

"Langston and I had a private joke. I would call him Punxsutawney Phil. That's how he'd look when I interrupted him in here. I'd often bring him a meal." She looked at me. "What about you?"

I realized she was offering to bring me dinner; I'd long overstayed my visit.

"That's not necessary," I said. "I was just leaving. If you don't mind, though, I'd like to bring some of your husband's paperwork home with me. There's still a lot I need to go through."

She gestured to the desk, indicating I could take anything I might want.

"I have all sorts of food in my refrigerator," Savannah said, "more than I could ever eat. You'd be doing me a favor by taking some of it home."

"That's kind of you," I said, "but—"

"I really do hate seeing food go to waste. And I've got some nice meat for that dog of yours. He's probably starving by now."

"He probably is," I said. "And I know he'd be nudging me now, telling me to accept your offer. So if you really don't mind, I'll happily take two doggie bags to go."

CHAPTER 33

THE GREATEST HUNTER ON EARTH

Writer Anne Tyler once wrote about humans coming home from the store with various cuts of meat, and the reaction of Fido to the appearance of this bounty: "Dogs must think we're the greatest hunters on earth," she wrote.

By this time I think Sirius knows I'm not the greatest hunter on earth, but that didn't stop him from offering me plenty of tail wagging at the food I brought home. Savannah Walker had been more than generous, filling containers with chicken, brisket, baked beans, potato salad, and corn muffins.

I cut up some of the chicken and brisket, mixed it with dry food, and then Sirius went to town. Then I made my own plate, nuked it, and had my late dinner. During the drive home, my stomach had awakened to the passage of time, and I was now hungry. Those who'd brought food to Savannah Walker had been making an offering of love to her and her late husband. As much as I enjoyed eating the food, the thought of it still left something of an aftertaste in my mouth. Had Langston Walker paid the ultimate price for my meal? I already owed him a dinner; now I owed him two. It was up to me to find a way to pay him back.

Before it got any later, I decided to make a call. I was fairly certain my contact was a single parent, and that his son would have school in the morning. Over the past two years, I'd spent a lot of time with Ellis Haines, more than was good for me. He'd caused a lot of upheaval in my own life, but that was nothing compared to what he'd done to the families and loved ones of his victims, like Art Epstein and his son Joel.

When Art answered his phone, I said, "Mr. Epstein, this is Michael Gideon. I hope I'm not calling too late."

"No, of course not, Detective," he said. "What can I do for you?"

"Something has been nagging at me," I said. "Detective Walker and I met for dinner after the last 187 Club meeting, and he arrived about half an hour late. I'm wondering what delayed him. He apologized for being late and told me that he'd had to 'put out a fire or two.' I know my curiosity probably sounds silly, but I'm wondering if you know what fires he had to put out."

"I wish I knew," he said, "but I left as soon as you finished speaking. Joel had a sitter, and I didn't want to keep her waiting."

"I can certainly understand that," I said, "and I'm sorry for bothering you."

"It was no bother. And if you'd like, I'd be glad to find out why Langston was late for your dinner. I'm friends with a few of the more active club members. They might have stayed to put away chairs and help, so they'd know."

"I don't want to put you out."

"I'd like to do it," he said.

"I'd appreciate it, then. I'm trying to tie up a few loose ends, and that's one of them."

"Detective Walker and the other club members helped me get through a very tough time," he said. "When I heard about Langston's death, I thought about what a godsend he'd been for me. I wish I'd told him that."

"A lot of people are wishing the same thing now," I said.

Then I gave him my cell number, and he promised to get back to me.

* * *

The ghost was elusive. It didn't pop out at me and say, "Boo!" It was lurking in the shadows.

I wanted to believe the Spook Town Compton Crips were Langston's ghost, but the more I looked into the Ceballos case, the less likely I thought it was.

Danny Ruiz of the South Bureau's Criminal Gang and Homicide Division had been the lead detective. I didn't know Ruiz, but I knew people who knew him. Reading through Walker's notes, I could see that he'd talked to Ruiz on multiple occasions. I decided to get in on the party line and called Ruiz's cell. After identifying myself and apologizing for not calling during office hours, I explained that I was following up on the late Detective Walker's inquiries into the Ceballos homicide.

Ruiz didn't hide his annoyance. "What do you want me to say?" he asked. "The case is what it is. We think we made our case. The DA still wants more. Barring a confession, and I'm not holding my breath on that one, we're stalled."

In L.A., more than two-thirds of homicides are gang related. Even if it's one of your own who's been killed, the rule is you don't talk to cops.

"I'm curious about Catalina Ceballos," I said. "According to what I've read, she insisted her husband wasn't a member of a gang, and also doubted that he dealt drugs."

"That's because Carlos didn't want to tell his new bride things that might upset her," said Ruiz. "And while it's true he wasn't an active gang member, he was an occasional dealer. Even Mrs. Ceballos has come to reluctantly accept that fact."

"Mrs. Ceballos says that she has been threatened by the Crips for continuing to press for an investigation. She fears that she and her family are being targeted."

"I wouldn't doubt it. But the gang knows we'd be all over them if they attempted any retaliation."

"Do you know if gang members threatened Detective Walker?"

Ruiz offered a disdainful laugh. "Cockroaches run from light, and so do gangbangers."

It was the reaction I expected, but it was still disappointing. Gangs operated on their own turf and generally didn't stray. The idea that a gang would ambush a retired cop on a rugged trail far from their haunts was far-fetched.

I had a few follow-up questions for Ruiz, then thanked him for his cooperation. He clicked off without saying good-bye.

For the moment I decided to put aside the Ceballos case; that made Walker's 187 Club folder noticeably thinner. There were still four other cases to look at, though. Maybe Langston Walker's ghost would still surface.

I read through the paperwork, paying particular attention to the police reports in the 187 folder. Why had Walker picked those five cases? From what I could determine, there were some 150 members of the 187 Club. In any given month, roughly a third of the membership showed up to the monthly meeting.

Walker could have had 150 cases in his folder, but he only had five. I cross-indexed the cases with the club members associated with them; all were loved ones of the victims. It was unclear if there was something about these particular cases that Walker didn't like. Maybe the loved ones, like Catalina Ceballos, had asked him to look into the homicides. I would have to contact them to find out if that was so.

There didn't seem to be any common denominator in any of the cases. All of them had ostensibly been solved, although three of them were "cleared others." I wondered if Walker had earmarked those cases because of that designation. The victims were black, Hispanic, and white. The murders had taken place in Carson, Hawthorne, Central L.A., Southeast L.A. (the outskirts of Compton), and Fairfax. Two of the victims had been shot, one had been stabbed, one had died of blunt-force trauma, and one had been hit by a car. Gang violence was suspected in two deaths; the other three involved a drug deal gone wrong, a bicyclist hit while riding, and the murder of a transgender female caught in a love triangle.

Write-ups in the *Los Angeles Times* detailed the deaths. Every year the paper puts out what it calls "The Homicide Report," providing a story for every victim. I thought about the old chestnut: *What is black and white and read all over?* In these cases it might be more accurate to say they were red all over.

Earlier in the day I'd looked at a map marked by five different *X*s, but unfortunately these cases didn't correspond to the locations on the map. The only potential map match was Andrea Rhodes, who'd been killed on her bicycle by a hit-and-run driver in central L.A. I remembered Walker's handwritten reference to a "comfortable street," and wondered if that could have any relevance to her death. The car that hit Rhodes had been registered to Donald Warren of Culver City. According to Warren, he didn't remember driving that night, but Warren was no stranger to blackouts. Over the years he'd had three DUI convictions and was an admitted alcoholic. Even cirrhosis of the liver hadn't stopped him from drinking, and apparently driving. It was that disease that killed him four months after his arrest. The case had never gone to court; Warren's timely death had spared taxpayers that expense. Because of that, the case was a "cleared other."

Sirius had been patiently waiting for me to finish working for hours. Dogs are great about overlooking the shortcomings of their humans.

I had kept him waiting for his dinner, and then had kept him waiting for his walk.

"Go get me the leash," I told him.

Sirius ran off to get his leash. Our use of the leash is infrequent, but for the sake of appearances, Sirius is willing to walk around with it in his mouth. Some people are scared to see a dog off-leash, and aren't assured that Sirius is a trained police dog. When that occurs, Sirius hands me his drool-laden leash and happily lets me buckle him up.

My partner deserved a long walk, and I gave him one. We took the roundabout way to the local park, and Sirius caught up on the day's news. I thought about Angie and tried to keep my blood from boiling. In a day or two she'd be coming home to us. I hoped her stay wouldn't be permanent. It wasn't only a selfish wish; it was a wish for the safe return of Heather Moreland.

On the bell lap to our house, familiar headlights came sweeping our way and caught us in their beams. Seth was returning home in his Jaguar, which had the personalized license plate SHAMAN.

He rolled down his window. Sirius ran over, braced his front legs in the open window slot above the driver's door, and managed to give Seth a kiss. It was a neat trick considering that he still had his leash in his mouth.

"Working late?" I asked.

"Weekend retreat," he said. "What about you?"

"Long day," I said.

"Up for a nightcap?"

"What took you so long to ask?"

CHAPTER 34

BEHIND CLOSED DOORS

He called himself *Kurios*, which was the ancient Greek word for "master" or "lord." He was Curious Kurios. She still resisted calling him "Lord," but he was bending her to his will. Unfortunately, the two of them would not have as much time together as he had hoped. Kurios couldn't take any chances, and as unlikely as it was that he'd be found out, it was best to be safe.

If everything had gone as planned the night before, he would have had more time to play with her. Mindful of cameras, he had parked half a mile from the house, but as soon as he exited his car, that damn dog had known he was there. The closer he'd gotten, the more the dog had barked. And when he'd neared the fence, the dog had gone crazy. Other dogs would have bolted down those chunks of meat he'd tossed over the fence, but not her. She'd wanted to bite *him* into chunks of meat. That fucking dog had almost managed to vault over the fence. Even when he'd gotten a stranglehold on her, she'd thrashed and fought and kept resisting.

He'd planned to kill the dog on the same night he took his slave. He'd brought along pepper spray that was supposed to be so toxic as to drive off grizzly bears, along with his twenty-million-volt stun gun. He planned to disable the dog, then inject it with enough ketamine to put her to sleep permanently. Both bitches were supposed to have gotten the ketamine, but he'd only had the opportunity to dose one of them.

The loose end of the dog bothered him. His slave's absence should have gone unnoticed for days, but the dog had gotten the cop involved. It was a good thing he'd noticed the tracker the bitch had tried hiding in her nightie. After all his planning, that one slipup had almost done him in. That's why he couldn't be too cautious. And that's why he would need to dispatch her much sooner than he'd planned. Get rid of the evidence, just like he'd gotten rid of the tracker.

Kurios wished he could have seen the cop's expression at the end of that wild-goose chase. He wondered if the cop could appreciate the thought behind where he'd taken him. It was unlikely, of course. The cop was cunning in his own way, but he was still a troglodyte. While the cop thought he was being so smart, Kurios had managed to turn the tables on him. He'd planted a much better tracker in the cop's car. It was the cop who'd taken him to Angie, even though he didn't know it.

At the moment, the tracker told him the cop was home. No doubt he was sleeping.

Kurios wasn't ready to sleep. Not yet. Tonight he had a few special prizes in store.

The entrance to the bomb shelter was hidden by a large garden shed in his backyard. The shelter had been built in 1962 at the height of the Cold War. The builder had spared no expense trying to escape the imminent nuclear fallout. The shelter went deeper underground than most. And the bunker had been built with ample insulation.

While it wouldn't have deterred radiation, it was perfect for silencing screams. Kurios had done all sorts of tests before getting his slave. Aboveground no one could hear what was going on down there.

Down there. He liked the sound of that. And he liked going down there to his own Eva Braun. It was a great dungeon for fucking. Kurios had known it would be. For the longest time he'd had to imagine how it would be. But now he knew.

Kurios unlocked the entrance to the fallout shelter, lowered the ladder, and began his descent down. Normally he liked to observe her through his closed-circuit television system, but not tonight. There was much to do.

He decided to announce himself before she was able to see him. Now what was that line? Oh, yes. It was a song his slut mother used to sing.

"Oh, no one knows what goes on behind closed doors," he said, speaking the words more than singing them.

The acoustics in the bunker were exceptional. You could hear a pin drop. And the sound quality of screams really couldn't be improved upon.

Kurios put on a mask. He hadn't yet decided whether or not to let her look upon his face before she died. It wasn't just that he was being cautious. The masks he wore allowed him a sense of freedom. He could be whatever monster he chose.

Tonight he was Frankenstein.

The slave tried to hide her fright, but he could read it on her, smell it on her. She stunk up the room. She smelled of waste, and his unwashed spilled seed.

"I brought you a present," Kurios said.

And then he showed her what he was holding in his hand. At first she didn't understand. He moved closer to her cage and tossed her what looked like a swatch of fabric. She bent down to look at it, and then realized what she was seeing.

Her expression of horror and revulsion made Kurios hard.

"No," she whispered.

"Tomorrow I'll bring you her heart," he said.

"No!" she cried. Tears streamed down her face. "Don't hurt her," she begged. "She's already had too much pain in her life."

"I won't hurt her," said Kurios. "I can't hurt her. She's already dead."

He watched as his slave's face began to melt. That's what it looked like. It was almost as if he'd put a match to wax.

He showed her the other thing he was holding. "I used this to take her ear."

In the gloom of the room, the razor-edge of the box cutter stood out. He lowered the box cutter to the cement floor, and then kicked it inside her cage.

"A word of advice," said Kurios. "Don't cut your wrists horizontally. That's an amateur mistake. You want to make multiple vertical cuts. That will do the job."

CHAPTER 35

FOR MEDICINAL PURPOSES ONLY

Seth and I slowly sipped a second drink. We were both tired and were talking less than usual, but between us was the comfort of an old friendship.

I took another pull on my bourbon and mused, "For medicinal purposes only."

That made Seth smile. "Is that so?"

"The proof is in the proof," I said. "When I was a boy, my mother used to take me on her visits to her sister Florence. Aunt Florence lived on the other side of the country in Portland, Maine. What I loved most about Aunt Florence's house was her collection of old bottles. She had hundreds of them, most from the nineteenth century. The bottles had these wonderful shapes and sizes and colors, far different than the glasswork we see today. Even on some of the so-called clear glass, there were hues of purple and green when they were touched by sunlight. On the bottoms of some of them were pontil marks indicating they had been handblown.

"My favorite bottles had writing on them. Lots of little towns back then used to have their own breweries and bottleries, and I'd take out an atlas and look those towns up on the state maps. But I found the products themselves even more interesting. I can remember names, such as Moxie Nerve Food, and Dr. Liebig's German Invigorator, and Dr. Jayne's Alternative, and Miller's Antiseptic Oil.

"We think modern advertising has a corner on hyperbole, but you should have seen some of the claims on her old bottles. They contained mostly booze, a much higher alcohol volume than anything being distilled today, but the contents were described as balms, tonics, purifiers, compounds, elixirs, and extracts. Nostrums, cures, refreshers, and remedies. Great vocabulary lessons. And there was one inscription on a number of these bottles that made me curious. And so I went to my aunt and my mother, and I asked, "Why do some of the bottles say 'For Medicinal Purposes Only'?

"They laughed and laughed. And then they explained how there was a time when some doctors really believed that alcohol had medicinal purposes, and how distillers capitalized upon that."

"For medicinal purposes only," said Seth and smiled. "I wondered how you would get back to that."

"Time in a bottle," I said.

"More like lightning in a bottle. Whatever happened to your aunt's collection?"

"When she passed, her children got it. I hope they kept those old bottles and didn't sell them."

"Did you ever think of starting your own collection?"

I nodded. "I've actually gone on expeditions to old dumps. So far I've found exactly one bottle—an old, rectangular apothecary container. But the digging and looking was a lot of fun. It was like searching for hidden treasure. And it was certainly a healthy way to hit the bottle."

"Another drink?" asked Seth.

I shook my head. "The first two drinks actually felt as if they were for medicinal purposes. I wouldn't be able to say that about the third."

As Sirius and I both got up to leave, I said what had been on my mind the entire time, but which I only now stated: "It was a week ago at about this time that Heather Moreland was taken."

Seth had known what was weighing me down, and gave me a sympathetic pat on my back.

* * *

I don't know if any old distillers ever made a nostrum they called a "dream tonic." It wouldn't surprise me if they did. And I might have been a believer in such a product, if not a buyer. The fire came to me when I wasn't seeking it, and for my sins known and unknown, I burned.

Haines was there to greet me. He was always a constant in my fire walk. Even when I avoided seeing him in my personal life, he haunted me. Langston Walker wasn't the only one with a ghost.

The gusting wind stirred up the flames, boxing us in. The fire was talking to me again. It wasn't only its crackling, popping, and sizzling; it wasn't only the howling wind, or the lamentations of the smoldering brush, or the taunts of the dust devils.

"Pay the toll," roared the fire. "Pay the toll."

"What is it?" asked the Strangler.

I wasn't sure if he was hearing what I was hearing, or if he was asking why I'd stopped and seemed to be listening to something.

"Pay the toll," I told him, and with a shake of my head signaled our direction.

"The fire," he said, as if I couldn't see it everywhere.

I cradled Sirius's limp form in one arm that refused to let him go, and centered my gun on the Strangler's chest.

"Pay the toll," I told him.

And then we walked through fire, and burned a little more.

* * *

My partner's excited barking was even louder than the fire, drowning out its voice. His barking delivered me from hell, and I sat up gasping for air.

The fire receded. With a hot, trembling hand, I reached for Sirius and stroked his nape. "Thank you," I whispered.

The moment after came; with it came the crazy stories. My oracle speaks in many tongues, and rarely allows for an easy interpretation.

Jacob Marley came in the form of Langston Walker. I stared into what looked like my mirror, and Walker materialized. Walker said nothing, but held up a sign that read "0 8 4."

He disappeared before I could ask him what that meant.

And then Angie appeared in my mindscape. She was excitedly sniffing something. She was telling me we had to hurry. But I still wasn't sure what she was saying. I did hear the voice of my one-time instructor, though: "You got to listen to your dog, Gideon."

Like Scrooge, I got a third ghost. An unholy trinity. Emilio Cruz, or at least a marionette that appeared to be Emilio Cruz, lectured me. His mouth opened and closed, as if pulled by strings.

"Point number one," he said. "I had nothing to do with my wife's disappearance. Point number two, I don't know anything about my wife's disappearance."

Cruz's mouth wasn't in sync with his words. He was lying, or he was a dummy, or both. His wooden choppers kept clicking, but they were at odds with the timing of his words. My sensory overload did its usual short-circuiting, and I fell asleep.

* * *

When I awakened in the morning, my body ached. My lips were cracked, and my skin was red and dry. It felt as if I was once more a harlequin that went around masquerading in a patchwork body of skin grafts. My steps were slow and painful, as if the fire was a recent event and not something in the past. I was dehydrated, and nauseated from the pain. After drinking two glasses of water, I went in search of some coffee. Imagine the worst hangover ever, combined with physical ailments that suggested recent burns. It was psychosomatic, I knew, but the mark of fire somehow manifested itself upon my body.

I sipped my coffee and took a chaser of aspirin. My recovery always takes time I don't want to afford it. Instead of thinking about my PTSD, I contemplated my visions in the order of their appearances. What the hell was Langston Walker telling me? And why was he suddenly silent and forced to communicate through signs?

The paper he'd held up had the numbers "084." I typed those numbers into my search engine and came up with a reference to a comic book wherein the code 084 meant an object of unknown origin. That wasn't something even my subconscious mind would have known, but I found it ironic that I was thinking about an object of unknown origin.

Angie's silence was more understandable. She was a dog. But I worked with dogs and was supposed to be able to divine what they were communicating. It was frustrating still not getting it. And what made it worse was Heather Moreland. Angie knew we had to hurry. At some level I knew we had to hurry. But that only made me all the more frustrated at my inability to figure out where to go and what to do.

Later, I would call Dr. Green and see how Angie was, but not now. There was other business I needed to tend to. I had to go call upon the dummy of my dreams. I had to go pull some strings of my own.

* * *

My shadow fell over Emilio Cruz. He was using a pressure blaster to remove paint and rust from a panel he was working on.

"What the hell?" he said, turning off the pressure blaster.

"I have some questions for you, Emilio."

"You're not allowed back here. This is a work area."

"The sooner you answer my questions, the sooner you can get back to work."

His face flushed red. "If you don't leave, I'm going to call . . ."

He stopped voicing his threat in midsentence. Threatening to call the police on a cop isn't usually much of a deterrent.

"I'm going to call your superior," he hissed, rethinking his warning, "and lodge a complaint."

"Are you sure you took anger-management courses?" I asked. "Your face is red and you sound furious."

"He who angers you controls you. I won't let you control me."

"The last thing I want to do is control you. Like I said, I just have a few questions. I'm sorry if that upsets you."

"I'm not going to give you the power to upset me. That would surrender my self-worth."

The jargon was getting thick, I thought.

"During all of our conversations, Emilio, you've never seemed very concerned about Heather. I thought she was the love of your life."

"I'm not her keeper."

"And you're not curious about what happened to her?"

"It wouldn't surprise me if Heather went off and ended her life."

"Really? That would surprise me a lot."

"People who die by suicide don't want to end their lives; they want to end their pain."

Most of the words coming out of Emilio's mouth were jargon he'd picked up in therapy. I was reminded of my conversation with Seth the night before, and how I'd talked about the purported remedies described in those old bottles—the nostrums, balms, and elixirs.

"Heather was all about overcoming the odds," I said. "Out of nothing, she made a life for herself. Her biggest misstep along the way was you."

Emilio clenched his hands into fists. The tattooed snake on his arm slithered and undulated as the muscles in his arms rose and fell.

When he didn't reply, I said, "I'm sorry. Is that a sore subject for you?"

"Anger is the only thing to put off until tomorrow."

"That sounds like one of those posters in Dr. Barron's office."

"Talk to my lawyer. I have nothing more to say to you."

"When we had coffee, you weren't inclined toward conversation either. So why did you meet with me?"

"You asked for the meeting."

"I asked for a talk. We never talked. You came with your piece of paper and your four points. Who dictated them to you?"

"No one dictated anything. I had a discussion that helped me to formulate my thoughts. The purpose of our meeting was to establish boundaries. I wanted to achieve closure. Your presence here is a clear violation of the boundaries I tried to establish."

"So what you're telling me is that Dr. Barron is the man behind the curtain?"

"He's my therapist. He cares about my well-being."

"That's right. You're one of his charity cases, aren't you?"

Judging by his bodily reactions, Emilio again had to rein in his temper and then weigh his words: "He chooses to work with me at a reduced rate."

One of Emilio's coworkers came over to join us. He was carrying a wrench, which might have been a tool of his trade, or it might have been a warning to me.

"Everything all right here?" he asked.

"I'm just leaving," I said. "I'm glad we were able to dialogue this, Emilio, but I'm afraid our time is up."

CHAPTER 36

BOOS AND BOOHOOS

When I left the body shop, my first call was to Dr. Barron's office. I waited five rings before hearing a recording telling me to please hold and that the call would be answered in the order of those waiting. I wondered if Emilio Cruz had called in immediately after I left, and if I was holding because of him.

After two minutes, a voice came on the line and said, "Dr. Barron's office."

"Are you the receptionist," I asked, "or are you Dr. Barron's answering service?"

"I work for Dr. Barron," she said, evading the question. "How might I help you?"

"This is Detective Michael Gideon of the Los Angeles Police Department," I said. "I need to speak to Dr. Barron."

"I am afraid that Dr. Barron isn't in today. May I take a message?"

"I need to talk to him directly."

"He's speaking at a conference in Sacramento, and I'm afraid he's unreachable."

"There has to be an emergency number."

"Dr. Strum is handling his emergency calls. Would you like her number?"

"What I want is Dr. Barron's number. This involves police business."

"I am afraid this is just a phone service, Detective," she said.

It had been a roundabout conversation to finally get my first question answered.

"So you're not actually at his office?"

"No, I am not."

"When is Dr. Barron supposed to return?"

"He will be back at work tomorrow morning. We do expect him to be calling for messages today if you'd like to leave one."

I repeated my name, and told her my cell-phone number.

"And your message?"

"Please have him call me when he gets this. It doesn't matter whether it's day or night."

"Anything else?"

I decided to offer up a commentary on therapists: "Samuel Goldwyn once said, 'Anyone who goes to a psychiatrist should have his head examined.'"

"How do you spell that name?"

* * *

My next call was to Dr. Green. Angie, she told me, was "much improved."

"Does that mean the patient is ready to leave today?"

"It does," she said. "What time will you be here?"

"What's the latest I can pick her up?"

"Dr. Avalos is scheduled to work until eight o'clock tonight."

I told her I would be there before eight, and Dr. Green said she would leave word with Dr. Avalos.

With the rest of my day cleared, I decided to spend time with Langston Walker's notes. I drove back home and found Sirius waiting for me at the front door at the same spot where I'd left him that morning.

"You can't fool me," I told him. "You were probably sleeping on the sofa, and when you heard me pull into the driveway, you ran to the door to make it look as if you'd been pining for me all morning."

Even if that were true—and I knew it wasn't—I was glad to be on the receiving end of an enthusiastically wagging tail.

Unlike Langston Walker, I've never had a space set aside solely as my office. Although I have a cubicle at Central, since becoming a detective, my dining room table has pretty much served as my office. Unless I need to use a terminal to tap into police records, I prefer working at home. My method is to fill the table with paperwork, and keep moving things around until a semblance of order is achieved.

I brought my laptop over to the table, piled up the paperwork next to it, and opened my notepad. Then I reached for the 187 Club folder. The day before I had put aside the Ceballos case; there were still four other cases Walker had chosen to single out.

The first case I looked at was the murder of DeShawn Adams, a transgender woman who went by the name of Dawn. The case notes alternately referred to Dawn as both "he" and "she," as well as Dawn and DeShawn, but I wasn't concerned with Dawn's name as much as I was her lover's: Nate "Casper" Johnson was a member of the 187 Club. The name Casper is certainly not common. I had only heard it a few times in my life. My association, and I assume that of most people, was through the cartoons and movies starring Casper the Friendly Ghost. I wondered if this Casper was the ghost that had haunted Walker.

J. R. Farley had been convicted of Dawn's homicide, but it had been ruled voluntary manslaughter. Farley was currently serving a sentence of twelve years. According to Farley, he and Dawn had been friends. The two of them had been drinking, he said, when Dawn began making sexual advances toward him. Farley said he warned Dawn not to touch him, but that didn't dissuade her. Dawn, he said, told him that the difference between a straight man and a gay man was "a few drinks." Farley said he "freaked out" when she came on to him, and that he physically beat Dawn, but insisted she was still alive when he left her apartment.

Farley's public defender had tried to paint Nate "Casper" Johnson as the more likely suspect in the homicide. It was Johnson who came upon Dawn's body. The lawyer said Johnson had exhibited a history of jealousy when it came to Dawn's behavior. He said a tipsy Dawn had probably told him what she'd done, prompting him to strike her with a blunt object. The murder weapon was never discovered.

There must have been enough questions in the prosecutor's mind for him to pursue a sentence of manslaughter instead of murder. That meant the prosecutor either hadn't believed there was the "malice aforethought" necessary to get a first-degree murder conviction, or had known it would be difficult to prove sufficient premeditation, deliberation, or planning with intent to kill.

The reports, case notes, and *L.A. Times* article didn't give me a good picture of Johnson. Could he have murdered Dawn? Was he Casper the Unfriendly Ghost? I found two phone numbers associated with his name, and called what was supposed to be his home number. Casper picked up on the second ring. After identifying myself, I asked him if he would be willing to answer a few questions pertaining to the Dawn Adams homicide.

Without any hesitation, he agreed to talk to me.

"I assume you've heard about Detective Walker's death?" I asked.

"I was sickened by the news," he said, his voice soft and concerned.

"I'm wondering if we've met, Nate," I said. "I was this month's speaker at the 187 Club."

"I'm sorry," he said. "I missed that meeting."

"Could we have met at the memorial service?"

"I missed that as well," he said. "I know myself; I don't do well at funeral services."

"I can understand that," I said. "Anyway, it's sort of fallen on me to put Langston's paperwork in order, and that's the purpose of my call. I found case notes that pertained to the homicide of Dawn Adams. Was there any reason for Langston to be looking at her case?"

The silence built, and then I heard sounds that at first I couldn't identify, then realized were breathy sobs.

"Are you okay, Mr. Johnson?"

"Give me—a minute," he said, and the sobbing gradually stopped. When he regained control of himself, he spoke again. "I asked Langston to look into Dawn's murder. He was doing me a favor. I wanted to see if there were any grounds to retry J. R. Farley."

"Why would you want that? Farley was found guilty."

"But only of manslaughter," he said. "I'm told in all likelihood he'll be out of prison in three or four years. That's not right. He murdered Dawn in cold blood, and he needs to pay for that."

"It might not seem like it to you," I said, "but he already is paying. I've seen murderers walk on cases that I thought were prosecutorial slam dunks, so I seriously doubt the DA would ever retry his case even if they had the grounds to do so."

"That's what Langston said. But he told me he would look at the case and do whatever he could to make sure Farley served his full sentence."

"I see," I said. Johnson was sounding credible, but I wanted him to keep talking.

"Farley told all sorts of lies. He claimed Dawn came on to him. Dawn would never have done that. She never threw herself on anyone. And she especially didn't do that after we began our relationship."

"Were she and Farley friends?" I asked.

"Dawn knew him," he admitted, "but they weren't friends. It was Farley who came over to her apartment with a bottle of Scotch. It was Farley who plied Dawn with drinks."

"Why?"

"Dawn had been saving up money for her sexual-reassignment surgery. I told the detectives that, and I told the prosecutor that. I also told them that I'd contributed almost three thousand dollars to Dawn's fund, and that she had saved up even more than that."

"What did they say about that?"

"They said there were no bank records showing that money, or any money. I said that of course there were no bank records. Dawn didn't trust banks. She had the money hidden in her apartment. That's why she usually locked up her place like it was Fort Knox."

"And you think Farley knew about the money?"

"He knew about how we were saving for her surgery; all her friends knew. Farley stole that money. If the police and the DA had done their jobs, they would have heard the same thing I did: on the night of Dawn's murder, Farley bought all the crack and smack in the neighborhood that he could lay his hands on. He was partying for days before he was finally arrested."

"Did Langston corroborate that information?"

"He did. Last month he even wrote me a letter with his findings. According to Detective Walker, Farley spent thousands of dollars on the drugs, and wasn't able to account for how he got the money. Walker said I could read his letter at future parole hearings."

"Could you make me a copy of that letter?"

"I'd be happy to."

"One more thing," I said. Johnson's claims sounded on the up-and-up, but L.A. has some world-class liars.

Speaking fast, trying not to allow him time to think, I asked, "How did you get the nickname Casper?"

In his calm, soft voice he answered, "I have vitiligo."

"I'm not sure what that is."

"It's a skin condition. If we were talking face-to-face, you'd see where I'm missing the pigment in parts of my skin. Michael Jackson claimed he had vitiligo, even though it didn't look like any vitiligo I ever saw. Most of my depigmentation is in the upper half of my body, especially my face. Even though I'm black, my face is white. In fact, it's close to being snow-white, almost the white of an albino. Because of that, everyone called me Casper when I was growing up. Some people still do."

"Some people are assholes," I said.

Nate Johnson agreed with me. I had found Casper, but I didn't think I'd found Walker's ghost. I thanked Johnson for talking to me.

* * *

The rest of my day was spent pursuing ghosts, most notably a stabbing in Hawthorne. The stabbing homicide had resulted in an arrest warrant being issued for Pablo "Diablo" Nuñoz for the murder of Juan Cuellar. It was Cuellar's widow, Ava, who'd been working with Walker. Word on the street was that Nuñoz had "gone ghost." That phrase had been written into the police reports, and the same words had been offered up by several of Nuñoz's friends. "He went ghost" was a street expression that had found its way into rap songs and gang slang. "Going ghost" meant going underground, or disappearing. In Nuñoz's case, it was thought that he'd made his way across the border and returned to his home state of Oaxaca in Mexico. As much as I tweaked that information, I still didn't think this case was Walker's ghost.

Including the Ceballos case, there were now three "boos!" And I had three boohoos.

I got up out of my seat and stretched. Sometimes the only way to work a case is to Super Glue your butt to a chair. The sun was already setting; another day was lost. I thought about calling Sergeant Reyes, but I knew if he'd turned up anything on Heather Moreland, he would have called. The last time we'd talked, he'd said he would be going door-to-door to see if any home surveillance systems had picked up anything around the time she was believed to have disappeared.

My cell phone rang, and I looked at the readout. Arthur Epstein was calling. My workday had dulled my senses, and it took me a moment to make the connection: Art Epstein, father of Joel, husband of Suzanne, whom Ellis Haines had murdered. The Weatherman, also known as the Santa Ana Strangler, was my tar baby. Even when I was away from him, his pitch couldn't be cleaned off.

"Thanks for calling back, Art," I said.

"No problem," he said. "I finally got something for you, or at least I think I do."

I'd asked him to see if he could find out why Walker was late for our dinner, what "fires" he'd had to put out.

"Shoot," I said.

"There were at least two people who stayed behind to talk to Langston at the last club meeting," he said. "One of them was LaToya Gibson. If I understand it right, there's this feud the Gibson family has with another family. It's like the Hatfield–McCoy feud. Anyway, that other family killed one of Gibson's sons, and apparently they're now threatening another one of her sons."

"Who was it that overheard this conversation?" I asked.

"Catalina Ceballos," he said. "She was putting away chairs, like she usually does after the meetings."

"And who was the second person who stayed behind?"

"James Rhodes," he said. "Catalina said Langston had asked him to stay after the meeting so that they could talk. She said it seemed like an intense conversation."

"Intense as in loud?"

"I don't think she meant it that way, but more that both of them seemed intent on what was being said."

"When I spoke at the meeting, Catalina and James seemed friendly. Are they an item?"

"I think so far they're just friends. I know for a fact James is interested in Catalina, but she's made it clear she's not ready for a relationship."

"How do you know that?"

"Over the past year I've gotten to know James pretty well. In fact, he was the first call I made on your behalf. It's a funny thing. James mentioned Detective Walker's talking with LaToya, but didn't mention their talk."

"And yet Catalina said it sounded intense."

"That's probably because James never realizes how intense he comes off. He could talk about the Dodgers and make it sound as if it was a life-and-death situation."

I thought back to my first encounter with James Rhodes at the 187 Club meeting. He had come across as an intense sort, although at the time I thought he was being protective of Catalina.

"What kind of work does James do?"

"He teaches calculus and physics at a JC."

"His wife was the bicyclist killed in a hit-and-run, wasn't she?"

"She was," Epstein said. "I'm always reminding Joel to be careful because of Andrea Rhodes. I don't let him go out riding without a helmet and pads, and still worry. Even a helmet didn't save Andrea."

The death of Andrea Rhodes was one of Detective Walker's 187 Club cases that I hadn't yet begun to work.

I thanked Art for his help, and within moments of hanging up, I began reading about the life and death of Andrea Rhodes.

CHAPTER 37

JUST A SHOT AWAY

"Promise you won't kill me?"

Lisbet laughed. "Okay, I promise, even though I'm already regretting that promise since I'm sensing you're about to cancel on me for the second day in a row."

"I'm not canceling. I intend to keep my promise of nibbling your ears. But I'm hoping you can accommodate my schedule."

"Which means what?"

"Can we hold off eating until around eight?"

"That does mean no later than nine, doesn't it?"

"It does."

"You raised your voice when you said 'does.' That means there's an unresolved 'but.'"

"I thought *I* was supposed to be the detective."

"I'm learning through osmosis."

"I have to pick up Angie from the vet's clinic before eight o'clock tonight," I said, "and prior to that, I need to check out a crime scene that relates to a case I'm working on. So I hope it's not asking too much for you to pick up dinner and that we eat at my place. And, yes, I know I'll owe you big-time."

"You know that when I agreed to not kill you, I didn't say anything about not committing grievous bodily harm."

"Talk mayhem to me," I said, breathing heavily.

"I'll talk food instead. What's your order?"

"What do you think about going with the papaya salad and the spring rolls as appetizers?"

"I concur."

"And please check to make sure they don't forget the peanut sauce."

"Yes, sir."

"And I'll have my pho with the flank steak on the side."

"Got it. The only thing we haven't worked out is my delivery charge."

"I will make sure matters are worked out to your satisfaction, madam."

* * *

It was dark by the time Sirius and I set out for Central L.A., and the sky made it look even later than it was. A rare April storm was threatening to descend upon Los Angeles. I programmed the address into the GPS, and we began our drive. For once I didn't have a tune in my head, so I checked what was playing on L.A.'s classic rock stations. I passed on an Aerosmith song, but then stopped my search when I heard the familiar tremolo of a rhythm guitar that was the opening for the Rolling Stones' "Gimme Shelter."

Mick's singing seemed to be a commentary on the darkening sky: a storm was on its way.

And then the voice of Merry Clayton did its best to make the little hairs on my neck rise. In her powerhouse emoting, her words were electrically charged; cracking with emotion she screamed of rape and murder.

And everything, all the madness, was just a shot away. It was close, too close. I could feel it.

I was on my way to a site where a woman had died, but my thoughts weren't only on Andrea Rhodes. Heather Moreland was also in my thoughts. Andrea Rhodes had been dead for years; I hoped Heather was still alive. I hoped she had found shelter.

We headed into the storm.

* * *

Even though it seems as if there are a lot of bicycle riders on L.A. streets, the city isn't very bicycle friendly. Among Langston's paperwork I had found maps of Los Angeles, and among that paperwork he had made the notation of a "comfortable street." I wondered if I'd arrived at the location of that comfortable street and the spot of the circled X on his map. When I'd originally looked at the maps, I'd never considered that they'd been designed for the city's bicyclists. The colored lines showed existing bikeway systems, proposed pathways, interconnections that were needed, and potential study corridors.

As L.A. streets go, Dalton Avenue was a quiet residential road east of Culver City. Because it wasn't a main thoroughfare and didn't directly lead to any major streets, it was less congested than most. There are lots of streets around L.A. that qualify as death traps for cyclists, but this wasn't one of them. The bicycle lane was well marked and roomy. Still, this was the street where a hit-and-run driver had taken Andrea Rhodes's life.

I drove along Dalton in search of the exact spot where Andrea had died. Even though she'd gone up and over a curb onto the sidewalk to try and escape being hit by the drunk driver, neither the sidewalk nor curb had stopped the vehicle. Supposedly the car was going close to fifty miles an hour, twice the residential street's speed limit, when it struck her bicycle. Although Andrea was wearing a helmet, her headgear wasn't enough to spare her. She was thrown into the air some thirty feet, and didn't survive the impact.

In the darkness I saw a white glow, and pulled over to the side of the road. Chained to a streetlamp was a whitewashed bicycle that gave off a spectral look.

Sirius and I jumped out of the car and walked over to the bicycle. Even the lock that was binding it to the streetlamp had been spray-painted white. The bicycle wasn't operational; it had no chain, seat, or gears. But it wasn't ornamental either. The bicycle was there for a purpose. Atop its crossbar a black Sharpie had been used to write the message, "RIP Andrea," along with the date of her death.

I took some pictures of the bicycle, and then I sat there staring at it. Near the front wheel I could see the remains of dried-out flowers. The white bicycle was a shrine.

Sirius and I went back to the car. I'd brought along my laptop and hot spot, and used them to call up a search engine. After typing in the words "white bikes in L.A.," I found myself staring at the first hit that came up: ghost bikes. My mouth fell open, and opened some more when I started scanning the other hits. I saw such entries as "Los Angeles ghost bikes, ghost bikes in L.A., ghost bikes memorialize cyclists killed on streets," and "ghost Bikes of L.A. art exhibit."

And then there was the search engine hit that said, "These photos of L.A. ghost bikes will haunt you."

They had already haunted me without my even knowing it. I was sure I'd found Langston Walker's ghost. And I became that much more certain when I clicked on a website showing the locations of L.A.'s ghost bikes. The map correlated with the Xs I'd seen on Walker's map. At each spot, ghost bikes had been left to memorialize those bicyclists killed by hit-and-run drivers.

"*X* marks the spot," I told Sirius. "I should have seen it. I should have known."

X was where Andrea Rhodes had died. She'd been killed on a street where she should have been safe. Andrea Rhodes had been targeted for death.

My oracle had told me. I had seen Langston Walker in a mirror, or through a mirror. It was better than Alice through the looking glass. He had held up a sign. The answer had been before my eyes. But what I had seen was o 8 4. The mirror had reversed the numbers. The LAPD police code for a felony hit-and-run that has caused great bodily injury or death is 480. Walker had noted the number in his paperwork, and my subconscious must have picked up on it.

I heard an engine start up, but my adrenaline was pumping too hard for me to take any notice of it. Langston had reopened the Andrea Rhodes homicide. The RHD detective who'd worked the case had arrested Donald Warren. It was Warren's car that had struck and killed Andrea Rhodes. But the suspect had died before the trial. Something had made Walker rethink that investigation. Doubts had surfaced. Maybe it was that Hamlet line he referenced, where he wrote about someone who was "protesting" too much. James Rhodes?

I suspected Andrea's husband had joined the 187 Club so as to appear an appropriately grieving spouse. In the normal course of most homicide investigations, if a wife is murdered, the husband is invariably the prime suspect. Rhodes would have done his best to keep up the fiction of pining for his wife. But something had made Walker suspicious. He'd gone so far as to talk with Rhodes on the night I spoke to the 187 Club. I suspected Walker hadn't been sure of his findings, but he'd probably told Rhodes he was reopening the case. Rhodes had known about Walker's Cactus to Clouds trek. Everyone in the 187 Club did. Walker's suspicions had likely gotten him killed.

The squeal of tires made me look up. A pickup truck, driving without lights, was flying toward my parked car. I had only a split second to react. I kicked off from the floorboard, propelling myself to the back-seat. I tried to throw myself over Sirius. I was trying to save myself; I was trying to save my partner.

And then there was impact, and I was a car-crash dummy. Because the ignition was off, the airbags didn't deploy, and I pinballed from one side of the car to the other.

Tilt. Game over.

I couldn't move. I wasn't even semiconscious. Thoughts didn't enter my head so much as sensations. Speech was beyond me; I couldn't form words. There was this din in my head, this static. I couldn't tune in to the station that was my brain. My eyes were open and my ears were functional, but it was almost like they belonged to another. I felt like a spectator watching from above, dispassionate and unmoving.

I heard footsteps running up to my car. A shadow moved outside, working its way from the truck to my vehicle. In some part of my brain, I could hear the tinkle of liquid. Then, through the broken glass, a head showed itself. A hand holding what looked like a baster extended its way toward me. *Why does someone have a baster?* I wondered. It wasn't Thanksgiving. The body in the car, the body that was mine, couldn't respond.

A snarl broke through my static. I could hear it even in my wilder-ness. I was lost, but it grounded me. It kept me from leaving, but I still couldn't move.

From above I watched the show, my reception improving. After the snarl came a scream, and the hand that had been advancing toward me was now trying to retreat through the window, but my partner wasn't letting it go. He was shaking it from side to side like he would have a poisonous snake. The body attached to the arm screamed, and screamed some more. There was more savaging of the arm, but I was only semiconscious. It was only the screaming that kept me from com-pletely going under.

At some point Sirius must have let go of the arm. While I drifted in and out of consciousness, my protector stood over me. He barked with deadly purpose, warning the world to stay their distance. His mouth foamed as he raged at the night. I remember waking once and seeing the blood on his fur, and hoping it belonged to James Rhodes, the man who'd tried to kill me.

I tried to say, "Good boy," but I'm not sure if I was able to utter the words before blacking out again.

CHAPTER 38

FIGHTING CRIME BY BITING CRIME

I opened my eyes and saw Lisbet sitting in a chair next to my hospital bed. Her eyes were closed, and she was praying.

"Where's my pho?" I whispered.

She opened her eyes and started laughing and crying, and then she said, "Michael, what am I going to do with you?"

"Unmentionable things, I hope." I tried unsuccessfully to speak with more than a whisper.

"No brain damage," she said, but then added, "Or at least no more than was already there. Thank God!"

Sirius awakened at the sound of our voices and struggled to rise.

"It's all right, buddy," I said, but he insisted upon getting up and planting his head right next to me.

It was then I noticed the IV tubes snaking into my arm, but that didn't stop me from scratching behind his ear.

"*So ist brav,*" I whispered to him. German is not usually the first language I think of when it comes to endearments, but he knew I was telling him what a good boy he was.

That was when Lisbet lost it, sobbing hard into her hands. I'm not sure which of us was more uncomfortable with her tears; both Sirius and I tried comforting her.

"They had to call me, Michael," she said. "Sirius wouldn't let the EMTs get to you. He kept everyone at bay, including the police and animal control. He was standing over you, and was ready to protect you with his life."

That's when I had to fight back my own tears, and poor Sirius didn't know what to do. He went back and forth between me and Lisbet, trying to comfort both of us, and it was his earnest efforts that enabled us to start laughing. At least that made my poor, confused partner happy.

"James Rhodes?" I asked.

"As far as I know, he's still in the ER being operated on," said Lisbet. "One of the doctors told me there are thirty-eight bones in the hand, and Sirius broke all thirty-eight."

"Rhodes was going to burn me alive," I said. "He was trying to mask the crime scene, just as he did with his wife and with Langston. I'm guessing he stole the truck, just like he stole Donald Warren's car. He was putting down a trail of accelerant between the truck and my car. I'm sure he studied up on car crashes to try and fool forensics. His only mistake was putting his hand into the car."

"That hand will never be the same," said Lisbet. "I was told Sirius broke fifteen of his sixteen wrist bones, and eight of his ten shoulder and arm bones."

"Only eight of ten?" I said to Sirius, adding a tsk-tsk.

He heard the love in my voice; that was all that mattered.

"When I walked up to your car, Michael, I was scared. There was blood all over Sirius. His ears were back and he was growling, and it was this throaty, scary sound I'd never heard before. I had to talk with him for a minute before he calmed down, and then it took me another minute to persuade him to let the paramedics see to you. I was afraid his loyalty might kill you."

I fought off tearing up again. *It's the drugs they gave me,* I tried to tell myself.

"Luckily, the doctors say you look worse than you really are. Having been thrown around like you were, they say you could have suffered traumatic brain injury, internal injuries, and paralysis, but it looks like you escaped with only contusions and cracked ribs."

"Does that mean I can go home?"

"It means in the morning the doctors can look you over from head to toe to get a better read of your condition. They told me that when it comes to car crashes, it's likely you'll feel worse the second day."

"I'm feeling okay."

"That's the drugs talking. The doctors shot you full of pain medication."

I fought back a yawn, but Lisbet noticed. "Don't fight off sleep. That's what your body needs."

"What time is it?"

She checked her cell phone. "It's ten thirty."

"It's past your bedtime," I said.

"You think I could sleep after what happened to you?"

"You're asking me to sleep after what happened to me."

"This isn't some negotiation."

"You know why you should leave? Because I'll have trouble sleeping knowing that you're sitting there."

"You need someone watching over you."

"Let Sirius take the first shift."

"Sirius needs someone watching over him as well. He was in your car with you."

I didn't tell her that I had shielded him, at least somewhat, from the impact. And as it turned out, trying to save him had saved me. My partner's head was still on my bed. His ears were up; he knew we were talking about him.

"If I know you're sitting in this room, I'm going to want to wake up just to talk to you," I said, "and maybe do a little canoodling."

"I hear the pain meds talking," she said.

"You hear the pitter-patter of my heart, and I'm not talking about the EKG machine."

I angled my head toward her, and Lisbet rewarded me with a kiss.

"So we either kiss all night, or you go and get some sleep," I said.

"Did I already mention that you're impossible?"

"You already did."

"Are you sure?"

"I am sure."

"All right; I'll be back here first thing in the morning."

"Maybe you'll bring me my bowl of pho," I said.

"Maybe I'll eat your bowl of pho," said Lisbet, and we kissed again.

She stood up and tried to get the kinks out of her shoulder. Done right, praying is a strenuous workout.

"Should I take Sirius home with me?" she asked. "Your attending doctor filled out paperwork saying that he was your therapy dog."

"I wish that wasn't true, but it is. So you better leave my therapy dog. I have some issues we'll need to work through."

"Dr. Padgett even stitched up Sirius, but we're not supposed to tell anyone because he says it could get him fired."

She raised a finger to her lips, and for some reason I found that funny. My amusement made her smile, and Lisbet took her finger from her lips and gently pressed it on my lips.

"Pleasant dreams," she said, and then tiptoed out of the room.

I fell asleep almost immediately, but I didn't have pleasant dreams.

CHAPTER 39

THE LAST RECORDING

It was late when Kurios arrived at the bunker. He controlled his urge to hurry down to see her. Delayed gratification, he knew, only made it better. He wanted maximum intensity. Besides, he needed to tend to business before pleasure.

He needed to make sure he was safe.

Kurios checked on the GPS tracker he'd planted on the snooper's car. The detective had gone here and there, but his vehicle hadn't moved for hours and was miles away.

There was nothing to worry about.

Still, he refrained from going to her. The anticipation needed to build, and the best thing for that was to put his workday behind him. It had started early and gone late. There had been a number of times during the day when she'd entered into his thoughts, but he hadn't dared to monitor her. Too many people were about. But now, finally, he was alone.

Kurios tuned into his live feed. She was against the wall, and her face was hidden from him. He zoomed the camera in, but couldn't detect any rising or falling of her chest. She didn't appear to be breathing.

He moved the camera's lens, studying the concrete floor. There was blood pooled around her, lots of blood.

He took a sharp breath, growing hard. It was just as he'd hoped. She'd used the box cutter.

He went from the live feed to what had been recorded, rewinding the footage back to the point in time when he'd left her with the box cutter and exited the dungeon.

Then he began watching, savoring every second of what he saw.

She had moved the box cutter far away from her, a feeble attempt to keep temptation at bay, but as time passed she had gradually moved closer and closer to where she'd left it. Finally she'd picked up the blade and examined it.

He had seen some of the light go out of her eyes when he'd presented the dog's ear, and then it had extinguished for good when he'd told her Bowser was dead. With her little baby gone, she'd lost the will to live.

Kurios watched as her last inner trial took place. He could see her thinking. She touched the blade, felt its sharpness. The promise of relief, only a few strokes away.

He paused the recording. He needed to tend to his own relief. And then he would return to the footage and watch her die.

CHAPTER 40

BLOWING IN THE WIND

I didn't have a burning dream, but during the short time I slept, I did have a troubled dream.

And I woke up even more troubled.

The pounding in my head didn't come only from a headache. In my dream I'd heard the music from earlier in the evening, with voices screaming for shelter.

It wasn't only Merry Clayton and the Stones clamoring for shelter. I was sure I heard Heather Moreland in that chorus. It didn't matter that I'd never heard her voice. I'd heard it in my dream, and even stranger, I was hearing it now. In my head she was calling for help.

I pressed a button for the floor nurse, and then began looking for my phone and my clothes. As far as I could determine, they weren't in the room.

The urgency welling up in me demanded immediate action. It was a war that couldn't be put off.

The floor nurse entered my room. Before she could speak, I said, "I need my phone right now."

"Detective Gid—"

"Now!" I said, interrupting her.

She read my voice and my expression and left the room. A minute later she returned with my phone, with security, and with what I assumed by his scrubs was my doctor. Everyone was looking at me warily. I had taken out my IVs and hadn't done a very good job of it.

The young man in scrubs stepped forward and said in an overly calm voice, "Detective Gideon, I'm Dr. Padgett."

"I understand I am greatly in your debt, Dr. Padgett," I said, "but right now I have to attend to a matter of life and death and need to discharge myself."

"You're confused, Detective. You're drugged, and not in your right mind. In this state, I can't release you."

"Phone," I told the nurse, extending a bloody arm.

She looked to the doctor, and he gave a slight assent. I took the phone.

"And I'm going to need my wallet," I said.

There was another exchange of glances between the nurse and the doctor, and then she left the room to get my wallet.

"You're bleeding everywhere," said Dr. Padgett. "Can I at least put some gauze on your wounds?"

"I would appreciate that."

Dr. Padgett didn't look much more than thirty. They keep making doctors younger and younger, or so it seems. With Sirius watching his work closely, the doctor did a quick patch job.

"You really are in no condition to leave this hospital," he said.

"And I wouldn't be leaving if it wasn't a life-and-death situation."

"Then why don't you call emergency services? They would certainly be able to respond faster than you, wouldn't they?"

"No," I said, "they wouldn't. Besides, it would be difficult for me to explain the situation to them."

"You're making my case for me that your cognitive abilities are compromised."

"You're making my case for me," I said, "that what I need to do can't easily be explained."

The nurse reappeared with my wallet. I found the business card of Angie's vet, along with Dr. Green's emergency number. Four sets of eyes—the doctor, the nurse, the guard, and Sirius—watched me as I dialed the number.

Dr. Green didn't use an answering service. When she picked up the phone at a quarter to midnight, she sounded tired, but not asleep.

"This is Detective Gideon, Dr. Green. I'm sorry that I didn't pick Angie up earlier, but there was a good reason for that: I was in a car accident."

"Are you all right?" she asked.

"I'm fine. And I wouldn't be disturbing you at this hour if it wasn't an emergency. A situation has arisen that requires me to get Angie out of your clinic right now."

"And it can't wait?"

"I would explain, but every second counts."

"I'll take you at your word, Detective. I'll call our evening vet tech and tell him that you're coming to get Angie."

The animal doctor was willing to believe in me, but the human doctor still had his doubts.

"You're really in no condition to leave," Dr. Padgett said, "and it would be unlawful for you to operate machinery."

I pointed to my phone and then hit the Uber app. After my account came up, I punched in the destination of Dr. Green's vet clinic. Uber electronically confirmed I would be paying with the credit-card information they had on file, and then gave me an amount and ETA of the driver.

"My ride is going to be here in ten minutes," I announced. "I'd like my clothes and my handgun."

"You are not getting your gun," said Dr. Padgett.

I took it as a good sign that he was no longer saying he wouldn't release me. The gun had been the bargaining chip I knew I would have to concede, but I pretended to be upset by his ultimatum, offering a long sigh and shaking my head.

"All right," I said. "I'll call in another cop with a gun to assist me. What about my clothes?"

"Your bloody clothing is being laundered," said the nurse.

"I'll need scrubs and my shoes, then," I said.

The nurse once again looked for direction. Dr. Padgett's sigh and headshaking were far more convincing than mine, but finally he said, "Go ahead."

The nurse and the guard both left the room, and Dr. Padgett made a last attempt to be the voice of reason: "I strongly suggest that you stay, Detective. You're leaving against medical advice."

"I understand that. And I'll sign whatever forms are needed that exonerate you and the hospital."

"We'll get them ready for you. And don't even think about walking out. We'll have an attendant wheel you downstairs."

* * *

I stripped and put on doctors' scrubs. The simple motions of undressing and dressing hurt like hell. I was already missing the drip, drip, drip of my pain medication. And I wasn't the only one moving gingerly: my guard dog was also limping.

"You can play the fife," I told him, "and I'll play the drums."

A pile of forms was dropped into my lap, and I signed my life away. Then my chariot showed up, and I was wheeled downstairs to the lobby. I felt guilty about my riding and Sirius having to walk. My attendant was a young, heavy-lidded Asian man. It looked as if he'd just been awakened. I knew for a fact that Sergeant Reyes had just been awakened, because I was the one who'd woken him up. I spent most of my wheelchair ride on the phone with him.

"You need to find a home address for me," I told him. "I might have something on our abductor."

"What's stopping you from getting the address?"

"Long story short, I had an accident and am just now being released from the hospital. Besides, I thought you wanted to be in on this."

"What's the name?"

"Dr. Alec Barron," I said, "with two *r*'s in the last name. He's a therapist, and has offices in Los Feliz."

"You think he's our guy?"

I had remarkably little in the way of evidence, but enough had added up. In my fire vision I had heard my instructor exhorting me, "You got to listen to your dog, Gideon."

The fire dream hadn't stipulated *which* dog. It was Angie I hadn't been listening to. I never took into account how alert she'd become when we neared Alec Barron's workplace. And when I came back from my meeting with Barron, Angie had all but patted me down with her nose. It wasn't a friendly sniff either. She was all business; she knew the scent of her enemy.

Emilio Cruz had finally admitted that Barron had authored his note. The therapist had to have been the one who suggested they meet. Barron must have been watching for me from the parking lot, and while I was preoccupied, had planted a tracking device on my car. It was the only way I could figure how he'd known where Angie was being kept. Barron had recognized what I'd failed to—Angie was a witness to his crime, or her nose was. He'd understood that she was a potential threat to him, and because of that he'd attempted to murder her.

Still, the evidence was sketchy. I had little more than a lost dog, a dream, and a gut feeling to go on, but for me that was enough.

"I do. He's certainly a person of interest."

"You're not exactly reassuring me, Gideon."

"I got to run," I said. "I'm making a stop along the way before calling on Barron. Call me when you get his home address."

"If it's going down, I want to be there," he said.

"Then you'd better find out where *there* is."

* * *

The Uber driver pulled up to the hospital's entrance. He was driving a Ford Focus. In a short while it was going to be a tight fit.

I got out of my wheelchair and told the attendant, "Thanks for the ride."

As Sirius and I approached the Focus, the driver rolled down the passenger window. He was a white kid who looked to be in his midtwenties. "I wasn't told about the dog," he said.

"It's not a dog," I said, "but a decorated police officer. And I'm his handler. We're on police business."

I flashed my wallet badge, groaned as I helped Sirius up into the back, and groaned some more as I took a seat in the front. The kid acted uneasy. That might have had something to do with my appearance in the wake of playing bumper cars. Or maybe it was my wearing doctors' scrubs while claiming to be on police business.

Uber driver Steven said, "Where are you going, sir?"

Judging from his appearance, Steven looked and sounded like a nerd. "We're going to a veterinary hospital," I told him.

"Is your dog all right?"

I reached back to my partner, gasped from the pain the movement caused, and then ruffled Sirius's fur.

"We were in a car accident tonight," I said. "But we're not going to the vet's office for my partner. We'll actually be picking up another dog."

Steven thought about that. "I'm not sure about transporting a second dog."

"A second police dog," I said. I decided to elaborate on my fabrication before Steven learned firsthand what a drooling machine Angie was. "And as you probably know, police dogs are afforded the same status as police officers and cannot be discriminated against. As you'll see, Angie is a trained bloodhound."

My Uber driver was looking that much more uncertain.

"Say, Steven," I said, "when you were a kid, did you like playing cops and robbers?"

* * *

Without asking Steven's permission, after we picked up Angie, I seated her in the front next to him. My neck was hurting too much for me to easily turn around, and I wanted to be able to monitor Angie's reactions.

My phone rang while I was getting into the backseat. The readout told me Reyes was calling.

"Good timing," I said. "What's his address?"

"I'm still working on it," he said. "His DMV address isn't where he lives. It looks like that's where he rents out a room in a house and collects his mail. His landlord says he uses it as a sometime office, but it's definitely not his residence."

"What about property records?"

"Nothing has popped out yet. And you know how some properties are in trust names or business names. Unraveling those takes time."

I cursed under my breath, and Steven's eyes widened. He'd told me he enjoyed playing cops and robbers as a kid, but I wasn't convinced. My menagerie was certainly out of his comfort zone; Steven was a grad student studying engineering at UCLA. His orderly world had been invaded by a cop in doctors' scrubs, my toothy partner, and a slobbering dog who was already drooling on him, not to mention his car's upholstery. Given his position, I might not be enjoying this particular game of cops and robbers either.

"Keep trying," I told Reyes. "And while you work on locking down his address, we'll be doing the same thing. We're going to be heading to Sherman Oaks."

"Why Sherman Oaks?"

"That's where I found Angie. She traveled a roundabout route from Burbank. I'm thinking she was following Heather Moreland's scent. I'm hoping by the time she collapsed in Sherman Oaks, she was getting close to her mistress."

"That sounds like a long shot."

"Until you get me Barron's home address, you got any better ideas?"

"Not a one," said Reyes. *"Vaya con Dios,"* he added, and then clicked off.

Go with God, I thought. That's what I hoped we were doing.

"Let's hit the road," I said to Steven.

"We can't proceed without a specific location," he said.

"We're going to my house in Sherman Oaks," I said.

Once more I had to lock and load the coordinates before we set out. For the first few minutes, we drove in silence. From the backseat I watched Angie's every movement. Her passenger window was halfway open, and she was sampling the breezes, but nothing seemed to have captured her interest.

Steven cleared his throat and then said, "I didn't mean to snoop, but I couldn't help but overhear some of your conversation."

"And?"

"So we're driving to Sherman Oaks with the hope of this dog picking up a particular scent?"

"That's right," I said. "A woman—Angie's owner—is missing under suspicious circumstances. We're looking for her. And we're looking for the man who might have taken her. So I guess we're potentially looking for two scents."

"Do you want me to put in my own two cents?"

He laughed at his own pun. It was a reminder to me of how I annoyed certain people.

"Go ahead," I said.

"When we get to Sherman Oaks, we should take into account the direction of the wind, and try to position ourselves accordingly to maximize our chances of the scent coming our way."

"I can't argue with that."

Angie apparently could. She violently shook her head, and froth and drool went everywhere, but Steven was the main target. He looked down to the splatter zone that was his shirt and pants and said, "Gross."

"Sorry about that."

He found a napkin and began dabbing at the mess. While working on the slobber, he took notice of Angie's bandages. "What happened to her ear?" he asked.

"I'm pretty sure the bastard we're looking for cut half her ear off."

"That's sick."

I liked the anger I heard in his voice. "Tell me again," I said, "your thoughts on matching up the wind to Angie's olfactory senses."

* * *

We had driven to one location in Sherman Oaks, and then a second. If I understood what Steven was telling me, he was establishing vectors on a wind map in the hopes of formulating a directional grid. That he was trying was enough for me. I kept paying for every ride with my credit card.

"If we're going with God," I muttered, "we're taking a circuitous route."

"Excuse me?" said Steven.

"Nothing," I said, but then added, "We need Angie to be Balaam's donkey."

"I don't understand," he said.

"I guess they don't teach religion in your graduate engineering courses."

"Of course not," he said, almost sounding offended.

"In the Bible there's the story of Balaam's donkey," I said. "I don't remember where Balaam was going or what he was doing, but whatever it was, somehow he displeased God. To intercede with Balaam, God sent down an angel. This angel stood in the middle of the road with a drawn sword, but Balaam couldn't see that. The donkey sure did, though, and being a smart creature, every time it saw the angel, it turned away from the road.

"Because of the animal's swerving, Balaam hurt his foot. Being a jerk, he took it out on the donkey and only stopped his beating when the donkey opened its mouth and spoke with the voice of the Lord, chastising Balaam. And then God opened Balaam's eyes so that he could see the angel that had been there all along."

I stopped talking. I hadn't beaten Angie, but I wondered if there were more similarities than not between me and Balaam. An animal had known what was going on. It had taken me too long to divine what was there.

"So Angie needs to see what we cannot?" said Steven.

"Or smell what we can't," I said. "The human species is so proud of the fact that we're at the top of the food chain that we forget the abilities that other species have."

Angie's head suddenly jerked and her body stiffened. She looked as if a jolt of electricity was coursing through her. Then she began breathing hard, almost like a wheezing asthmatic, desperate to take in some rare air.

"What do I do?" said Steven.

"Follow the wind."

CHAPTER 41

THE TRUMPETING OF A HAIRY ANGEL

As Kurios made his approach to her cage, he tried to hide the sounds of his footsteps. He was sure she was dead, but he wasn't going to take any chances. As he had fast-forwarded the footage, he was able to see that for hours she had remained curled up and inert in a pool of blood. That couldn't be faked.

Neither could the smell. He raised his hand up to his nose and tried to ward off the odor. The foul creature had soiled herself when she died.

It appeared rigor mortis had set in, but because she remained in the shadows, it was difficult to get a good look at her. She had been remarkably uncooperative in death. She'd kept her back to the camera. When she'd cut her wrists, he had observed the flow of blood, but hadn't seen her rend her own flesh. Kurios had felt cheated by that. Next time he'd set up multiple cameras so as to be able to see everything.

He felt the electricity running through him. He had hoped it would be like this. It was what he expected, and more. For so long he'd listened to their lurid stories, to men talking about how they put their women in their place. His clients had never known how much Kurios enjoyed hearing how they beat and bloodied the oppressive women in their lives. Growing up, he had watched his father beat his mother. She had always deserved it. And then his mother had abandoned both of them when he was only eight. His father was right: women should have a bounty on them.

Kurios looked into the cage. It was too dark to see the purpling of livor mortis, but he wouldn't be surprised if there was purge fluid along with her feces and urine. She had been disgusting in life, and was even more disgusting in death.

Now all that remained was for the trash to be put out.

He unlocked her cage, holding his breath. The stench was revolting. He had bought a huge roll of polyethylene, what the worker in the hardware store had called painters' plastic sheeting. After coating the body in lime, he'd wrap her up in the sheeting. Then he'd find a spot in the desert to bury her so that she would cook in her own foul juices.

He stepped closer and bent down to see her face. Her mouth was set in a gargoyle's rictus.

This time there was no mask obscuring Kurios's vision. He could see the filth for what it was; the bad thing was that he had to smell it.

The box cutter came at him before he could react. Kurios heard it better than he saw it. The blade sliced upward but missed his throat. The sharp edge didn't go thirsty, though; it cut through to the bone of his jaw. Blood began streaming down his shirt.

Kurios backed up, instinctively raising his hands. She sliced open his palm and kept coming at him. He found himself screaming. It wasn't only the surprise and the pain; she looked inhuman. Her face was white, her flesh pallid, and there were wounds all over her body. She had acted dead, and looked dead. She was growling and making subhuman sounds.

She lunged at him again with the box cutter, and Kurios almost fell over. For a moment he thought about running away. He could escape and lock her in the tomb forever. But there was no need to run. She was panting, and weak. Losing all that blood had taken its toll.

No, he wouldn't run. He was the lord, and she was the lowest of the low. She had thought she could escape her cesspool, but he'd put her where she belonged. He would disarm her and then break her. She was a pile of shit, and he would wipe her from the bottom of his shoes forever.

She went for his face, but he threw his head back and she was only able to nick his ear. It was a movement that exposed her, and he grabbed her arm. She tried swinging the box cutter, but his grip gave her no leverage. Squirming, biting, and kicking, she did everything possible to free herself. But he wouldn't let loose. He bent her arm to the point of breaking, forcing her to drop the box cutter.

Without a weapon, she tried to use her nails, tried to rake his flesh, but he was taller than she was and had longer arms. His hands wrapped around her neck, choking the life out of her.

* * *

Stars came to Heather's eyes. She had done everything she could, but her last desperate gamble hadn't worked. She had completely humbled herself, had lain in her own waste, but even that ruse had failed. Lack of food and water, and her own spent blood, had done her in.

She heard something over the rushing sound in her ears. It was some kind of trumpeting. Were the angels coming for her? She hoped that was so. But no, it wasn't trumpeting. It was a different kind of triumphant sound. It was baying.

That sounds like Angie, thought Heather, and passed out.

CHAPTER 42

UNLEASH THE HOUNDS

The driver and I were both holding our breath. Angie seemed to be on the scent again. From the backseat, I was keeping her from jumping out of the opened passenger-side window by holding on to her leash. She was pulling hard, ready to run after the scent. But then her body suddenly went slack, and she settled back into the front seat.

"Shit," I said. Steven joined my chorus.

It had been stop, and start, and stop again. Angie had caught the scent, and then lost it, and then locked in once more before losing it.

Steven wet his index finger and then raised it in search of the wind. It had come to that.

"Not much wind," he said. "And what's there isn't consistently coming from one direction or another. Maybe that's why she lost the scent."

"Head that way," I said, signaling with my hand. "I think that was the direction she was pulling."

He began driving, but I think he was watching Angie more than he was the road. I was more obvious in my staring. And I was gauging her leash like an anxious fisherman might his fishing line. Angie hadn't given up on her sniffing, but she couldn't find that elusive scent.

"It's not like the movies, is it?" said Steven.

I shrugged dispiritedly. Maybe it was like the movies. After all, the bloodhounds had come up empty in *The Shawshank Redemption* and *Cool Hand Luke*. Of course I'd been glad the hounds had come up short in those films. I wasn't so glad now.

"She'll pick it up again," he said.

It might have been lucky that Angie had picked it up at all, I thought. Neither Heather Moreland nor her abductor had walked this route. Their spoor wasn't on the grass or brush.

"I hope so." Heather's elusive scent was out there in the ether.

"Maybe we need to get Angie out of the car," he said. "It's possible her being in an enclosed space makes it difficult to pick up the scent."

"That didn't stop her earlier."

Angie's nose had taken us throughout much of Sherman Oaks before she'd lost the scent.

"But you might be right," I added. "Let's wait a minute or two, though. Walking would slow us up."

I didn't add that I wasn't even sure if I was up to the task of acting as her handler. My accident had caught up with me. Just breathing was causing me pain.

We came to a stop sign. "Where to now?" he asked.

My fish wasn't pulling. I pointed in the direction of North Hollywood and said, "That way."

We started down a quiet road in a residential section of Sherman Oaks. The leash was still slack. My bobber still wasn't bobbing. I watched Angie's nose twitch, saw her breathe in, but the air offered no secrets.

The foreboding that awakened me at the hospital had grown worse. I had this feeling something bad was either happening or imminent. The anguished tune in my head kept playing.

"The war is coming, and there's no shelter from it," I said.

"What do you mean?"

I didn't have to explain. Angie did that for me by suddenly going ballistic. Her earlier baying was just a warm-up for the big show. I had to hold tightly to her leash. There was a whale on the line. Angie had radar lock-on. The target was fixed, and she wanted the missile to fly. I could barely hold her inside the car.

"Stop," I said.

Steven braked hard. I was losing the tug-of-war, and Angie was trying to jump out her half-open window. "Hold the leash!"

Steven grabbed it, and that gave me the chance to throw open my door and step up to Angie's door. With Sirius at my side, I inched open the passenger door, getting a grip on her leash and collar.

Then I made the mistake of opening the door all the way.

Angie leaped out and almost pulled my arm out of its socket.

I ran as fast as I could, but it wasn't anywhere near fast enough for Angie. She began dragging me, and I had to let go of the leash. Sirius came to a stop next to me, but I had enough breath to go German on him: *"Voraus!"* He heard my command to "go" and didn't need to be told twice.

There had been a reason Dr. Padgett had advised me to not leave the hospital. My cracked ribs were now on fire.

"Are you all right?"

Steven had caught up to me. It hurt too much for me to reply, so I let the dogs do the talking. Sirius and Angie were running around an eight-foot-high privacy fence that ringed a home's large backyard. Angie was desperately looking for an entrance into the yard.

"Help the dogs over that fence!"

Steven assumed I knew what I was talking about. He sprinted to the dogs. I watched him lift Angie high enough for her to scrabble over the fence, and then he began hoisting Sirius. I arrived on the scene just as my partner disappeared from view.

"Now me," I said.

He interlaced his fingers, offering me a stirrup. I stepped up and he gave me a boost. His lifting up my body was bad enough; the torque of my swinging over the fence made me scream, but my cries of pain were covered up by the urgency of Angie's baying.

I didn't need to take any time figuring out where to go. Angie was scratching at the door of a backyard shed. Unfortunately, it was locked. Whether I kicked it in or hit it with my shoulder, it was still going to hurt. I took a step back.

And then I heard a sound coming from behind me and watched as Steven rammed into the door. Maybe he really did like playing cops and robbers. The door flew open, and the dogs jumped over his downed form. I moved around him and joined Angie. She was scratching at a throw rug, and I pulled it aside. The shelter dog had found the underground shelter.

I gripped a metal ring and lifted the hatch up. The rungs in the concrete walls had lost their battle to time, but had been replaced by a portable fire-escape ladder that extended to the floor below. The drawbridge was down. It was time to storm the castle.

I started down the ladder. Maybe I should have first consulted with Angie. Going down second apparently wasn't to her liking. It didn't matter that there wasn't room for the two of us. I was only halfway down the stairs when she jumped through the opening. I tried to catch her with one arm and hold on to the ladder with the other, but succeeded only in falling. Luckily, I cushioned her landing, but at the expense of my own body. I would have screamed, but the wind was knocked out of me. From above I could see Sirius's anxious face, and knew he was ready to do his own high-wire act.

"No!" I gasped, and then found breath enough to say, *"Sitz! Bleib!"*

I began to rise gingerly, but that was before a man began screaming. His terror not only got me to my feet, but got me running. I ran toward the sounds and saw Dr. Alec Barron trying to fend Angie off. Most dogs have to be taught to bite. It's not in canines' nature to clamp down on humans. But Barron was on the wrong end of Angie's teeth, and she showed no signs of letting up. His hands and arms were bleeding from multiple wounds, sacrificial victims to the shielding of his neck and trying to keep his jugular from being torn apart.

"Angie!" I yelled. "No!"

She ignored me and continued lunging at Barron.

"Angie!" I yelled again, trying to get her attention.

I didn't want to have to hurt her, but wondered what else I could do to stop her from ripping Barron apart.

And that's when a form raised itself from the shadows and began violently coughing. That got Angie's attention a lot more than my shouting.

And then Heather Moreland whispered, "Angie, come!"

Angie forgot her prey and bounded over to the still-coughing Heather. Then the woman threw her arms around Angie and held on as if she was the world's largest life preserver. Heather began sobbing uncontrollably, and all the while Angie desperately tried licking away what she perceived as Heather's sorrow.

The mother-and-daughter reunion was almost too personal to watch. The two survivors consoled each other and let their love speak. It would be a memory, I knew, that would sustain me for the rest of my life; it would be my own perpetual night-light that I could call upon to stave off the darkness that sometimes comes upon me.

Out of the corner of my peripheral vision, I saw Alec Barron trying to crawl away. I didn't let him get very far. I read him his Miranda rights and then secured him with flex cuffs.

He said only two things to me: "I need a doctor. And I need a lawyer."

I was glad he chose not to say much. Glad that he seemed to be in even more pain than I was. And I had the ready relief that he didn't. All I had to do was look at Heather and Angie. That was better than pain meds. That was better than anything.

CHAPTER 43

ANSWER UNCLEAR, TRY LATER

"You want to go for a ride?"

It was a question I needn't have asked. Sirius always wants to go for a ride.

"We're going to see a friend of yours," I told him.

That was reason for more tail thumping. Just being alive, Sirius knows, is reason enough for tail thumping. My partner reminds me of that every day, and shares his contagious joy. He keeps me from being a grump, which qualifies him as a miracle worker. I would nominate him for sainthood, but the Catholic Church has always discouraged any canine veneration.

The weeks since the car crash were supposed to have been a time of healing, but work had conspired against that. Sometimes the aftermath of a case proves to be more problematic than the solving of it, with a flurry of required reports and meetings.

As I drove, I tried to get comfortable. The car crash had thrown my body out of alignment. I sang my woes to Sirius: "Your backbone connected to your shoulder bone, your shoulder bone connected to your neck bone, your neck bone connected to your head bone."

My cell phone rang, and I looked at the display. Lisbet was calling. *Uh-oh,* I thought. And then I finished the lyric: "I hear the word of the Lord."

I suspected I was busted but pretended otherwise in my best mellifluous on-air voice: "This is the love doctor, and right now I'd like to give a shout-out to a special L.A. lady named Lisbet."

"And I'd like to ask the love doctor why a certain L.A. cop didn't go to physical therapy today," said Lisbet.

"Temporary insanity?" I waited a moment for her to laugh, and when that didn't happen, I said, "I had to take a conference call with the assistant DA."

"You can't keep putting off the therapy. You have to prioritize it."

"I'll make it tomorrow," I promised.

"Why is it that the bad guys have time for physical therapy, and the good guys don't?"

"Thanks to Sirius," I said, "James Rhodes needs to do *a lot* more PT than I do. Of course, his scumbag defense lawyer is trying to claim that his client's wounds were a result of excessive force."

"Saving your life constituted excessive force?"

"When you have a client looking at the attempted murder of a police officer with special circumstances, assault with a deadly weapon, and assorted other charges, lawyers tend to grasp for any straws they can. And we're not even taking into account the premeditated murders of Andrea Rhodes and Langston Walker."

After the fact, we'd learned that James Rhodes had run down his wife when he discovered she was having an affair. On the surface it was a crime of passion, but scratching that surface showed all the planning that had gone into her murder. Rhodes had targeted a problem drinker, and stolen Donald Warren's car after determining the man was in a drunken stupor. After running down his wife on a residential road as she was biking home, Rhodes had returned the damaged car to where he'd stolen it. There was a reason Warren had no memory of having driven his car on the night Andrea Rhodes was killed—he hadn't driven it, after all. It wasn't a blackout like everyone had assumed. Warren's death from cirrhosis of the liver was the only thing that had spared him a trial and a jail sentence.

"I'd rather you cared more about yourself than your cases," said Lisbet. "You think I can't see how much you're still hurting?"

"It's not that bad."

"Then why is it you've worn loafers ever since the crash? You can't even bend down to tie your shoes."

It was nice having a girlfriend who cared, but there were times I wished she wasn't so observant.

"I promise I will be better about going to physical therapy," I said.

"Good," she said. "I hate having to act like a schoolmarm."

I found myself laughing at her use of the word "schoolmarm."

"Schoolmarm," I repeated, and then attempted an urchin voice and said, "I have been naughty, teacher."

"Yes, you have," she said, "and I'm not about to be bought off with an apple."

"Then how can I go about currying your favor?"

"You can bring over a variety of kebabs for dinner. While you grill them up, I can make some rice pilaf and a Greek salad."

"Do you want some falafel with the kebabs?"

"That sounds good, but baklava sounds even better. In fact, I'm already salivating. What time will you be over?"

"Six," I said, and then added, "I think. It's possible I'll be late, but no later than eight. Then again, I might even be early."

Now it was her turn to laugh. "Was that you, or the Magic 8 Ball, being ambiguous?"

"Reply hazy," I said. "Try again."

"You do plan on showing up sometime tonight?"

"You may rely on it," I said.

"And it will be sometime between five and eight?"

"It is decidedly so."

"Do you think you'll get lucky?"

"Signs point to yes," I said.

"I think you must have an old Magic Eight Ball," she said. "Mine says, 'Answer unclear, try later.'"

* * *

Even before I reached the door, Angie began barking. I rang the doorbell and waited for the door to open, listening as deadbolts and locks were unlatched.

Heather Moreland offered up a big pretend smile, and I was reminded of how I'd presented the same faux cheeriness while recovering from my fire walk. My mantra had been, "Fake it 'til you make it." I was sure that's what Heather was doing.

Despite wearing makeup, she was pale, and under her eyes were deep, dark circles. She wasn't quite as haggard-looking as when I'd found her three weeks earlier, but she still hadn't regained the weight she'd lost. She had proved her resilience, but her ordeal had taken its toll. Now she looked worn and fragile. Handle with care.

I hadn't seen her since our time together in the dungeon. That night she'd clung to Angie and had clung to me. She'd wanted to clean up before being taken to the hospital, but the best I could do was wrap a coat around her. The cardinal rule of investigation is to preserve evidence and not contaminate a crime scene. Sometimes that means you can't be the human you want to be.

Heather extended a hand to shake. I think that was her way of making sure I didn't try and hug her. We shook and she said, "Thank you for coming, Detective."

Sirius had already invited himself in, and he and Angie were romping around the living room.

Heather gestured for me to come inside. "Please take a seat wherever you're comfortable."

I chose an armchair, and Heather sat in a rocking chair, but only for a second. "I didn't realize the room was so dark," she said, getting up and opening the curtains halfway.

She stood in the light, blinking, and then said, "Can I get you something to drink? I have lemonade and cookies already made."

"Lemonade and cookies sound great."

She hurried off, first returning with a plate of oatmeal cookies, and then coming back with a pitcher and glasses. Only after pouring did she sit in her rocker again.

"I've heard the rocking chair is a uniquely American invention," I said. "Some European said only Americans would be crazy enough to invent a chair that requires you to work while you sit."

"I suppose that's right," said Heather.

She looked preoccupied. Her chair moved up and down, but I don't think she was aware of that. I took a bite of one of her cookies.

"Yum," I said appreciatively. "These have to be homemade."

"They are. And if you like them, you have to take all the rest with you. I've been doing all sorts of baking. It keeps me busy, but I don't know what to do with all the extra food."

"I'm sure Angie is willing to be your test kitchen."

Heather offered up her first real smile of the afternoon. "She's more than willing, but I try to make sure she has a healthy diet."

We both sipped our lemonade. "I meant to have you over before now," she said. "I wanted to thank you in person. I know I would be dead if it weren't for you."

I shook my head. "I was just the guy holding the leash. It was Angie who tracked you down. I just wish I'd let her do that sooner than I did."

"I know how tirelessly you worked to find me. My friends tell me you were calling them night and day."

"I was doing my job."

She nodded, and her rocking chair slowed. "I had an ulterior motive for asking you over here. It wasn't only that I wanted to thank you. I also wanted to ask your advice."

"I don't know if that's my strong suit," I said, "but ask away."

Heather took a nervous breath. "You've been in the spotlight before. I was living in Los Angeles when you and Sirius captured the Weatherman. I remember how everyone was afraid you might die from your burns and wounds, and how every day there were reports on your condition."

"The good thing about being in the burn unit," I said, "is that I was spared from the media onslaught. You weren't afforded that luxury."

The media had been relentlessly pursuing Heather's story. That partly explained her acting like a recluse.

"How long did it take you to get your life back?" she asked.

I shrugged. "After I was released from the hospital, I went around for about a year saying, 'No comment.'"

"But your silence didn't stop the media from reporting on you."

"Not completely, but I wasn't an active participant in their non-sense. The department had me do some talks for PR purposes, which the local stations used as fodder for slow news days."

"Have you put all of that—craziness—behind you now?"

I thought about her question before admitting, "Probably not."

Then I found myself unconsciously touching the keloid scarring on my face. Heather noticed what I was doing.

"I have scars of my own," she said, "even though they're not visible like yours."

"I have those kinds of scars too, but I'm sure they're nothing compared to yours. I hope you're getting help."

"I am, but every time I sit down and talk with my therapist, I think about the therapist who abducted me and raped me. It's an irony that doesn't escape me, or that I can't seem to escape from."

"Things get better."

"Do you promise?"

"I promise."

"There are days when I find myself shaking and feeling scared. I know Barron is behind bars, but it feels as if I can't escape his evil."

"It takes time. The grip of fear lessens."

"You know this?"

"All too personally," I said.

"I'm afraid of being targeted by another Barron."

"You beat Barron," I said. "You took him on after he'd raped you, and enslaved you, and done everything imaginable to break you down physically and mentally. And in the end, you still had the presence of mind to open your veins and soil yourself to make it appear you'd died, just to have the chance to live. And then, as weak as you were, you took him on. That's why your story is so inspirational. You never gave up. And ultimately, do you know how you won? It was love that won out. The love that you gave Angie, and the love that she gave you, were not to be denied. The good guys actually won."

"Did they?" asked Heather. "Sometimes I wonder. I thought I would never have to see Barron again, but now I'm told I'll be facing him in the courtroom. And I'll have to listen to his lies. Do you know he claims that all he was doing was fulfilling my sexual desires? He's trying to suggest that I wanted my abduction to happen, and that it was a form of role-playing between us."

I took a picture out of my coat pocket and handed it to Heather. She looked at the glossy of a cut-up, battered, and bleeding Dr. Alec Barron, and then at me.

"The jurors are going to see that picture," I said. "The jurors are going to see lots of pictures. They'll know it was never a game. That doesn't mean Barron won't stop telling his lies. He will. But for the rest of his life, and let's hope that won't be too long, whenever Barron looks in the mirror, he'll think of you. *You* beat him, Heather. That was all you and Angie. Against all odds, you destroyed the monster. And he will always know you beat him, and that hard truth will haunt him day and night. That's the story people will take away from this, because that's the real story."

Heather handed the picture back to me, but I had a sense she was now breathing a little easier and feeling less anxious.

"Why is it that you never agreed to a book deal," she asked, "or a movie deal?"

"That wasn't for me."

"I'm not sure what I should do. There's this part of me that wants to tell my story, and this part of me that just wants to go into hiding. I've been listening to offers, though. All these publishers and studios are after me, and they're offering crazy money. I'd never have to work again."

"What do you think you're going to do?"

She shook her head. "I've always been a private person. It's hard for me to imagine putting all my dirty underwear on display. And as you know, I'm talking both literally and figuratively. If I'm going to tell the story, I'm going to tell everything."

Heather gave me a sad smile; I tried to give her a supportive one.

"Maybe it would be therapeutic if you told your story," I said. "Everyone has demons. Writing about what happened might be a way of exorcising yours. Isn't confession supposed to be good for the soul?"

"Do you practice what you preach?"

"Not to the extent I should. And maybe that's why I haven't healed as well as I should have. I am absolutely a case of do as I say, not as I do."

"I loved my job, but now I'm not sure if I can go back."

"Give it time."

"Everyone says I have to act now or I'll be yesterday's news."

"It's not so bad being yesterday's news, but that doesn't mean it's what you should want."

"I'm leaning toward taking the money."

"Do you have your tropical island picked out?"

"That wouldn't make me happy. But opening a no-kill animal shelter would."

I smiled. "Your friends told me you were a sucker for happily-ever-after stories."

"That's true. And I guess I've always been searching for mine. What do you think of the name Angie's Rescues?"

CHAPTER 44

MONDAY, MONDAY

When I left Heather Moreland's house, it was a little after four. I stopped at a Greek takeout and picked up some kebabs, falafel, and baklava. I also got some lamb shavings. Sirius made quick work of those in the car.

The decision left to me—the decision I'd been avoiding—was whether to take the direct route to Lisbet's apartment or make a detour along the way. All day I'd tried to ignore the date on the calendar. No, that wasn't quite true. All week I'd been trying to not think about the impending date. Wasn't my work done? Hadn't I done my job and more? I couldn't even carve out enough time in my schedule for physical therapy. Putting more on my plate wasn't in my own self-interest.

I could surprise Lisbet by not being late for once. The two of us could drink an unhurried glass or two of wine. I would tell her how excited Heather Moreland got talking about her plans for Angie's Rescues.

"Besides," I told my partner, "I'm overdue for my pain medication, and I'm really feeling it. That's another reason to drive straight to Lisbet's."

Sirius listened.

"The road to hell was paved with good intentions," I said.

Sirius stared me down.

"Yes, it's the second Monday of the month," I said. "So what?"

My partner let the silence build.

"Yes, this is when the 187 Club meets. That has nothing to do with me."

I wanted to believe that. I didn't want to believe that.

"Monday, Monday," I said, and took a deep, indecisive breath. "When you think of sixties music, it's hard to do better than the Mamas & the Papas. And you know what they sang about Monday?"

Sirius was listening intently. That was good enough for me. "That's right," I said. "You can't trust it."

My partner made a little conversational *grr* sound.

"And let's not forget the Carpenters and 'Rainy Days and Mondays.' Karen Carpenter only sang upbeat songs, but even she admitted that Mondays got her down."

I wondered if Langston Walker had specifically chosen to meet on Monday because it's a day most of us have the blues, and the purpose of the 187 Club was to deal with those blues. Or maybe it was just a date that worked on his calendar.

Sirius rested his muzzle on my shoulder, offering his touch of reassurance. "Let it be," he was telling me, "let it be." He said it even better than Paul McCartney sang it.

"Let it be," I agreed.

Our course was decided.

* * *

As I neared the Jim Gilliam Recreation Center, I saw at least seventy-five people milling around the front of the building. That was almost enough to make me turn around. All the parking spaces were full, and

I tried to tell myself that was another sign from the fates, but at that moment, faces in the crowd recognized me, and people began waving.

"They think we're the cavalry," I told Sirius.

I used a cop's prerogative and parked illegally. And then with Sirius at my side, I began to slowly walk toward the gathering. I tried to not hobble, tried to stand up straight, and tried to not grimace from the pain of every step.

One person began clapping, and then another, and another, until everyone was cheering. To my ears the applause sounded overly loud, and I could feel myself flushing. Sirius wagged his tail, enjoying the moment.

The overflow crowd opened up a path for the two of us, guiding me to take a place at the top of the steps. It was clear too many club members had shown up to be accommodated in the community meeting room, and everyone had been milling around the front until now. They'd been waiting, even if they weren't sure for what.

I looked down at the expectant eyes, and then took a deep breath while trying to collect my thoughts. Sirius barked. I wasn't sure whether he saw a squirrel, or whether he was calling the meeting to order.

"I'm no Langston Walker," I said. "His shoes are too big for anyone to fill. But the reason that all of us are here is that although Langston is no longer with us, we can't let his dream die."

Heads in the crowd nodded; faces encouraged me to go on.

"At last month's meeting, Detective Walker said that everyone came to this monthly meeting for different reasons. Tonight, though, we are all here for Langston."

I told them how the case against his murderer was proceeding. Everyone already knew what James Rhodes had done, but heads still shook, and faces expressed shock and bewilderment. I spoke to that pain. I'm not much of a public speaker, but words started pouring out of me. Where they came from I'm not sure. My words assumed a kind of poetry that I was sure I did not possess. I think Langston Walker spoke through me, offering one last address.

"We have all been betrayed by a murderous Judas," I said, "but we can't let him tear down what we have built. This club was formed so that it might lift its membership up. All of you share a bond. All of you are members of a club that claims a terrible price and unimaginable dues. No one wants to join this club, and yet we must retain this refuge for those in despair. We cannot let this light in the darkness be extinguished."

The clapping started up again. It wasn't for me; it was for the survivors of the 187 Club.

I had found my ghost, and it had found me.

"Let us bow our heads now," I said, "and offer up a moment of silence to remember Langston."

I lowered my head and did my remembering of Langston, and then directed a thought his way: "You better help me, because I don't know what the hell I'm doing."

Then I lifted my head, and waited a few more moments for everyone else to raise their heads.

"Now it's your turn," I said. "I want to hear Langston stories and memories that make us laugh and cry. Who is going to start us off?"

A tentative hand went up. I smiled and acknowledged the woman behind the hand, and she began to talk.

ACKNOWLEDGMENTS

When I first envisioned the Gideon and Sirius novels, my good friend and longtime agent, Cynthia Manson, encouraged me in the writing of them. And then Cynthia asked me to take a chance on a new publisher. Andy Bartlett of Thomas & Mercer bought *Burning Man* along with some titles from my backlist; I'll always be grateful to him.

Once again I have to thank Caitlin Alexander. She is a wonderful editor, and a wonderful person.

And speaking of editors, Gracie Doyle has done a great job of transitioning into her new position. I have never heard anyone say a bad word about Gracie. In the publishing business, that should qualify her for sainthood.

My kudos go out to all of those at Thomas & Mercer who have allowed me to flourish as a writer. Thank you, one and all.

I would also like to thank Jean Jenkins, a friend of mine who happens to be a fine editor and rewrite consultant, for sending me an article about the unfortunate death of a cop on the job and the reaction of his loyal K-9 partner. The loyalty that dogs often exhibit is astonishing.

My thanks also go out to Dr. Sue Spray for her veterinary insights on display in this novel (any mistakes are mine and not hers!). "Dr. Sue," as she is known to all her two- and four-legged friends, offers her wonderful mobile veterinary service (PetDoc2U) in the North County of San Diego. Our three dogs give their beloved vet three enthusiastic paws-up.

I would also like to offer a tip of the hat to retired police Sergeant Brian Kutney. Brian and his wife, Janee, have been kind enough to send pictures and tell stories of their wonderful K-9 charge, Aja, a beautiful female German shepherd police dog. And thanks again to Bob Connely, who is always available to answer my dog-training questions.

Finally, I'd like to thank my readers. It's great hearing from you. Please keep your notes and those cop–K-9 articles and stories coming. You can reach me at my website, www.alanrussell.net, through my email at alan@alanrussell.net, or by "liking" me on Facebook at Alan Russell Mystery Author.

ABOUT THE AUTHOR

Critical acclaim has greeted bestselling author Alan Russell's novels from coast to coast. *Publishers Weekly* calls him "one of the best writers in the mystery field today." The *New York Times* says, "He has a gift for dialogue," while the *Los Angeles Times* calls him "a crime fiction rara avis." Russell's novels have ranged from whodunits to comedic capers to suspense, and his works have been nominated for most of the major awards in crime fiction. He has been awarded a Lefty, a Critics' Choice Award, and the Odin Award. A California native, Russell is a former collegiate basketball player who these days plays under the rim. The proud father of three children, he is also an avid gardener and cook, and fortunately is blessed with a spouse who doesn't mind weeding or washing dishes.